The Cursed Sword

Book One of the Nine Worlds Trilogy

By

Debbie Champion

Text copyright © 2016 Debbie Champion

All Rights Reserved. No part of this book may be used or reproduced in any manner whatsoever without the written permission from the author.

ISBN: 978-1537350363

This novel is entirely a work of fiction. The names, characters and incidents portrayed in it are the work of the author's imagination. Any resemblance to actual persons, living or dead is entirely coincidental.

For my family....you know who you are!

Prologue

The ancient ring of stones cast long shadows across the grass as the sun dipped behind the mound. As the sun disappeared a final ray caught the top of the central stone, highlighting the runes and the deeply engraved snake.

As darkness settled the snake writhed and stretched around the stone, searching once more. Tonight felt different and the snake slunk down excitedly to the base of the stone its tongue flicking in and out, tasting the air. Mist gently oozed from the snake's mouth and curled around the stones, seeking the source of power the snake could sense, the gentle thump, thump of a beating heart.

The mist gradually spread out encasing the valley in a deep grey fog. White fingers formed and stretched out seeking the source. When it reached the hospital, the tendrils swirled up a drainpipe and slipped into an open window.

The new born baby lay tucked up tight against his sleeping mother's side. The mist swept across the floor, seeking the tiny heart beat that thrummed in the air. As it reached the bed it snaked up the covers and gently stroked the baby boy's cheek. His eyes flickered open and he let out a small cry. The mist recoiled hissing with pleasure and slunk back through the open window, back through the valley to the sleeping granite stones. As the mist seeped back into the central stone the runes on the top most edge started to glow.

Finally, after a thousand years the curse had been triggered. The gate could now open and Hel could break loose from her bonds and seek revenge on those who had sought to contain her in the Underworld. A deep chuckle sounded from within the depths of the ground and the runes burned brighter, a beacon to those who had been waiting in the shadows for a millennium. It had begun....

*

A hand curled around the door to the maternity ward and a pale face peered around the edge. Loki muttered a spell under his breath and the mother sighed deeply and turned over on her side in a deep sleep. He waited a moment and then approached the edge of the crib where a baby was sleeping peacefully.

"Ew gross," he sneered, curling his lip up into a grimace. "Looks puny, nothing like his father," he whispered, to his companion.

"He'll grow," he replied.

"Not if I can help it and there's nothing my darling brother can do about it."

Loki grasped the edge of the blanket and moved it across the baby's face, brushing his cheek with his finger.

Suddenly a flash of bright white light burst from the crib and flung Loki back slamming him into the wall.

"What the...?" he spluttered.

His companion sniggered. "Loki, your hair is smoking."

Loki cast him a murderous look and pushed himself off the floor. "Sneaky devil. He's protected the little rat. Magnus, you try."

"Seriously? Look I'm your right-hand man but I like my hair, I'm not going anywhere near it."

"Do it, or you'll have more to worry about than your hair."

"Loki seriously, look in the mirror, he nearly killed you."

"I'm immortal you moron, I am a god, a son of Odin. I am

invincible."

"Exactly. I'm not."

Loki grabbed the smaller man by his neck and held him up in the air.

"Do it...now...or you'll be paying an early visit to my daughter in Hel," he snarled.

"I can't breathe..okay..okay..put me down," Magnus wheezed.

Loki flung him forward towards the crib. "Quickly, before someone comes."

Magnus gingerly poked the baby's cheek and jumped back.

"Come on, it's fine," hissed Loki.

"It tingled," Magnus whined, rubbing his index finger.

"Man up, at least it didn't fry you. Go on...kill it. We need to get out of here."

Magnus crept towards the crib again. "It's awake...I can't do it when he's looking at me."

"Oh, for Odin's sake, just cover the face, then it won't be looking at you." Loki threw his arms into the air in despair.

"Look he's staring right at me. He knows," Magnus whispered out of the side of his mouth.

"He won't care in a minute if you just get on with it," Loki hissed, in his ear.

Magnus reached down into the crib and the baby waved his arm up into the air and grabbed Magnus's little finger.

"Ah he's cute you know, look at that. Strong little begger."

"For the love of Odin kill him," Loki screeched.

The sudden shout startled the baby and he started to cry loudly.

"I'm out of here," muttered Magnus, as he scooped up the

baby.

He tucked him inside his heavy coat and ran towards the door.

A concerned looking midwife bumped into him as he flung the door open.

"What?...What are you doing in here?" she shouted, angrily.

"Loki....do your thing quick. I'll sort this out later," said Magnus, pointing inside his coat and sidling out of the door.

Loki took in a deep breath and raised his eyes to the ceiling.

"I seriously, seriously hate humans," he hissed, between clenched teeth.

"Come here then love," he said, flinging his arm over the midwife's shoulder and drawing her closer to him.

He turned her so she was facing him eye to eye.

"Now then, there's nothing to see here is there? The baby in this room went home with his mother today and you forgot to do the paperwork. Best get on with it now eh love, and then you won't get into any trouble? Go on then, off you go and sort it out," Loki murmured, softy into her ear.

"What the hell are you talking about?" she asked, pushing away from him.

"Er that's not meant to happen," he said confused, gripping her head in both hands and staring into her eyes.

She was wearing contact lenses.

"Get off me you weirdo," she screamed, kicking his knee hard.

"Seriously? Did you just seriously kick me? You sniveling excuse for a human, you dare touch me?"

"Let me go," she screamed, twisting her head away from his powerful grip.

"Fine, we could have done this the easy way. You could have done what you were told, gone home, had a nice cup of tea, tucked your kiddies up in bed. But no, you have to be difficult, like my day hasn't been bad enough. Oh, I'm done."

Loki twisted her neck in one swift motion and there was a sickening crunching noise. She slumped to the floor in a heap.

"Well that didn't quite go to plan," he murmured to himself.

He stood up smoothly, straightened his hair and then his jacket and cruised out of the door humming softly to himself.

*

Magnus sat in his car and plucked the baby out from inside his coat.

"So, you're the one eh little man?"

The baby gazed up at him with big blue eyes and reached up with his hand to grab Magnus's finger.

"I reckon your uncle is just a weeny bit jealous of you. Well he can stick his immortal godliness up his you know what," he whispered, stroking the baby's cheek.

"Reckon it's time for us little folk to show them what's what eh? Come on littleun, time to get you somewhere safe."

Magnus placed the baby in the foot well of the front seat and tucked the blanket firmly around him.

"For such a little one you sure stink," he mumbled to himself, making a note to stop off and get some necessary baby items....

Chapter One

Eighteen years later

9.10 a.m. Monday 21st June

The sound of a mobile phone vibrating under his pillow made Alex turn over in bed. He reached under the pillow and put the phone to his ear and grunted into the receiver.

"Dude, where are you? We're about to go, your gonna miss the coach man."

"What? Who is this?" Alex fumbled with his phone, looking at the screen to see the caller ID.

"Matt? What's up? It's way early," he said, sleepily.

"Dude its gone nine o'clock and Franklin is really freakin' out, you better get your butt over here quick," said Matt.

The phone cut off and Alex looked over at the clock by his bed.

"Dammit."

He swung his legs out of bed, grabbed the jeans and t-shirt he had worn the day before then ran down the stairs and out of the front door. He tore open the garage door and swung his leg over his bike and peddled frantically down the road. It was at times like this he wished he had the money to buy himself a car or come to think about it had even passed his driving test.

Dark clouds gathered overhead as he darted between cars and a rumble of thunder echoed over the valley.

"You friggin' kidding me?" he yelled, as he glanced up at the rain cloud.

A flash of lightning lit up the sky and the thunder crashed closer. A raven swooped towards his head making him duck towards his handlebars and he swerved to a sudden stop.

"What the hell?" he cried.

Lightning lit up the sky again and the sharp smell of sulphur filled his nose. His phone buzzed in his pocket and he grasped it to his ear.

"Come on man, they're loading the coach, where are you?" said Matt, worried.

"Two minutes, delay them, I'm nearly there," gasped Alex, breathlessly.

He gripped the handlebars and pushed off towards the school. The coach doors closed just as Alex tore into the car park.

"Hey wait up," he shouted, chaining his bike to the rails.

The coach pulled up next to him and his history teacher Miss Franklin stood in the stairwell glaring at him. The door hissed open and Alex stumbled in pushing past Miss Franklin.

"Alex Thornson, that's the third time this term you have been late, I appreciate you need your beauty sleep, but...."

"Yeah whatever," he growled, making his way to the back of the coach where Matt was sitting.

It was easy to spot him, he was the second tallest in the class and he had jet-black short wavy hair which stuck up uncontrollably.

"Oh no sunshine you're sitting up at the front with me," she smiled, pointing to the seat next to her by the window.

Alex stopped in his tracks and swung round, his blue eyes shooting daggers at her. Thunder crashed overhead and everyone ducked in their seats. Alex sneered and flung himself into the seat by the door. This day really had not started very well.

It was at this point he noticed his t-shirt really didn't smell too good and he had left the house without showering or brushing his teeth. He looked and felt gross and to top it all he was starving and needed coffee. Thunder crashed overhead again as his black mood settled in for the day.

*

Two hours later they arrived in the city and pulled up in the coach park of the museum. Alex was the first off and stood by the door waiting for Matt. He glanced up and Sasha Piper tottered down the steps; her skirt rolled up so high she looked like she was wearing a black belt.

"Hey Alex, are you going to give a lady a hand?" she asked, looking down at him and pouting prettily.

Alex sighed. This day really wasn't getting any better. He was sick to death of Sasha always hanging around him. Over the last two weeks he had noticed every time he turned around she was there watching him.

He wandered towards the rear of the coach trying to catch Matt's eye. As he glanced up he caught the eye of Becca Rodgers instead. Now he wouldn't have minded helping her off the coach. She looked past him as he gave a weak lame wave and tossed her long dark hair over her shoulder.

Alex groaned to himself. "Please tell me that did not just happen."

"Dude it happened, she completely blew you out," Matt sniggered in his ear. "Sasha's waiting for you lover boy, she told Franklin you wanted to be her partner for the day."

"Seriously? The chick's a stalker, this isn't funny anymore," cried Alex exasperated.

"She's the hottest chick in the year and you don't want to know. Man, you're weird. At least put in a good word for me," laughed Matt, punching him lightly on the arm.

"I can't stand her, she's so thick if I asked her for a penny for her thoughts I'd get change back. Nah she's all yours," sneered Alex, walking off.

Becca jumped off the coach and surreptitiously glanced over to where Alex was talking to Matt. She had blown it, what was the matter with her? As soon as she had seen he was looking at her, she had quickly looked past him completely embarrassed. She just couldn't deal with him. He was sheer perfection. Tall, blonde tousled hair, icy blue eyes and muscles everywhere, even in places she had no right looking. He looked her way again and she plucked her phone out of her pocket and selected some music. Plugging in her earphones and tucking her long hair behind her ear she turned her back on him and followed the others who were making their way to the museum entrance.

"Face it man, she's icy, I would rather date Sasha any day," laughed Matt.

"Yeah well you can have her," Alex muttered, following the back of Becca and admiring her long legs.

"Roll call," shouted Miss Franklin, waving her clipboard in the air.

As she called out names Alex scratched the back of his neck. He just couldn't shake the feeling someone was watching them. He peered around the car park and caught Sasha's eye.

"Damn it," he muttered, looking down at his shoes.

She wandered over to him and squeezed his arm.

"Alex darling we're buddies today, make sure you behave yourself, I don't want people talking," she said smiling, showing off her perfect white teeth.

"Trust me Sasha you couldn't be safer. Perhaps you would prefer to partner Matt today if you're worried," he said, shaking her off his arm.

"Oh no sweetie, we're going to get on just fine. I've been so looking forward to getting to know you better," she giggled into her hand.

Alex rolled his eyes towards the sky and saw a big black bird circling overhead.

"Weird," he muttered to himself. "What is it with birds today?" He stalked off towards the entrance in a foul mood and a rumble of thunder sounded in the distance.

The group of students entered the foyer and Miss Franklin handed out work sheets.

"Okay class, you've one hour to complete the sheets. Stick to your buddies and don't go outside," she warned.

"Right where's the cafe?" asked Alex, looking at the map.

"Cool let's get a coffee and chat," said Sasha brightly, looping her arm through his.

"No, I'm starving, oh and by the way I haven't showered or brushed my teeth today so you might want to give me some room," he said, moodily.

"Ew gross....wait, you're kidding aren't you?" asked Sasha.

"Nope, that smell is one hundred per cent pure sweaty male," he said, grinning.

"Oh my god, you're so gross. Don't you know how to take care of yourself?" she asked, with raised eyebrows.

"I'm outta here," muttered Alex, pushing her away firmly. He strode off following the signs to the cafe.

"Alex wait up," called Matt. He jogged up with Becca tagging along behind.

"You two buddies today?" asked Alex.

"Yep, wanna swap?" asked Matt, hopefully.

"Too right," Alex grinned.

"Nah better not, we don't want Frankie getting all tetchy and I don't think Sasha would be too pleased," Matt grinned back.

"You sir are no friend of mine," Alex shook Matt's arm off his shoulder and headed off quickly towards the cafe.

"Okay, okay, we'll hang out together. Man, you're in a bad mood. What is it?" asked Matt.

"Dunno, didn't sleep well and I just feel really weird today. I want to explode, I'm so wound up," said Alex, running his hand through his hair.

"Save it dude, let's get some munchies into you and then you'll feel a whole new man," said Matt, grabbing Alex in a headlock and pushing him along the corridor towards the cafe.

*

"So, Becca isn't it?" asked Sasha, hooking her arm through Becca's.

"Sasha I've been in your class the whole year, you know my name," said Becca, annoyed.

"Sorry I've been distracted, oh my god he's such a hunk," she giggled into Becca's ear. "What do you think he would look like with his shirt off?"

"Er semi naked? Sasha I really don't think he's into you," said Becca.

"Oh, so you're after him are you?" asked Sasha, unhooking her arm.

"No, no I'm not, look just forget I said that, of course he must be into you, half the school are," Becca laughed.

"Ladies, come on our table awaits," Matt called over opening the door to the cafe.

*

Alex tucked into his all-day breakfast feast with relish, stopping occasionally to gulp down some coffee.

"Alex, you're a pig, slow down or you'll give yourself heartburn," Sasha whined, stirring more sugar into her coffee.

"I could eat a horse," he said, with a full mouth.

"You probably are," said Becca, eyeing up his sausages dubiously.

"Right what's first?" asked Matt, plucking the crumpled worksheet out of his bag.

"What are we even here for?" asked Sasha, studying her nails.

"Vikings," said Becca. "They found a new burial barrow and the contents are amazing, fully preserved pots, helmets, swords, coins, jewelry, that type of thing."

"Old pots, great, that's an hour of my life I'm never going to get back," moaned Sasha, looking into her pocket mirror and touching up her lipstick.

Alex glanced up at Becca as he scooped the last bit of egg into his mouth and grimaced as egg dribbled down his chin. Not cool, he thought and he quickly wiped it away with the back of his hand. She reached over and passed him a paper napkin. He was really regretting not taking that shower now. At least he managed to grab some mints from the counter and he popped one into his mouth.

"Okay, I'm done let's roll folks," said Alex, rolling his shoulders and stretching. "Ah I feel human again."

The sudden loud cawing of a bird made them all jump and look toward the window.

"Is it my imagination or is that bird looking at us weirdly?" asked Alex, standing up and backing away from the table.

"Define weirdly?" asked Matt, tapping on the window and making the bird hop off the window ledge.

"Hey leave him," said Sasha.

"Forget it, this is just a really weird day," said Alex, walking over to the door.

"Okay we need to take the stairs to the left and head to the right," said Becca, looking at the map.

"Lead the way milady," Matt opened the door and bowed.

Chapter Two

They all trooped up the stairs checking their phones for any missed text messages.

"Oh my god, my legs ache, don't they have any lifts in here?" asked Sasha.

"Exercise...you should try it sometime, might do you some good," said Alex, who had bounded to the top of the stairs and grinned down on them.

"Dude where do you get your energy from? I'm gonna need my inhaler in a mo," wheezed Matt, as he climbed the final stair and bent over double trying to catch his breath.

"All in the genes my dear friend, all in the genes," laughed Alex.

"You don't even know what genes you have. Bet your dad was a puny little dude who always got picked on and your mama was a big hairy wrestler who bullied him into marrying her," said Matt, dodging out of the way as Alex swung a playful punch in his direction.

"Yeah, then they abandoned me when I was a baby cos they knew I would be way too awesome for them to bring up. I would just show them up," said Alex, grabbing Matt's arm and twisting it playfully behind his back.

"Wait are you an orphan?" asked Becca, her eyebrows raised in surprise. "I didn't know that."

"No, I'm not an orphan, to be an orphan means your parents are dead. My parents are out there somewhere, but where is anyone's guess, their loss I reckon," he shrugged his shoulders and wandered off down the corridor.

"Totally, anyway your new foster mum is well hot," said

Matt, grinning.

"Matt that's so gross shut up," Alex smacked him on the back of the head and stalked off.

"Guys come on we don't have long, the room is right here," said Becca.

She led them off to the right and headed into a dimly lit room.

A red velvet cordon kept the public away from the main exhibition in the middle of the room, which was a reconstructed Viking burial, complete with the remains of a long ship and a discoloured skeleton gripping a long rusty sword. Arrows directed them to go around clockwise so they went the opposite way.

"Oh my god this is so lame, it's like just a boat and some old pots," Sasha moaned. "Ew, that's a dead body," she grimaced, pointing to the skeleton.

"How embarrassing for him," said Becca, looking at the skeleton sadly.

"Yeah bet he never thought he would become the centre piece of a display," said Matt. "It's not very respectful, is it? There he was all tucked up safe underground in his boat and the next he's got all his bits on display."

"It's a fake you moron," said Alex, laughing. "They're just trying to show you what it would look like. It's just plastic."

He shook his head and left them debating as to whether the skeleton was real or fake and wandered over to a small glass display case in the corner of the room. He felt drawn to it for some reason and his ears started to buzz drowning out their arguing. He shook his head to clear it and scanned the questions on the worksheet in his hand. It was very dark in the room and there was a crackly recording of someone chanting in a language he didn't recognise. He held the sheet up to the light in the case so he could read it.

"Copy the runes on the gold torc and the translation provided," he read out loud.

"We could have like Googled this and stayed in the cafe," muttered Matt, over Alex's shoulder.

"Hey this is cool, just think some guy was wearing this over a thousand years ago. This is hard core old, bet it has a few stories to tell," said Alex.

"Yeah, like how many poor kids have to stare at it and write down useless crap," said Sasha, over Alex's other shoulder.

"Do you reckon it belonged to the dead guy over there?" asked Matt.

"You write and I'll read it out," said Alex, irritably.

The bright light from the cabinet was making his eyes hurt and he felt the burning need to get out of the room and into some fresh air. The repetitive chanting was getting on his nerves now.

Alex studied the torc closely and he could clearly see the runes etched deeply into the gold. They seemed to stand out to him and glowed a dim yellow. His eyes glazed over and he intoned in a low voice.

"When day becomes night and the sword of Tyrfing is wielded by the last-born son of Porr, Hel shall be cast down and will no longer be able to wreak havoc ever again."

The lights in the room flickered off and on and an icy blast of air washed over them.

"Brrr okay that's creepy," said Matt, nervously looking

around.

"It's just the air con regulating. They need to keep the artifacts at a certain temperature," said Becca, peering into the glass case.

"Alex what were you reading? This card doesn't say anything about a sword," she said, looking at the notes she had just scribbled down.

Alex shook his head, he felt sick and dizzy and his legs felt wobbly.

"What are you on about? I just read it out," he said, looking closely at the torc. The light had stopped reflecting off the runes and Alex could barely make out the scratching's engraved in the gold.

"Hmm that's weird," he said, glancing at the card pinned next to the torc.

The inscribed torc remains the subject of a considerable amount of academic interest. There are a number of theories as to the origin, the most prevalent being that the torc contains a prophecy and belonged to a Volva (Nordic term for a witch) who practiced Seidr (magic) in the 9th century a.d.

The actual translation is impossible to complete but academics have identified the runes for the words

"When day....night", "....last born son of Porr" and "Hel...havoc".

Porr is one of the names given to the Norse god Thor and Hel is the goddess who rules over Helheim, the underworld.

Alex grabbed Becca's notebook and read what she had written.

"Well I guess I got carried away and filled in the blanks," he said, jokingly making his way to the door.

He had no idea what had just happened and was keen to get out of the room.

"Hold up, we haven't finished the rest of the sheet yet," said Becca, who was making her way over to the other side of the room where there was the partial remains of a Viking helmet and iron cauldron in a dimly lit display case.

"I'm done, come on let's get out of here, we can Google the rest on the coach," said Alex, over his shoulder as he walked out of the room.

"Wait up, I'm coming," called Matt, as he stuffed his worksheet back into his bag. "Girls you coming or what?" he added.

"Might as well, this room is well creepy. I hate museums, they smell funny," said Sasha, tossing her bag over her shoulder.

The four students made their way back to the entrance to the museum and joined some of the others from their class.

"Hey Sasha," called over Pete Parsons. Alex looked over to see a slim, short boy with curly back hair and glasses waving at Sasha.

"You're coming tonight right? I'll meet you by the gate at eleven thirty," he said, winking.

"Oh my god I totally forgot. You guys just have to come," she cried excitedly, grabbing Alex and Matt by the arm.

"You too Becca," she added. "This is going to be awesome," she said, jumping up and down on the balls of her feet.

"What's going on tonight?" asked Alex, moving back warily out of Sasha's reach.

"Like Pete heard old man Withers talking to Miss Franklin about a ceremony or something going on tonight at the henge. It's like super-secret or something and he told her to bring the myrrh oil. They are so going to have a sex party or something. A bunch of us are going up there to record them," she said, grinning.

"Are you serious? Old man Withers? What is this some sort of Scooby Doo movie? They are not going to get away with it cos of us pesky kids," laughed Matt.

"Who the hell says things like that, eh Daphne?" he asked.

"He's the creepy school janitor, the name fits perfectly thank you ....Shaggy," she retorted.

"Nah, I'm more of a Fred, the cool one," replied Matt, smoothing back his hair with both of his hands.

"Stop goofing around you two, what henge are you on about?" asked Alex.

"You haven't been to the henge? Seriously?" asked Becca.

"Obviously, if I have no idea what you're on about," said Alex irritably. He hated feeling like an outsider. He had been living with his current foster family for a couple of weeks and had yet to explore the surrounding countryside.

"You've been at our school for like a year now," said Sasha. "How can you not have seen the henge?"

"Where is it?" he asked.

"Lokson's valley, this side of the river. You've been living over the other side so I'm not surprised you haven't come across it," said Matt.

"This sad boy doesn't get out much. He's pretty good at Minecraft though, made a whole town and everything...super geek!" said Matt, ducking the punch Alex aimed in his direction.

"Minecraft is cool, I've got my own server and everything," said Becca, shyly.

"Shut up," said Sasha waving her arms around.

"This is like Geekville, get me outta here," she moaned.

"Seriously? What's your avatar name?" asked Alex, turning his back to Sasha.

"Darkangelxx1," said Becca, gigging nervously.

"No way, you're Darkangel? That is so awesome, you totally trashed Hellxboys house."

"Oh my god you saw that? He was totally stalking me, creepy kid. What's your avatar?" asked Becca, excitedly.

"Guys you can out geek each other later, are you coming tonight or what? Pete's snagged some beers from his dad's fridge, we can have a bit of a party," asked Sasha.

"Yeah sure why not?" said Alex, looking at Becca out of the corner of his eye.

"You're coming too right?" he asked.

"Sure, could be fun," she answered, shyly.

"Most excellent, dudes," cried Matt, looping his arms over Alex and Becca's shoulders.

"And I'm the geek? Someone's been watching too much Bill and Ted," laughed Alex, as he made his way out of the museum towards the coach.

He was glad to be out in the fresh air and he raised his head to the sky, which was now bright blue with a smattering of wispy clouds. He felt great and took a deep breath. Finally, a date with Becca. Okay Sasha would be there too but he was sure Matt could work his charms and win her over.

Chapter Three

Alex glanced at the clock on his bedside table; it was a quarter past eleven. He took a last look at himself in the mirror. Yep looking good, he thought to himself. You couldn't go wrong with jeans and a plain white t-shirt. The t-shirt clung to his broad chest and he flexed his muscles. He had no idea why he had such a good physique. He rarely went to the gym. "Oh yeah, I'm just a freakin' god," he said peering into the mirror and ruffling up his hair.
His phone buzzed in his pocket. Must be Matt, he thought to himself.

"Hello, this is the God of Awesomeness speaking, mister, I have totally got a better six pack than you," Alex answered, still playing with his hair in the mirror.

"Er, Alex?" asked a female voice.

"What the...?" Alex stammered, looking closely at the caller ID.

Unknown number was displayed.

"Alex is that you? It's Becca."

Alex swore quietly to himself and butted his head against the mirror.

"Hey Becca, sorry about that, I thought it was Matt," he said, wincing.

"Well I should hope so, I know I've put on some weight but I don't have a six pack," she laughed.

"What's up, are you still on for tonight?" Alex asked, looking at his watch.

"Sure, I was just wondering if you still were and if you could meet me at my house? It's a bit dark out there and I don't want to walk there on my own," she replied.

Alex cursed his stupidity, of course he should have thought of that himself.

"Of course, are you ready? I'll swing by now," he said.

"Yep, I'm good to go. It's the house on the corner of Eddington Road, number 42."

"Cool I'll be there in a sec." Alex hung up the phone and collapsed onto his bed.

What an idiot, he thought to himself covering his face with his hands. He rubbed his eyes, sat up and grabbed his leather jacket from the hook on the back of his door. He paused on the landing checking to see if he could hear anything from his foster parent's bedroom. All was quiet and he slipped down the stairs and carefully shut the front door behind him. He looked up at the sky. It was a clear night and hundreds of stars winked down on him. He took a deep breath, messed up his hair a final time tucked his hands into the pockets of his jeans and strode off in the direction of Becca's house.

She was waiting on the corner, looking about nervously.

"Quick, let's get out of here. My mum will kill me if she finds out," she said, walking off down the road before he had even reached her.

"I think she's asleep but I didn't check, I just snuck out," she whispered, looking towards the top front window of her house.

"Where are we meeting the others?" Alex asked, as he jogged up behind her.

"By the main entrance to the henge. There's a wooden gate, we'll have to climb over it," she replied, walking quickly.

"This should be interesting, bet Sasha's wearing a skirt and heels," Alex laughed.

"You do know it's all an act? She's actually really intelligent and aces all her subjects," said Becca.

"Really? Why the blonde bimbo act then?" asked Alex.

"She can't bear the thought of people thinking she's a geek. She wants to be one of the popular ones, all made up, wearing the latest fashion, you know what I mean?" she said.

"Yeah you get a gang of them in every school, along with the nerds, geeks, nearly popular ones and the normals," said Alex, crossing over the road.

"So, what are you then?" asked Becca, looking at Alex sideways.

She was jogging now to keep up with his long stride.

"Ha, I said it earlier, I am the God of Awesomeness, I don't fit into any category, I make my own," he laughed, winking at Becca.

"Yeah right," Becca giggled, brushing against his arm and pushing him off the path.

"Anyway, what's tonight all about?" asked Alex, wishing he had the courage to take Becca's hand.

He was pretty sure she was into him but he didn't want to make a move too early until he was sure.

"Well it's the summer solstice tonight, I Googled it earlier. I guess it has something to do with that. Probably some druid ritual," said Becca.

"Yeah where they sacrifice a new born baby and drink its blood, mwah ha haaaa," Alex laughed.

"I think Sasha wants to catch Miss Franklin in a compromising position. These pagan rights normally get a bit you know...." Becca said, nudging Alex on the arm again.

Alex grinned "We have so got to get this on video and put it on Instagram."

"No way, we would get expelled," said Becca, shaking her head.

"Been there seen it done it, never got the year book as I never managed to make it to the end of the year."

"Really?" I thought you were the God of Awesomeness, you know Mister Perfect?" she laughed.

"That's right, too awesome to be told what to do. Let's just say I had a few issues growing up."

"You over that now then?" she asked.

"I think my last foster family would say no...I still have a few issues," he said, shrugging his shoulders.

"What did you do?" she asked, looking at him curiously.

He didn't look like a troublemaker.

"I have a bit of a sleep walking problem."

"They kicked you out because you slept walked?" she asked, incredulous.

"Well it was a bit more than that. The last time when they found me my feet were covered in blood and I had a kitchen knife in my hand,"

"Crikey, where were you?"

"In the baby's room looking in the crib,"

Becca stopped in her tracks looking horrified.

"Nah just kidding," Alex laughed, holding up his hands.

"Thank god, you had me going there, that's not funny," she said, relieved.

"I did sleepwalk a lot, I just don't think they could handle having a moody teenager in the house anymore. Anyway, they called in social services, said it wasn't working and I got moved onto the Bakers. Pretty lucky they're more or less in the same area. Let's just say I've been around." Alex sighed. He really hoped he didn't mess up this time. Though creeping around the woods with a young, pretty girl wasn't going to get him any points. He grinned wryly to himself and looked up into the distance. He hadn't realised they had walked so far. They were following a grassy path running between dense overhanging trees. Luckily there was a pretty full moon so they could see where they were going easily.

"Really glad you picked me up. I'm not sure about this now. It's a bit creepy," said Becca, sidling closer to Alex.

"Hey don't worry, my godlike powers of awesomeness will protect you," he grinned.

They came to a wooden gate at the end of the path and looked around for the others.

"What's the time?" asked Becca.

Alex looked at his watch. "Eleven thirty, they should be here by now."

The sound of someone giggling made Alex look up and peer into the bushes.

"Dudes if you're going to jump out on us, you need to be a bit more ninja than that," called out Alex.

"Sasha, you're so lame. That would've been so funny," moaned Matt from behind a tree.

"I couldn't help it sorry. I think it's nervous laughter. I'm really not sure we should be here now," said Sasha, emerging from behind a large leafy bush.

"Where's Pete?" asked Alex, looking around.

"Behind you," whispered a gravelly voice in Alex's ear.

Alex jumped and whipped around, grabbing Pete by the

throat.

"Hey man easy there, it's only me," Pete gasped trying to prise loose from Alex's steely hold on his neck.

Alex released his hold and Pete bent over double coughing and spluttering. When he recovered, he stood up and pushed his glasses back up his nose.

"Dude it's not cool to creep up on someone," Alex hissed, between his teeth.

He was feeling really edgy for some reason and was starting to think he shouldn't have bothered. Especially when he looked over at Becca, Matt and Sasha who were struggling not to laugh.

"Grow up all of you," he growled, marching over to the gate.

He put one foot on the first strut and leaped nimbly over.

"Ooh touchy. Come on give us a hand. Some of us need to brush up on our ninja skills as you so kindly pointed out," said Sasha, grinning.

Alex helped the others over the gate and peered into the gloom.

"Where is everyone else? I thought you said there were others coming from our class?" Alex asked Sasha.

"They bottled it, they didn't want to get caught out on a school night," said Sasha.

"So, what's the plan then?" asked Alex.

"Let's get closer to the henge and check out some hiding places. They will be here soon, we don't want them seeing us," Sasha whispered, loudly.

They fell into single file and crept along the path, looking behind them when they heard the slightest noise.

"Christ this is such a Scooby moment," Matt chuckled and poked Alex in the back. "I'm Fred, Sasha's the gorgeous Daphne, Pete's Shaggy..."

"Dude if you say Becca's Velma I'll break your legs," Alex cut in.

"No, she's like Daphne's sister, you're Velma!" laughed Matt.

Alex grabbed Matt in a headlock.

"Hey I could have said you were the dog," Matt laughed, pushing himself out of the headlock.

"Guys, keep it down," hissed Becca. "We're there."

"So, where's the henge? There's just one stone over there?" asked Alex, puzzled.

"There are smaller stones surrounding the central one, they're hidden in the grass," Becca replied looking around cautiously.

"Geez was this built by dwarves or something?" Alex looked very unimpressed and moved forward to take a closer look.

"Ouch," he cried, hopping on one foot.

"Shush," the others all hissed at the same time looking around the clearing.

"Hey I just stubbed my toe on a stone," he moaned.

"Man up dude, come on let's find somewhere to hide. Pete, have you got the beer?" Matt asked.

"Sure do, shall we split up? You and Daph can take that tree over there," Pete said, reaching into his bag and tossing a bottle of beer over to Matt.

"Cheers mate, are you going to open that? It's going to explode," Matt asked, holding the beer gingerly.

"Nah, pleasure is all yours. I'll bunker down over there with Scooby and Daph two," said Pete, as he reached into his rucksack for another beer.

"No let's stick together," said Sasha, moving swiftly to Alex's side and holding onto his arm.

"Alex, you could have picked me up," she pouted prettily, tossing her long blonde hair over her shoulder.

"Well you should have called me like Becca did," Alex muttered irritably, shaking Sasha's arm off and striding over towards the dark bushes on the far side of the clearing.

The others jogged after him and crouched down behind a thick bush.

"Matt move over, I can't see anything," moaned Sasha, elbowing him in the arm.

"Alright keep your hair on," he grumbled, shifting over slightly and peering around the edge of the bush.

"If we get caught, this is going to be so embarrassing. What should we say?" whispered Becca.

Pete grinned, "That's easy, we're checking out the night wild life. Studying the nocturnal habits of the.."

"Shush!" hissed Alex "Someone's coming."

They hunkered down and tried to peek through the dense leaves without making any sound.

"Over there," Alex whispered pointing towards the gate.

He could see the light from several torches flickering between the trees and bushes.

"Nine," he whispered, quietly.

"What?" asked Sasha.

"Keep it down, there are only nine of them. I thought there would be more," Alex replied, parting the leaves of the bush to get a clearer view.

The light of the moon cast long shadows on the grass as the nine people gathered into a close group on the edge of the stone circle. They began pulling items out of rucksacks and carrier bags and they whispered quietly to each other. Each movement was precise and organised, it was obvious to all watching they had been here before. A tall broad-shouldered man swung a heavy looking fur cloak over his shoulders and stood to one side of the group, cocking his head to one side as though he was listening for something or someone. The group stopped their preparations and glanced over at him expectedly.

"Friends it is time," he called out, raising his hands to the sky. "Take your places, midnight is nearly upon us."

Sasha stifled a giggle and Matt put his hand over her mouth glaring at her in warning.

She pulled his hand away and whispered, "It's Mr Ericson, you know, the head of the history department."

The nine people had donned cloaks too, they pulled up their hoods and stood before a ring of burning candles which one of them had placed at the base of each of the outer stones. Mr Ericson stood in front of the big carved monolith in the centre of the ring and placed his hands on either side of the stone.

"Nancy, the oil," he called not taking his eyes off the stone.

Sasha snorted "OMG, look it's Miss Franklin," she whispered, pointing to the woman called Nancy. "Someone video this quick I've got no charge on my phone."

Pete grabbed his phone from his pocket and set it to record.

Nancy moved forward and rotated around the circle

dipping her hand into a bowl and flicking a liquid towards the monolith. She was chanting something in a low, deep voice but Alex couldn't make out any of the words. When Nancy had completed a full circuit, she returned to her place on the outer edge. Suddenly Mr Ericson roared out to the sky.

"Hail bright one of Asgard,
Favourite one, who came to ashes.
You who fled your destiny
Only to see it come true.
Help us bright one, to protect the gateway,
Help Garm and Modgud keep the souls at bay from our world
And be our torch in the darkness."

His voice reverberated across the clearing and the hair on the back of Alex's neck stood up. He shivered and ran his hand over the back of his neck.

Then there was silence.

Alex looked at Becca raising his eyebrows. "Is that it?" he whispered.

"I don't know, I was kind of expecting something a bit more," she whispered back.

The nine people stood silently with their heads bowed and hands clasped in front of them as though they were deep in prayer. Suddenly, a massive cracking sound came from deep within the circle and the ground trembled.

"What in Odin?" cried Mr Ericson, losing his balance and falling to his knees.

A white mist hissed from a crack in the ground by the

central stone and snaked up the side of the monolith. It oozed into the deep carvings making the runes stand out. The carving of the snake shimmered and started to writhe around the top of the stone.

"Nancy...Nancy... the oil quick," called Mr Ericson, scrambling back on his heels away from the stone.

Nancy looked frantically by her feet. "Alan, it's all gone, it tipped over," she cried.

"Oh Odin help us. Everyone, quickly the prayer of Baldur again, all together. Hold hands," he shouted.

The sound of beating wings echoed from deep under the ground and a cold wind whipped around their ankles. The leaves of the trees rustled fiercely and Alex ducked his head shielding his eyes from the grit that had been blown up into the air.

The nine people held hands around the central stone and shouted out the prayer.

"Hail bright one of Asgard..."

Their words were lost in the wind and their cloaks flapped wildly whipping around their legs. A sudden crack of thunder crashed overhead and a jagged fork of lightning struck the top of the central monolith. The nine were blasted onto their backs and the smell of sulphur filled Alex's nostrils for the second time that day. He coughed several times and staggered to his feet.

"Oh my god they're dead," he shouted, running towards the circle.

He tripped over a stone buried deep in the grass and he sprawled onto his hands and knees.

Alan was lying on his back. He raised his hand to his face

and groaned. "What happened? Hey is everyone okay? Nancy?" Alan croaked, reaching over to his right and gently shaking Nancy's shoulder.

She groaned and rolled over onto her elbow.

"Alan, my eyes, I can't see anything," she whimpered.

"It was the light, just give it a moment," Alan said, gently.

He could barely hear her through the persistent hum in his head. He either had tinnitus or they were about to be attacked by a swarm of bees he thought to himself as he raised himself gingerly to his feet and looked around warily. Suddenly he winced in pain. He reached under his shirt and pulled out the amulet, which was strung, around his neck. The amulet was burning his skin. He held it away from his chest and it glowed a deep pulsing yellow.

"What the?" he cried, looking around at Nancy.

"Check your torshammere quickly," Alan shouted.

The others already had their amulets in their hands, they had all been burned and all of the amulets were glowing a bright yellow.

"Alan, what is happening?" Nancy asked, holding onto Alan's arm.

He drew her protectively towards his chest.

"I don't know," he said, looking worried.

Alex stood up slowly wiping mud from his hands onto his jeans.

"Who's there?" called Alan, peering into the darkness towards Alex.

Alex started to move forward when suddenly the amulet in Alan's hand flew towards Alex and slammed into his chest. Alex was flung onto his back by the force, a fierce burning engulfed his chest and he struggled to breathe. His eyes flickered and he slipped into unconsciousness.

*

The mist curled around Alex's prone form and tendrils broke off and snaked towards the village as though they were searching for something....

Chapter Four

"Alex....Alex...can you hear me?" said Alan, as he gently shook Alex's shoulder.

Alex groaned and rubbed his hand on his chest. He felt like he had been hit by a ton of bricks.

"What happened?" he asked, groggily. "Where am I?" he looked around puzzled.

He was lying on top of a bed with crisp white sheets in a room with plain white walls. The only other furniture in the room was a chair by the side of the bed. Alan was sitting in it looking at Alex with a worried expression on his face.

"Is this a hospital?" Alex asked, sitting up slowly and swinging his legs over the side of the bed.

He winced as he felt a muscle pull tightly in his chest.

"Agh, my chest," he said looking down and rubbing his hand over a red raised lump in the middle of his chest bone.

"What's that, it stings? Hang on where has my shirt gone? What's going on around here?" he asked, looking around confused.

"Alex you've been unconscious for hours, you've had us really worried. We're in York at our headquarters we...."

"York? That's like two hours away," Alex cut in.

"Yes, well we couldn't have people asking questions about what happened to you. We have a great medical facility here, you have been in good hands, don't worry. It's probably best if we go join the others now if you're up to it, we have a lot to discuss. You can clean up through there," he said, standing up wearily and nodding towards a door on the right.

"We found some clothes which should fit you, they're in

the bathroom. When you're done come and join us, we'll be in the room at the end of the corridor," said Alan.

Alan left Alex alone and Alex opened the door, which Alan had indicated. It was a bathroom. He stripped off his dirty jeans and turned on the shower. Standing under the powerful hot stream was bliss and he sighed deeply running his hands through his hair.

When he was clean he stepped out of the shower and wiped the steam off the mirror. He took in his reflection and he thought he didn't look too bad considering he had been knocked unconscious. His eyes drifted to his chest to the red mark, which was irritating him. It was shaped like an upside-down anchor and throbbed constantly.

"Weird," he muttered, to himself.

He grabbed the green combat trousers he found sitting on the side and pulled a dark t-shirt on over his head. Alex left the room and made his way along the corridor to a door at the end. He opened it a crack and peered around the edge.

"Great you're ready come in, come in," said Alan, coming over to the door and opening it fully.

Matt, Becca and Sasha were seated on a comfy looking leather sofa and they all jumped up as soon as Alex entered.

"Oh my god, you're okay," cried Sasha, crossing the room in two strides and flinging her arms around his neck.

"We thought you were in a coma or something, it's been hours," she sobbed into his neck.

"I'm fine guys, just a bit of a sore chest," he said, rubbing his hand over the red mark.

"Welcome back buddy," said Matt, walking over and punching him on the arm gently.

"Come on, sit down, we have a lot to discuss and I'm sure you're eager for answers," said Alan, sitting himself down behind the large desk in the centre of the room.

Miss Franklin, or Nancy as they now knew she was called, hovered to the right of him leafing through a large book. She looked up at Alex and smiled.

"Good to see you awake, you really had us worried there," she said, closing the book and taking a seat to the side of Alan.

"Can someone please explain what is going on? The last I remember is the henge being struck by lightning," said Alex, sitting on the sofa next to Becca.

She smiled up at him, reached over and squeezed his hand. Alex felt his stomach dip and he smiled back squeezing her hand gently.

"This is going to be really hard to explain. I need you all to keep an open mind," said Alan.

"Hang on, I should really call my foster family, they're going to be really worried and you guys, have you been here the whole time?" Alex asked, looking at his three friends.

"That's all been taken care of," cut in Nancy. "Your foster father was there at the henge, he's, er, one of us," she said looking sheepish. "He was here earlier to check in on you but he had to get back to the henge to help the others. I just called him to let him know you had come around."

"Seems like all of our parents are involved in some shape or form," said Becca. "Amazing what goes on right under your nose."

"Well perhaps if the youth of today bothered to tear themselves away from their computers and phones once in a while they might notice a bit more," said Alan, testily.

"Yeah good point, we're all ears now though so perhaps you could enlighten us," said Alex, sitting forward on the sofa.

"Okay, let's start at the henge. What you guys saw was a ritual we and our ancestors before us have performed every year for generations and generations. It goes right back to when the Vikings first settled in the area. It's basically a ceremony held each summer solstice where we ask Baldur, son of Odin to help the guardians of Helheim, to contain the dead. Baldur lives down in the underworld and he keeps Hel, his niece in check. Do you know anything about the Norse gods? You must have seen the Avengers films surely?" he asked, looking around.

"Too right, Thor is soooo hot, I love that scene where he takes his top off, he is totally ripped," said Sasha, bouncing up and down on her seat.

"Oh yes," agreed Becca, her eyes shining "Tom Hiddleston as Loki is pretty hot too," she added.

"Can you please stop lusting over a bunch of overpaid actors and let me hear the rest," said Alex, frustrated.

He glared at Becca and released her hand. Becca shrugged apologetically.

"Great well at least you know of some of the gods. They are not fictional by the way, they're very much in the here and now though quite a distance away. Anyway, as I was saying, Baldur helps keep order in Helheim. It's not his job, he does it to wind up his niece," said Alan.

"Sorry you've lost me; Thor and Loki are real? Are you serious? And Helheim is what exactly?" asked Alex, looking thoroughly confused.

"I'm very serious. Helheim is the world where spirits of

people who die of old age, disease or not in battle live. You're probably more familiar with Valhalla, where the spirits of those who die in battle live, where they feast with warriors they have fought in their lives and recount their great battles. Helheim is the opposite, a miserable land where spirits roam trying to find their way back to the living. Hel is the goddess who rules this land but she's not terribly reliable. You see she really doesn't want to be there and thinks it's all a bit unfair."

"So, she's like Hades?" asked Becca.

"You could look at it like that I suppose.....though....never mind, it's all a bit complicated," said Alan, pushing his glasses further up his nose and running his hand through his sparse grey hair. "Anyway, as I was saying, she thinks she has a bit of a raw deal. You see there was a prophecy that her and her siblings would cause great mischief for the gods. She's the daughter of Loki and Angrboda and they had other children, Angrboda gave birth to the wolf Fenrir and a serpent they named Jormungand."

"She gave birth to a wolf and a snake, that's so gross, what is Ang whatever her name is?" asked Matt, horrified.

"Angrboda is a giantess. Gods and giants do not make a good combination and their children basically turn out to be monsters. Their daughter Hel is a girl and she looks relatively normal from her waist upwards. You would think she was a human at a quick glance. She's always miserable though and rarely smiles," said Alan.

"Like my older sister then?" asked Matt, laughing.

Alan ignored him and continued. "The bottom half of her body is a different story; her skin is green and black and her flesh looks like it's rotting off her. She is certainly not the type of girl you would want to take back home to meet your parents," said Alan, chuckling at his attempt at a joke.

He glanced at Alex who was looking like he didn't believe a word he was saying.

"Anyway," Alan continued. "The other gods knew there would be trouble and they asked the Norns to confirm it. They did and so Odin got a hit squad together and sent them to Jotunheimr where the children lived with their mother. They stole the children and brought them back to Odin. He dealt with the serpent first and he threw him into the sea thinking to drown him. He didn't drown though, he just got bigger and bigger as he ate more and more fish. He is so big now he could wrap himself around the Earth."

"Yeah right, if it's that big someone would've seen it by now," said Alex.

"He is careful not to be seen and he doesn't cause us any bother so we just leave him alone. He does pop up every now and then in strange places....Loch Ness for example, that's caused a stir a few times," said Alan, smiling at them.

"What about the others?" asked Becca.

She was fascinated with the story and was sitting on the edge of her seat eagerly.

"Odin dealt with Hel next. He banished her to Niflheim and told her to look after everyone who was sent there. She renamed it Helheim, as it's her world now, but she's a bit upset she can't go back to Asgard. I mean you can't really blame her, being surrounded by dead people for eternity is bound to be a bit depressing. She is constantly trying to escape and return home and she causes all sorts of trouble by encouraging the worst souls, who really annoy her, to escape.

When Odin heard she was doing this he sent Modgud and Garm to provide some protection. Before you ask....wait, I have a picture let me show you."

Alan leafed through the book on his desk and opened the large volume at a double page. The group crowded around the desk to get a good look. On one side of the page there was a picture of a giant woman, standing guard before a bridge with a golden roof.

"That's Modgud," said Alan pointing to the giantess. "She's a Jotnar, a giant from Jotunheimr, one of the Nine Worlds and she guards the Gallarbridge.....the bridge leading to Helheim. She's actually quite decent. Her job is to ask people why they want to cross the bridge and enter Hel. It's a bit lonely down there and it can take days before she will let people pass."

"Yes, she's a bit of a talker," added Nancy.

Alan pointed to the left-hand side of the page. "That's Garm" he was pointing at a picture of a monstrous dog which had multiple eyes and sharp protruding teeth which were dripping with blood and saliva."

"Hmm nice puppy," said Matt, grimacing.

"Garm guards the Gate of Hel. It's a bit of a way beyond the bridge. He's a bit of a mean hound, you don't want to mess with him." Alan closed the book and they sat back down on the sofa again.

"Even with these two guarding the entrances, we've still had some problems, some souls have managed to sneak past Garm and Modgud in the past so Baldur lends a hand maintaining order. He is the only one Odin can trust and he is his favourite son. Loki has always been jealous of him. He couldn't stand it that Odin loved Baldur and even Thor more than himself. He had borne a grudge for centuries and he loathes him. He made it pretty obvious to Baldur but it didn't bother Baldur until the day he and his mother had the same dream. They both dreamt he would die at the hand of his brother Hodr. His mother naturally became anxious and she wanted to protect her son. She made every living thing in the world vow to not hurt him and she asked everything except mistletoe. You see she considered mistletoe to be too young and would not understand. Big mistake. Anyway, Loki somehow found out about this and being the sneaky devil he is he made a spear, which was coated with mistletoe. All of the gods were enjoying a new game of 'let's throw everything at Baldur and see who can hurt him'. They were basically throwing whatever they could find at Baldur and the items kept bouncing off him, he didn't even have a scratch. Loki gave the spear to Baldur's brother Hodr and persuaded him to hit Baldur. It was a bit of a joke as Hodr was blind. The gods were rolling around laughing and Hodr took his shot. Unlucky for Baldur, the spear struck true, whether it was just a lucky shot or if Loki guided the spear we will never know. So, Baldur died of the poisoned spear and as he didn't die in battle he was taken to Helheim. He now takes great pleasure in annoying his niece at every opportunity he can. He was especially annoying after she agreed to release him if every object alive or dead would weep for him. Everything did except the giantess Pokk. It was Loki in disguise. He's not a nice fellow, certainly not someone I would want to cross."

"He's a pig," cut in Sasha.

Alex looked at her with raised eyebrows.

"Well he sounds it, doesn't he?" she asked, shrugging.

"So, what were you doing at the henge then?" asked Becca.

"Our little ceremony gives thanks to Baldur. We remind him he is not forgotten and ask him to help protect the underworld. Tonight was strange though, nothing like that has ever happened before. We normally complete the ceremony and go down the Dog and Duck for a few pints. The noises, the ground shaking and the lightning, well that was new and something we have been trying to figure out. Nancy, did you find anything in the books?" Alan asked, looking over at Nancy.

"Wait a second, you're talking as though this Baldur and Hel are real. They're just myths, you know stuff we learn in primary school to fill out the curriculum," said Alex.

"Actually, they're all real, I know it's a bit much to take in but we're pretty sure you're involved in what happened last night somehow. The torshammere, the mark on your chest and I understand there was an incident in the museum?" said Alan.

"Remember the torc Alex, you went all funny and read out something that wasn't on the card," said Becca.

"Yeah, I remember," he said rubbing his hand through his hair. This was ridiculous but some strange things had been happening recently and he couldn't deny what he saw at the henge.

"So, what has this got to do with me?" he asked.

"Well I haven't managed to find anything in the books so you'll have to ask one of the Volvas," said Nancy.

"Oh dear, I was hoping to avoid that," said Alan, standing up and moving to the window.

"Hang on it said something about a Volva on that card in the museum," said Sasha. "Something about the torc belonging to a Volva or something like that."

"That's right. We know about the torc of course but no one has ever been able to read the runic inscription. The markings have worn down too much. We have our best analysts working on what Alex saw but to be honest I think Nancy is right, you're going to have to speak to a Volva," said Alan.

"Sorry I'm lost, what's a Volva?" asked Matt, looking very confused.

"Best way to describe her would be a seeress. The one we know practices the art of prophecy and she's actually quite good. I should also add she's quite a powerful wand carrier...a witch. You don't really want to get on the wrong side of her," Alan replied.

"And I have to go see the creepy, powerful witch because....?" asked Alex.

"Because you're the one with the torshammere engraved on your chest. She'll want to see that. She will also probably only talk to you about what you saw on the torc. She can be a bit funny sometimes," said Alan.

"Reading between the lines you really mean neurotic, crazy, old bat," said Matt.

"In a nutshell, yes," said Nancy, her eyes twinkling.

"Okay so I need to ask some crazy old witch what happened at the henge and why I have a hammer on my chest? Does that sound crazy to anyone else or is it just me?" asked Alex, as he paced around the room in frustration.

"You got it," said Nancy, rising from her chair and moving

to the door. "I'll make the arrangements," she said, leaving four very confused teenagers in the room.

Becca glanced at Alex's chest. "So, can you show us this magic mark?" she asked raising her eyebrows.

"Ha, of course he will, any chance to show off his abs," snorted Matt.

Alex glared at him, stood up and peeled off his t-shirt. The red hammer was still pulsating red.

"Ooh weird," said Sasha, reaching out her hand to touch it.

"Don't," snapped Alex, stepping out of reach.

"Calm down," she pouted, sitting back down.

"Look we don't know what it is yet. Best leave it alone until we find out more," he said, sitting down again.

Becca was staring at his chest, she couldn't take her eyes off him. How can someone be so perfect? She wondered to herself, feeling very disappointed when he pulled his shirt back on. She was dying to touch his smooth chest.

"So where is this wicked witch?" asked Matt. "Don't tell me, she lives in a cave up a remote creepy mountain."

"Not exactly. Manhattan, New York," said Nancy, coming back into the room carrying a folder.

"Right you're all set, we've booked you on the last flight out of Manchester airport. Your ESTA visas are being sorted now and your passports will be at the desk waiting for you," she said, handing the folder to Sasha.

"What the? That's just not possible, it takes ages to get a Visa doesn't it?" asked Becca. "What about our parents...school? We can't just go running off to New York," she cried.

"Needs must Becca," said Nancy. "What you saw at the

henge has never happened before, something is very wrong, I can feel it and we need to know what is happening."

"Hang on, are we all going?" asked Becca.

"No, Nancy and I are needed here," said Alan, gathering some papers on the desk.

"We can't go to America on our own, we're minors," said Becca, pacing up and down.

"Well that's not strictly true, one of you is now legally an adult," said Nancy, looking through the notes in her hand.

"You what? We're all seventeen," said Matt.

"Alex?" asked Nancy looking over at him.

"Yeah well, I would've said something, it just never came up," he said, sheepishly.

"What?" asked Matt.

"I got held back a year in my previous school. I turned eighteen a week ago," he said.

"And you didn't say anything? Mate that is not cool. We totally missed out on a party there." Matt said, disgruntled.

"It's not a big deal, I didn't want to make a fuss. I'd just been moved to my new home and I told them not to bother," said Alex, shrugging his shoulders.

Suddenly Matt's phone started vibrating in his pocket. Removing it, he looked at the caller ID on the screen.

"It's Pete," he said, putting the phone to his ear.

"Pete? God yeah, I wondered where he was," said Alex.

"He said he had some things to do and would be back," said Sasha.

"Okay mate, calm down, hang on I'll put you on speaker," said Matt, fiddling with his phone.

"Guys I'm freaking out here, there's some really strange

stuff happening," Pete's voice echoed through the receiver.

"What's going on?" asked Sasha, moving closer to the phone.

"People in the town are going nuts, like they're possessed or something. Mr Baker, you know, the school cook? He stabbed Sandy Cooper in the head with a knife. It was sticking out of his head. He just dropped dead in front of everyone. Mr Baker says he can't remember anything. The cops arrested him and took him away. Then there was Brian from the fish and chip shop, he stuck his head in the fat fryer...."

"Oh my god I'm going to be sick," cried Sasha.

"No, it's cool, the fryer wasn't on, he just got like really greasy. Kept saying over and over 'die...die' Skegs was there said it was well creepy. God if that fryer had been on..."

"This is worse than I thought," said Alan, taking his phone from his jacket.

He dialed a number and said urgently into the receiver, "We've got a problem. Yes, the henge, I think we have a breach. Not a full one, the whole world would have known by now if she had escaped. Send your guys in, we need containment fast."

"This all sounds a bit Men in Black," snorted Matt.

"Matt this is serious. Your father heads up the containment team, he could be in a lot of danger if they can't contain the breach quickly enough," said Alan.

"Yeah right, my dad works for the Government, this is crap," said Matt.

"Yes, he works for the Government but he also works for the Asguardians. We have people in many important roles, hence the visas being sorted so quickly. The American ambassador is one of us," said Alan, whilst texting a message to someone.

"Hang on don't Asgardians live in Asgard?" asked Sasha, twirling the end of a long lock of hair around her finger.

Alex looked at her with his mouth open.

"What? It's in the Avengers film," she said, quickly.

"We're the guardians to the secret of Asgard, hence Asguardians. The gods want to keep a low profile; they think it's for the best. Nothing good has ever happened when they meddle with Midgard. That's what they call Earth," explained Alan, when he saw their blank faces.

"Guys...guys...you still there?" echoed Pete's voice down the phone.

"Sorry Pete, look you need to get to Manchester airport, we'll explain when you get there," said Matt, into the phone.

"It's okay if Pete comes isn't it?" he asked, looking at Nancy.

"Of course, he's part of this too, I arranged a ticket," she replied. "Okay guys are you ready? The car is waiting in the basement. I've sorted a bag for each of you with some essentials. You can buy anything else you need on the way," she said, handing an envelope to Becca.

"Cool we get chauffeur driven to the airport," said Sasha, walking out of the door and following Nancy.

"Hang on, I'm starving," said Alex, rubbing his stomach. "Is there any food around here?"

"You can stop off at a service station on the way. We have a canteen here but you really need to get moving or you'll miss your flight," said Alan, ushering them out of the door.

Nancy led them to an elevator and took them down to the

basement car park. An old battered Honda pulled up.

"Er where's the cool black SUV?" asked Matt. "You're a super-secret organisation, you must drive around in blacked out SUVs..."

"Budget cuts," said Nancy. "And who said we were secret?" she smiled, opening the door for Matt.

"Ben, take them to the airport and come straight back, I'll need a ride back home," she said, to the driver.

Ben sighed; this was going to be one long day for him.

Chapter Five

Alex settled into the front seat, laid his head back and closed his eyes. He was feeling very tired and completely confused. What Alan had told him made no sense at all but something deep down told him he was hearing the truth as crazy as it sounded. Real gods, an underworld, monsters, witches, the Asguardians. It was all too much for him to take in. His stomach grumbled loudly and he looked over at Ben. He looked like he was not much older than they were and looked out of place in his ill-fitting black suit and tie in the battered old car.

"I really need to eat something, I haven't had anything for ages," moaned Alex.

"Sure, the Bilbrough services are the closest, I'll pull in there but you'll have to be quick," said Ben, pulling onto the dual carriageway.

Alex turned and looked at the others cramped in the back. Matt looked smug sitting between the two girls.

"So, what do you make of all this?" Alex asked them.

"Totally stark raving bonkers," said Matt, shaking his head. "If I hadn't seen it with my own eyes I would say Miss Franklin was on drugs and that guy Alan needs to see a psychiatrist, he is a complete loony," he added.

"I suppose it would sound rather unbelievable to you if that was the first you had heard of the gods but it's all true, Odin, Thor, Asgard....the whole lot," said Ben. "It's pretty cool really. I haven't met any of them but Alan has."

"So where do you fit into all of this?" asked Alex.

"Alan's my dad," said Ben, looking in the rear-view mirror

at Matt and grinning.

"Awkward," said Matt, under his breath.

Becca dug him in the ribs and Sasha giggled.

"It's okay, I thought he was a loony too when he told me everything about what he did. He took me to meet Lit though and that kind of changed everything," said Ben.

"Who's Lit?" asked Alex. "Another god?"

"No, he's an immortal dwarf. He's the only one who can come out into the light, as he's immortal. All the others would turn to stone if they're exposed to sunlight," said Ben.

"Hang on, now you're telling me there are dwarves who turn to stone in the sun?" asked Matt, leaning forward and resting his elbows on the back of the seats. "Why do they turn to stone?"

"One of them annoyed Odin centuries ago so he got a Volva to place a spell on the entire dwarf race for eternity. He basically banished them underground so he would never have to set eyes on them again," said Ben.

"Wow, that's harsh," said Matt. "What did they do to annoy him so much?"

"A dwarf named Gelgus cut off Odin's beard when he was asleep. He thought it would have magical powers and he wanted to test it to see what it could do," said Ben.

"Odin was furious when he woke up. He is rather proud of his beard you see and he was just left with a few straggly bits. He found Gelgus and fed him to Loki's son, Fenrir the wolf. Then he got the Volva to curse all dwarves so they would turn to stone if they ever came out into the sunlight."

"He sure likes his curses," said Alex.

"He likes power and he likes to be obeyed," said Ben

seriously. "Take my advice, never get on the wrong side of him. Oh, and if you get to meet a dwarf watch yourself with them, they're moody little buggers so be careful. Lit's pretty cool though, he acts as our go between and passes on messages, between the worlds."

"So why is he immortal and the others aren't?" asked Becca, leaning forward too.

"Well he was at Baldur's funeral. I take it you know about him?" he asked, looking into the rearview mirror. The three in the back nodded slowly. "Well he was messing about in front of Thor doing this little death dance ritual. Thor lost it and kicked Lit into the funeral pyre. As Baldur's wife Nanna had also thrown herself into the fire because she was so upset, there was some serious immortal mojo going on in the flames and it made Lit immortal," said Ben.

"I don't get it, if Baldur is a god, then he's immortal surely? How could he have died?" asked Alex.

"They're not immortal, that's a common misconception. They eat golden apples from the orchard of Iduna, the Goddess of Spring. They eat them to preserve their youth. So, you would think they're immortal and to be honest they consider themselves immortal as they will live forever.... providing they keep on eating the apples," said Ben, as he indicated and started to pull over onto the inside lane. "The services are the next exit, we're okay for time at the moment but don't hang about in there," he said, steering the car towards the exit.

Alex jumped out of the car as soon as it was parked and he jogged into the service station. He had seen a McDonalds sign and his face lit up, he could kill a couple of Big Macs. The others drifted after him and they made their way to the burger counter. Alex placed his order and Becca lifted her eyebrows when she saw how much food he had ordered.

"What? I'm a growing boy?" he laughed, tucking into the fries, which had been placed in front of him. "Are you guys getting anything?" he asked.

"I'm okay, we ate earlier," said Becca.

Matt placed an equally large order. "Matt, you pig, you've already had dinner," said Sasha.

"That was just a snack. We won't get any proper food for ages. Plane food sucks," he said, grimacing.

"McDonalds is not proper food Matt," said Becca.

"Oh, but it tastes soooo good," he said, with his mouth full.

Alex laughed and took an equally large bite of his burger, turning around and heading out of the restaurant. A large man knocked into his shoulder and made him drop his bag of food.

"Hey watch it," Alex shouted.

"Get out of the way then moron," snarled the man over his shoulder.

"Are you serious, you just knocked into me. I think you need to apologise mate," said Alex, really annoyed now.

The man turned around slowly and walked towards Alex menacingly.

"I think you and your buddies need to respect your elders," he said, pushing Alex in the chest.

Suddenly a flash of white light snaked out of Alex's chest and punched the man in the stomach. He was lifted off his feet and he slammed heavily into a table behind him. He lay on the floor dazed, his shirt smoking.

"Oh my god Alex what did you do?" cried Becca, running

over to the man.

His shirt had a scorch mark on it and wisps of smoke drifted up from his stomach. He groaned and tried to sit up.

"You punk, what was that?" he mumbled. "Did you just freakin' Taser me?"

"Alex quick," said Matt, pushing him out of the door.

Alex grabbed his bag of food off the floor and they all sprinted back to the car.

"Oh my god...oh my god" said Sasha, as she ran.

They jumped into the car surprising Ben.

"Go, go, go," yelled Matt, punching the back of Ben's seat.

"What the?" asked Ben.

"Get us out of here," said Alex looking around frantically.

The man was staggering out of the door holding his stomach and a group of people were following him and pointing towards their car.

Ben started the car and screeched out of the car park in a panic. He followed the signs back onto the dual carriageway.

"Would someone like to explain what that was all about?" he asked, looking into his rear-view mirror.

"I've no idea," said Alex, pulling back the neck of his t-shirt to look at his chest.

The hammer mark was pulsing a deep red and it felt itchy.

"Dude you totally fried him. Was that electricity?" asked Matt, peering over Alex's shoulder trying to get a look at the mark.

Alex pushed Matt back and shrugged. "Honestly, I've no idea, I thought I killed him," he said.

He felt really shaken and wasn't sure he could handle any more.

"Guys, tell me what happened," said Ben.

"This man tried to pick a fight with Alex in the burger bar and he pushed him in the chest but something like electricity came out of Alex's chest and hit the guy. He went flying and hit a table. He was smoking, I mean literally smoking," said Sasha.

"He was okay though, just a bit singed," added Becca.

"Interesting," said Ben, looking in his mirror again and increasing his speed.

The sooner he got them to the airport the better; someone was bound to have taken down his number plate. He wasn't sure how he was going to explain this one.

An hour later they pulled into the drop off zone at the airport and they got out of the car as soon as Ben stopped.

"Hey say hi to Cassie for me," Ben said, through his open window grinning. "Her address is in the folder Nancy gave to Becca. Take care of yourselves and call my dad after you have met her. He'll want to be fully briefed on what she says."

"Sure, thanks for the ride," said Alex, as he hoisted the rucksack Nancy had provided onto his shoulder.

They made their way into the airport and found the British Airways check in desk. Pete was there already pacing up and down and looking at his watch.

"Guys, hey, what the hell is going on?" he asked.

"Hang on let's get the tickets first," said Becca, opening the folder Nancy had handed to her.

"What's in there?" asked Matt.

"Flight details, a big wad of US dollars, ooh a credit card, oh it's for Alex," she said, disappointed.

"Cool," he said, plucking it out of her hand and popping it

into his back pocket wandering what the credit limit was.

They went up to the desk to arrange their boarding passes and collected their passports, which had somehow managed to get there before them. They must have some serious contacts, Alex thought to himself.

"First class?" Sasha asked Becca hopefully.

"Economy, not even Economy Plus, this is going to be a long flight," sighed Becca. "Nancy wasn't wrong about budget cuts I guess," she added.

They made their way through security and went straight to their gate as the flight was about to board.

"So, anyone care to explain to me why we're jetting off to New York?" asked Pete, as he joined the queue waiting to board the plane.

"Man, it's a really long story," said Matt, joining him. "There is stuff you're just not going to believe."

"My dad already told me about the gods, which is just crazy by the way. I mean do you seriously believe all that? I just don't get why we're going to New York. There was some crazy stuff happening back home, surely we should be there trying to figure this out," said Pete.

"Well apparently there's a crazy witch in Manhattan who can tell us what happened at the henge and what's going on with Alex," Matt replied. "Personally, I don't care if they're all super psycho, I'm getting a free trip to the big apple, this is going to be awesome," said Matt, grinning widely.

Whilst they waited to board the plane Becca filled Pete in on everything he had missed whilst they had been at the headquarters and the journey to the airport.

"This is so cool, I'm meant to be taking a history test

tomorrow and I'm going all James Bond instead," said Pete, handing over his boarding pass.

"I'm not sure Miss Franklin will be bothering with school right now," said Becca.

"My dad said she would cover for us. I think we have all been signed off sick with some sort of virus or something," said Pete, settling into a window seat.

"We really need to speak to our parents, I can't believe they have not said anything about this before," said Becca, taking the seat next to him.

"All would have been revealed when we turn eighteen apparently. They have a ceremony to initiate the next generation," said Pete.

"None of it makes sense. Why all the secrecy? Why don't the gods just say hi, we're here, worship us?" asked Matt, from the row behind.

"It's not as simple as that. My dad said they wanted a break from humans. Apparently bad things kept happening when they mixed with our race so they leave us alone. He didn't tell me much more, there wasn't time. Said we would catch up when I got back," said Pete.

"Well let's just hope the wicked witch of the east has some answers," said Alex, closing his eyes and settling back into his seat.

His legs were cramped already; it was going to be a long night he thought to himself.

Chapter Six

When they arrived in New York, Matt hailed a taxi and gave him the address Nancy had provided in the folder.

"It's a bit late, isn't it?" Sasha yawned, as she got into the taxi. "Don't you think we should find a hotel and get some sleep first and see her in the morning?"

"You reckon you could sleep after all we have been through?" asked Alex.

"Personally, I can't wait, the sooner we see this witch and find out what is going on the better."

The taxi set off and pulled up a short time later outside a smart apartment block. They got out of the taxi and stood together looking up at the impressive building.

"Very nice, not quite what I was expecting," said Sasha, looking up and down the street. "What's the number?" she asked Becca, as she walked up to the door and looked at the buzzer system.

"Apartment ninety-nine," replied Becca.

Sasha pressed the buzzer and they waited. Nothing happened so she pressed it again.

"Come on up, it's the ninth floor," called a female voice over the intercom.

The door buzzed and they entered a hallway.

"She's a bit trusting, isn't she? This is New York, we could be a bunch of weirdos," said Sasha, stepping into the lift in the foyer.

"She's a seeress, she probably saw us coming before we even got on the plane," Becca laughed, as she followed Sasha into the lift.

The door to apartment ninety-nine was ajar and Alex called out as he pushed it open, "Hello, anybody there?"

He saw a petite girl about their age with long red straight hair preparing drinks in an open plan kitchen. He pushed open the door and entered the apartment. He was immediately struck by how large and stylish it was. Everything looked white and the walls were covered with modern art that looked straight from a gallery.

"Finally, you took your time," she said, bringing over a tray. "I thought you would be here an hour ago."

She handed out glasses of lemonade and motioned for them to sit on the white plush sofas in the main part of the luxurious apartment. Alex sat down gingerly in a white armchair. He was worried about getting anything dirty in this immaculate apartment. It really was not what he was expecting a witch's house to look like. He couldn't see any bubbling cauldrons anywhere.

"We got held up at security. Four minors travelling to the states with an eighteen-year-old is bound to raise some questions. They wanted to know our life stories," said Alex, looking at Cassie appreciatively.

She was very slim and her long red hair hung below her waist.

"I'm Alex by the way, pleased to meet you," he said, smiling at her.

She didn't seem crazy and he wasn't sure why Alan would think she would be difficult, she seemed very pleasant.

"I know who you are Alex," she said, looking at him closely. "Hmm Nancy was right there is quite a resemblance, but your hair is a different colour...interesting."

"What do you mean? Resemblance to who?" Alex asked, looking puzzled.

"Your father of course," she smiled and took the seat opposite him.

"My father? You know who my father is?" he asked, shocked sitting forward on the edge of his chair.

"Of course I do. The Norns have been really having fun with you. I asked them to cut it out but they never listen to anyone. I imagine you're feeling rather confused right now," she said, smiling at him.

"That's putting it mildly," said Alex, seething.

He was at the end of his tether and was getting angrier by the minute. Nothing was making sense today, he was tired, hungry and now this strange girl was telling him she knew who his father was.

"Okay, before I tell you anything I need you to calm down Alex," Cassie said, wandering over to a large window and looking up.

Sheet lightning was flashing in the sky lighting up the city.

"You're doing that you know. It's fantastic but not necessary tonight thank you," she said, glancing back at Alex.

"You what?" he spluttered. "Don't be ridiculous."

"The lightning, that's all you. It's happened before hasn't it, quite recently?" she asked, beckoning him over with her hand.

Alex had no idea what she was talking about and he joined her at the window and peered up at the sky. Flashes of lightning flickered through black clouds, which were roiling around, covering the starlit sky. The air felt oppressive and the smell of ozone crept into the room choking him.

"When you have been feeling moody or angry recently you

have been creating lightning. Thunder too when you've really lost it. Quite a talent you have there, your daddy will be very pleased," she laughed.

Alex thought back to the day at the museum when he was late for the trip and the strange storm, which had come out of nowhere.

"No way, that's crazy," he said angrily, turning his back on the window and flinging himself back into his seat.

The sky lit up with a huge bolt of lightning and a massive crash shook the building.

"Calm down, take deep breaths," she said, dropping onto her knees in front of him.

She placed her hands on his knees and looked deeply into his eyes. Alex immediately felt calmer and he sank back into the seat relaxing. The lightning stopped immediately and the sound of thunder rumbled in the distance. Cassie looked out of the window and the clouds began to disperse.

"What are you doing to me?" he asked, sleepily through half closed eyes.

"I'm calming you down. You're dangerous when you're angry. There that's better," she said, stroking his knees gently.

"Wait that felt good," he said, dreamily.

He leaned forward and looked into Cassie's eyes. They were a bright green and very pretty. They almost seemed to glow. Alex took in her face appreciatively. She was cute, about the same age as Becca and had a heart shaped face, clear creamy skin and a rosebud mouth he really wanted to kiss right now. A lock of her long red hair fell over her eye and he tried to lift his hand to tuck it behind her ear. His arm felt too heavy to move though, he was so lethargic he could just go to sleep right now. She was not quite the witch he was expecting to meet. He focused his energy and leaned further forward. The action making her hands move higher up onto his thighs. Alex groaned and moved further forward.

"Did you just put a spell on him?" asked Becca sharply, standing up and moving to Alex's side.

"I just used a little of my influence to make him chill out," Cassie murmured, still looking deeply into his eyes.

"Alex," barked Becca, shaking his shoulder.

She really didn't like the way he was looking at the beautiful petite red head. She liked where the red head's hands were resting even less.

Alex blinked and shook his head. "What the?"

Cassie laughed and stood up in one graceful movement and sank back down into her own armchair smiling into her drink.

"I've no idea what that was but you can do it again anytime," he said, relaxing back into his own chair.

He was completely relaxed and hadn't felt this good in a long time.

"Alex," shouted Becca and Sasha in unison.

"So, you know Alex's dad then?" asked Matt, quickly changing the subject.

"Thor? Yes, I do. Handsome guy, though Alex's pretty cute too. Like a blonde little sexy version of him," she said, flirtatiously looking Alex up and down.

Alex shot up out of his chair suddenly very alert. "Thor? As in the god Thor? Are you freakin' out of your mind? Don't mess with me like that, it's not funny."

"I'm not messing with you. You know it's true. You have

even been marked as one of their own," she replied calmly, sipping her drink again and peering at him over the edge of her glass.

"One of their own what?" he asked, coming over to her chair and standing over her.

"Calm down handsome, we have had enough lightning tonight," she said, standing up and stroking a long finger down his bicep.

"The mark on your chest, let me look at it. From what Nancy described it's the mark of Mjolnir. Only Thor would mark his son like that, which makes you, my handsome, a demi god."

Alex looked around at his friends. They looked just as bemused as he was.

"Come on then, let's see it," Cassie said, reaching for the bottom of his shirt.

"Hey hands off," he said, moving out of her reach.

He pulled his t-shirt off and Cassie darted forward and ran her hands over his chest around the mark.

"Don't touch it," he warned. "The last person who did got a nasty shock."

"That's because he probably meant you harm. I on the other hand...." Her hand brushed over the mark and Alex shivered.

"Yes, it's as I thought. Thor has marked you as his own. The Mjolnir is protecting you. Anyone who means you harm will basically get zapped," she said.

"Man, that's so cool, you're like a god?" said Matt, in awe.

"You don't seriously believe this crap, do you?" Alex sneered, pushing away Cassie's hand and putting his top back on.

"No leave it off, I haven't finished my examination," she purred, winking at him.

"We're done with the examination thank you," he said, putting his hands up as she tried to move closer. "Okay so say my dad is Thor, what about my mum then, do you know who she is too?"

"Your mother is human. Thor fell for her straight away, she was quite a looker when she was younger."

Pete stood up and placed his finished glass on the coffee table. "But my dad said the gods kept away from humans, it always caused problems when they mixed together," he said, confused.

"True on both counts. In fact, Odin made the gods swear to not visit Midgard again after the last fiasco."

"Why what happened?" asked Becca.

"Loki is what happened. He was up to his usual tricks and thought it would be funny to interfere in the love life of Ran, the goddess of the sea. You see she was having an affair with a human behind her husband's back. Loki told Aegir, her husband, she was meeting a human and where she was. Well let's just say Aegir found her in a compromising position and he lost it. He was so angry he created a great flood across the whole world. He nearly destroyed this world but luckily there were enough humans and animals who found shelter and they could start rebuilding again. Poor Ran was devastated, her young lover was drowned and she's never been the same since. Anyway, Odin had had enough, he made all of the gods swear to never interact with humans again. If they did then a curse would be triggered which would release Hel from the underworld to finally finish off the human race. No one really wanted that as it would ruin the balance of the Nine Worlds. Nine is our lucky number you see."

"Hang on, if Thor got it on with Alex's mum, then what you're saying is this curse was triggered?" asked Matt.

"Correct, but it only triggered when Alex turned into an adult at eighteen."

"This is nuts, so you're saying my dad's a god, I'm a demigod and when I turned eighteen last week I triggered a curse which basically means the end of the world?" Alex paced around the apartment with his hands in his hair.

"You got it handsome. The Norns were working overtime when they wove that idea into Odin's head," Cassie said, following Alex's every move with her eyes.

"What about my mum then where is she? Can I meet her?" asked Alex.

"Well that could be tricky at the moment. She lives in an asylum. They think she's crazy you see. When you went missing from the hospital she was frantic. She told anyone who would listen you were a demi god and had to be protected or the end of the world was nigh," said Cassie.

"She knew about the curse then?" asked Alex.

"Well not until after your dad had his wicked way with her. He wasn't going to get her in bed by saying, hey let's have sex and make a baby who will be the end of the world would he?"

"Oh god, I can't take this in," said Alex. "I have to see her, I have to get her out of there. How did I go missing from a hospital?"

"I'm not sure, I didn't see it happening which is strange because I saw your birth. You made your mum's eyes water when you came out big boy," she laughed.

"You saw me being born but not being taken? What sort of seeress are you?" Alex said, his eyes flashing dangerously.

"If you're going to insult me you can leave now," Cassie said frostily, crossing her arms.

"Look I'm sorry. This is just all too much, I can't handle it," he said, miserably.

"Apology accepted don't do it again though," she warned, wagging her finger at him.

"We lost track of you the day after you were born. You caused quite a stir and Odin was furious, he couldn't believe Thor would disobey him. Anyway, we were watching you to see if the curse triggered but someone must have put a concealment charm on you at the hospital. We couldn't see you the next day; you just vanished into thin air. No one knew you were even alive until you turned eighteen. The charm must have broken when you became an adult. Now no offence but no one knew about you as we had given up looking, Hel hadn't escaped so we thought the curse had not been triggered because you were dead. No one thought about the curse triggering on adulthood. That only became obvious when the Asguardians completed their ritual at the henge."

"What about my mum and dad though, surely they wouldn't have given up looking for me?" Alex asked, distraught.

"They thought your mum was crazy, she kept saying you had been stolen but no one believed her. She is still in the hospital now. Alan has the details and he will contact her for you. Your father thought you had died. When we couldn't track you he thought you had been murdered. He tried to find out what happened but there were no leads, you just disappeared. I'll try and contact him as soon as I can. I'm not sure what his reaction will be. You know, having a son who could end life on earth as we know it. I suppose I'll have to move back to Asgard which will be a total bore, no pizza, no Starbucks, it will suck," she complained.

"Cassie please stop. I'm not going to end the human race just because I was born and have now turned eighteen," said Alex.

"Wait," said Sasha, "there must be a get out clause, that's how the Norns work isn't it?" she asked.

"Clever girl, you hit the nail on the head. Of course Alex can break the curse. You even know the answer yourselves," said Cassie, clapping her hands together.

They all looked at each other blankly.

"Hang on the torc," said Becca excitedly, digging into her bag to get her worksheet from the museum.

She read out her notes. "When day becomes night and the sword of Tyrfing is wielded by the last-born son of Porr, Hel shall be cast down and will no longer be able to wreak havoc ever again."

"Well I can't see how that helps," said Pete, grabbing the notes from Becca and reading them.

"Porr is Thor," said Cassie. "Alex is the last-born son of Thor so whilst his very being will open the gateway to Helheim, if he fulfills the prophecy, he can stop it from happening and can ensure Hel stays in Helheim forever."

"Okay so that's weird, why bother with the curse in the first place?" asked Becca.

"The Norns like to have their fun, put a little twist in every now and then to keep everyone on their toes. They probably also didn't relish the thought of Hel being free and no one looking after the dead. It would cause all sorts of havoc. The gateway has already been breached that's what you saw at the henge. A few spirits escaped and unfortunately possessed some of the locals. Alan has his containment team in place to stop more coming through, but it's a temporary measure. The protective seals cannot hold much longer. Alex, you're going to have to fulfill the prophecy, find the sword and seal the breach once and for all before Hel escapes and takes her revenge," said Cassie, seriously.

"Okay so let's say for one moment I believe all this rubbish, where am I meant to get the sword of...what's it called Becca?" he asked, looking at Becca.

"Tyrfing," she said, taking the notes back from Pete.

"Sword of Tyrfing, right," he said.

"Well that's easy, you just need to ask the dwarf who made it," said Cassie.

"Right of course. I need to ask the dwarf who made the sword, where it is so I can seal a breach to the gateway to Hel to stop the end of the world," Alex laughed hysterically. "You're on drugs lady, this is complete madness, I'm done with this, I'm out of here. Come on guys, we're wasting our time, let's get back home. There is just no way I'm buying this crazy rubbish."

"Alex this is your destiny," said Cassie.

Her green eyes grew brighter and she seemed taller somehow.

"This isn't Star Wars you nutcase. Thor is not going to appear in the middle of the room and say, "Alex I'm your father…This stuff just doesn't happen," he shouted angrily.

A rumble of thunder sounded in the distance.

"Alex, if you do not fulfill the prophecy then you will all die, you and the entire human race," said Cassie, angrily.

"Hey no pressure dude," Matt joked.

"Shut up Matt, come on I want to go." Alex strode over to the front door and wrenched it open.

The door slammed in his face and locked.

Cassie snarled. "How dare you walk away from me. Find the sword of Tyrfing or face your peril," she shouted furiously.

"Open the door you crazy witch, we're done," Alex snarled back.

She may be stunningly beautiful and he was very attracted to her but he had to get out of there and clear his head. This was far too much for him to take in. A shriek split through the air and they all clasped their hands to their ears. Alex turned back towards Cassie and she literally flew across the room at him. Her hands were outstretched and she picked him up by his neck and held him high in the air with her hands.

Alex gasped struggling for breath. He looked down at her and wished he hadn't. She had completely transformed into a hideous being. Her eyes were deep black pools, the skin on her face was putrid, rotting and peeling away from her skull. Her teeth were pointed, razor sharp and dripping with blood and her grey hair hung matted about her shoulders. She screamed again into his face and her breath made his eyes sting.

"You arrogant, conceited fool. You dare disobey me?"

She shook Alex by the throat and he kicked his legs helplessly, clawing at her gnarled hands. The others stood in shock, their mouths wide open.

Becca suddenly snapped out of it and cried. "Stop it please, you're killing him, he can't breathe."

Becca grabbed Cassie's arm and tried to pull her away but the witch was too strong. She shoved Becca with her elbow and Becca went crashing into the sofa.

Alex pulled at her hands again and gasped, "I'm sorry…I'm sorry…please."

She looked into his desperate eyes. "Okay but you had better be," she said, dropping him to the floor.

Alex rubbed his throat and looked up. Cassie looked normal again and she tossed her long red hair over her shoulder.

"Sorry about that," she said apologetically. "It happens when I get a little moody."

"Moody? Christ what happens when you get really mad?" asked Matt, helping Alex get back up to his feet.

"You really don't want to know darling," she said, looking Matt up and down.

"Now, where were we? Oh, yes you're going to fetch the sword of Tyrfing and then take it to the henge. You will need to plunge it into the stone in the centre. That will seal the breach. You'll need to find Dvalin and ask him what happened to it. He's one of the dwarves who made it you see and he keeps track of its whereabouts."

"Where do we find this Dvalin then?" asked Alex.

He decided it was best just to go along with whatever she was saying. There was no way he was going to annoy her again, but as soon as he could he would get out of there and go home.

"Svartalfheim," said Cassie.

"Svar what?" asked Alex struggling with the pronunciation.

"Svart...alf...heim, you may be more familiar with the Black Elves, they were in the last Avengers Thor film. They got it all wrong though; their elves didn't look very much like dwarves. I can't stand it when films get the details wrong. Detail like that really matters. The Manhattan dwarf branch were most upset."

"There is branch of dwarves in Manhattan?" asked Becca.

"Yes, they live below the subway, nice guys most of them. I'm sure they'll be able to tell you where Dvalin is."

"And we get below the subway how exactly?" asked Alex, sarcastically.

"I'll open a portal for you. It will take a little time to prepare so I suggest you get some sleep and you can see them in the morning. I have spare rooms you can stay in tonight, unless you want to share my bed Alex?" asked Cassie, winking at him.

Everyone looked at each other warily, it was obvious no one wanted to stay but no one wanted to tell Cassie that either. Alex shrugged his shoulders, it was only one night and the girls were looking really tired.

"That's great thanks, but I'll take my own room thanks," he said, hoping she wouldn't go into a rage again.

Matt mouthed "What?" to him but he just shrugged again and followed Cassie through a door leading off the main room.

They all followed muttering under their breath.

Cassie showed Alex into a large double bedroom. "See you later handsome," she whispered, winking again.

Alex pushed her out of the door quickly and turned the key in the lock. Not that that's going to keep her out he thought to himself. He was just considering whether to haul the dresser over to the door to block it when there was a gentle tap on the door.

"Alex, it's me Becca," he heard through the door.

Alex opened the door and pulled Becca in by the hand. He drew her in close and whispered in her ear.

"Shush, if she knows you're in here she'll probably freak out and turn us into frogs or something."

"I just wanted to check you were okay," she whispered back. "It's been a crazy day, I'm not sure if I understand what's happening let alone how you're feeling about all this. I mean your dad....your mum? None of it makes sense."

"Tell me about it," he said pulling her over towards the bed.

He sat on the edge and drew her down next to him.

"We just need to go along with it until we can get out of here. I've a horrible feeling Cassie fancies me," said Alex, grimacing.

"Well you did encourage her...," said Becca, nudging him in the ribs with her elbow.

"Seriously?" he asked.

Becca laughed, "No, oh my god she's hideous. She must use a glamour or something."

"Oh, I don't know, I thought she was pretty hot," he said, nudging her back and smiling.

"You're welcome to her."

Becca stood up as though she were going to leave and Alex grasped her wrist and pulled her back down onto the bed.

"You're prettier of course," he murmured, looking deeply into her brown eyes and holding her hand in his lap.

"Gee thanks, I don't think it would have taken much, I...."

Alex cut off what she was about to say by brushing his lips gently over hers. His hand moved to her face and he cupped her cheek gently. A tap on the door made him pull away guiltily. He jumped up quickly and opened the door. Becca's mirror image stood there smiling seductively.

"Thought you might be lonely," she said, looking deeply into his eyes.

Alex sighed and held the door open, revealing the real Becca, who was blushing furiously sitting on the bed.

"Nice try Cassie," he said, grinning.

"Damn it. Can't blame a girl for trying," said Cassie, spinning on her heel and returning to her room.

"That was close," said Alex, laughing.

"Time for me to leave," said Becca, smiling. "I think you'll be safe now."

She brushed past Alex out of the door.

"Becca wait," he called after her.

She looked over her shoulder, smiled again and went into the room opposite. Alex shook his head wearily, closed the door firmly and crashed out on the bed fully clothed.

He looked up at the ceiling and grinned to himself, "Demi god...oh yeah."

His last thoughts before he caved in to sleep were whether he should demand sacrifices from his minions.

Chapter Seven

Early the next morning they gathered together in a tight group around the entrance to the Cathedral Parkway subway entrance. Cassie had given Alex a vial of purple liquid with instructions to pour it in a circle near the subway entrance. She hadn't explained much more than that, just told them to "ensure all their bits and pieces were in the circle," whilst she was looking at Alex's crotch.

"You guys ready?" he asked looking around.

They were getting some funny looks standing so closely together. Just as he unstoppered the bottle his phone pinged in his pocket.

"Hang on he said," holding the bottle in one hand and juggling his phone in the other.

"Damn it," he said, looking at the screen.

"What's up?" asked Becca.

"Cassie just sent me a Facebook request," he groaned and Matt snorted.

"Awkward," laughed Pete.

"Dude delete that one," said Matt.

"Are you kidding, after what happened last night?" he said, clicking accept and tucking his phone back into his pocket.

"Stalker witch, is better than angry witch. Okay guys gather close, let's do this," he said, pouring the liquid around them in a wobbly circle.

They stood there holding their breath but nothing happened.

"What do we do now?" whispered Matt, looking at Alex.
"It's not exactly a circle, is it? She specifically said a circle. Try

it again," he said.

"It's round enough," said Alex looking at the floor. "I did what she said, do you think she's having us onnnnn....." he yelled, as the ground opened up beneath them.

Alex's stomach flipped as he fell down into a deep dark chasm. They all screamed as they fell, desperately flailing their arms and legs in the air. Alex couldn't see anything, it was pitch black. He felt someone kick his head and he was pretty sure he just punched one of the girls in the stomach. The air rushed past him and then suddenly he found himself bouncing up and down on what felt like jelly. He bounced up and down a few times and then lay to rest on his back. He took a deep breath and felt beneath himself to see what was going on. The floor was rough to touch but solid.

"Okay, that was weird," he said, getting slowly to his feet. "Welcome but weird. My life just flashed before my eyes then."

Alex brushed dust and small bits of rubble out of his hair and looked around.

The others were all getting to their feet dusting themselves off. They were standing in a large stone circular cavern, which was lit with fluorescent lights, which flickered on and off randomly.

They were alone and Matt's voice echoed off the walls, "Now what?"

"Hello....anyone there?" called Becca.

Her voice echoed back and then there was silence.

"Can anyone see an exit?" asked Pete. "It looks like these walls go all the way around," he said peering into the gloom.

Becca moved to the rough stonewalls and started to edge

her way around, tapping on the rock every now and then.

"Becca what are you doing?" asked Sasha, puzzled.

"Well there must be a way out. Cassie wouldn't have thrown us into a hole for nothing. Come on take a look," said Becca. "There's probably a hidden doorway somewhere."

"You want to bet? She's probably going to sweep in on her broomstick to whisk Alex out of here. Then we'll be left to rot," said Matt, moving to the opposite side to Becca.

He began rapping his knuckles on the stonewall too.

"Ouch," cried a voice, from the rock.

"What the?" cried Matt, jumping back in fright.

"You smacked my dose," cried a small man emerging from the rock in front of Matt.

The top of his head reached up to Matt's waist and he had long droopy muscular arms.

"I'm bleeding you moron," the man complained, holding his face with his hands.

"Oh my god, I'm so sorry are you okay?" Matt asked, bending down on his knees in front of him.

The man grabbed the back of Matt's neck and he took a swing at Matt's face. A loud crunching sound echoed around the chamber.

"What? You freakin' freak, you nearly broke my nose, you son of a...."

"Matt," shouted Alex, in warning.

He didn't want to have a fight on his hands with his first encounter with a dwarf. Matt backed off touching his nose tenderly and Sasha took his hand away to take a look."

"There's nothing there, you baby," she said, reaching up to kiss the end of his nose. "There all better now."

"Where's mine?" asked the dwarf, sidling up beside her and touching her leg.

She looked down at him and flicked his hand off her leg. Each finger on his hand had at least two jewelled rings, which sparkled in the light. Even his long brown hair, which was pulled back into a ponytail and his long beard, had gems woven into them.

"Er, please keep your hands to yourself," she said, moving back out of his reach.

"Come on I want one," he pleaded. "It's the least you can do after your boyfriend nearly knocked me unconscious."

"He's not my boyfriend," she said, quickly.

The dwarf's eyes lit up and he moved closer to her.

"Look I've no idea who you are. I'm not kissing a stranger," she said, holding her hands out to fend him off.

"Well we can change that. My name is Sven, pleased to meet you," he said, reaching out his hand to shake Sasha's hand.

"Hello Sven, my name is Sasha," she said, politely shaking his hand.

"Okay now we know each other, you can kiss me," he grinned, puckering up his lips and leaning towards her.

"Oh, ignore Sven, he's a pest," echoed a gruff voice from behind them.

Alex spun around and saw another dwarf emerge from the rock.

"Cassie just texted me to say you would be here. I'm Half, pronounced ha-lf, not harf, yes I know it would be funny if my name was Harf, but it's not," he glared at them, expecting them to snigger.

He was slightly taller than Sven, had long blonde hair and a short neat beard. He was dripping with jewels as well. They were on his hands and in his hair and he even had gems embedded in his blue dungarees.

"Right well, I'm pleased to meet you all, now would you please follow me. Don't touch anything and do not wander off. If you do then I will not accept any liability for anything which may happen to you."

He spun around on his heel and disappeared into the rock. They all stood there looking dumbly at the solid stonewall and then they looked at each other. Half's face poked back through the rock.

"Come on we don't have all day," he said impatiently and then he disappeared again into the rock.

Matt pushed Alex forward. "After you..."

"Why me? You go," said Alex, shoving Matt towards the wall.

"You're the god around here, this is all your show buddy," said Matt, moving backwards and bumping into Sven.

Sven growled and glared at him. Alex shrugged, he put his hand out in front of him and poked a finger into the rock face where Half had disappeared. The surface shimmered and rippled under his finger, it looked like liquid silver. He pushed his hand fully into the rock and pulled it out slowly. It came back and didn't look any different so he decided to go for it and he stepped through the wall slowly. His skin tingled and his hair stood on end for a moment and then he was through the wall. He opened his eyes cautiously and looked behind him. Becca came next and bumped into him so he moved quickly to one side. Then Sasha and Pete came through together.

They waited for Matt but he didn't emerge.

"Where's Matt?" asked Alex.

The wall rippled and then Matt came stumbling through the wall rubbing his forehead.

"You okay?" asked Becca.

"That little devil did something to the wall. I went to follow Sasha and Pete but I hit solid rock. Have I cut my forehead?" he asked, touching his forehead and looking at his hand.

Alex sniggered. "No, it just looks a bit red."

Sven stepped through the wall whistling and looking a picture of innocence.

"Have you got a problem with me Dopey?" asked Matt, standing in front of Sven threateningly.

"Get moving punk or I'll bite your ankles," Sven snarled.

"Oh no, now you've started something," said Half sighing. "Top tip of the day my good people, do not insult a dwarf by calling him by one of the seven dwarves names."

Matt growled at Sven and brushed him out of his way.

"Come on guys calm down." Alex stepped between the two of them. "Let's get going, we're wasting time. Where are we?" he asked Half, looking around.

They were standing in a long, dark stone tunnel with perfectly smooth walls. Electric light bulbs lit the tunnel and Alex could hear the sound of tapping reverberating off the walls.

"We will be passing through the worker's caverns. It's the quickest way to the Grandmaster's office," said Half, walking off down the gloomy tunnel.

They all followed him peering through open doors as they passed. Dwarves were in each room and were bent over large tables piled high with gold and silver cups and plates.

"These fellows are working on a new dinner set for Freyja, Odin's missus," said Half, over his shoulder. "Don't disturb them and keep up, the Grandmaster is waiting," he said, impatiently.

They turned a corner and came to a dead end.

"Stand back please," said Half, shooing them backwards with his hands.

He drew a doorway with his index finger, muttered under his breath and a wooden door suddenly appeared. He reached out turned the doorknob and opened the door. He stepped to one side and gestured they should enter the room.

"Cool," said Matt, stepping through the door.

They entered a large circular room filled with odd pieces of furniture. Bookshelves lined the entire room and were packed with dusty books and scrolls. Thick multi coloured rugs were strewn across the floor haphazardly and a large leather chair with soft comfy looking cushions was nestled to one side. An ancient looking dwarf, with a white beard reaching down to the ground, appeared from behind a large wooden desk, which was piled high with books.

"Ah you made it, wonderful, wonderful," he said, stepping forward and holding out his hands in welcome.

Tripping over his beard, he fell flat on his face. They all went to move to help him up but he waved them away.

"It's okay, I'm fine. Blast this beard," he said, getting up quickly and tucking his beard into the already bulging waistband of his green trousers.

"Welcome, it's an honour to meet you. I'm Lit," he said, pumping Alex's hand vigorously.

"My, my, what a fine young man you have become, your father will be most proud, yes most proud," he said, his eyes brimming with tears.

"Lit? Ben told us about you. You're immortal, right?" asked Becca.

"Yes, yes, that's me. How is dear Ben I haven't seen him for a while?" asked Lit happily.

"Hang on, you know my father?" asked Alex.

"Of course, of course. He comes every Saturday night for a game of Tafl and a few pints of mead. I'm the only one he can't beat you see and he does love a challenge. Well that's what he says, personally I think he just likes to get away from his wife for a few hours," he said, winking.

"Does he know about me, that I'm alive?" asked Alex.

"Yes, yes of course. Cassie managed to get hold of him this morning. He's sorting out a bit of a problem in Asgard at the moment, otherwise he would have come to Midgard to see you," said Lit.

"Problem? What problem?" asked Alex.

"Finding the one who stole you," said Lit, looking at Alex over the top of his half-moon glasses, which were perched on the tip of his bulbous red nose.

"Cassie said when she told him you were alive she could hear the thunder he created in Asgard all the way in Manhattan. That's a long way away; our worlds are not close at all. He was furious no one had told him sooner. He told Cassie he has his suspicions about who hid you so he's following up on them. There is also the small matter of his wife. I expect she is a little bit upset. She didn't know about you, you see, so it must have come as a bit of a shock."

"His wife?" asked Alex, shocked.

"Yes, yes, lovely lady though a bit of a nag that's probably why...."

"So, who does he think did it?" interrupted Becca, moving to Alex's side and taking hold of his hand.

He looked down at her and squeezed her hand tightly.

"Cassie said he wouldn't say but we discussed it and we're pretty sure it was Loki. It's the sort of 'joke' he would play," said Lit, making speech mark gestures with his fingers. "I'm sure we'll find out soon. Thor isn't one to forgive lightly."

A young looking dwarf who was clean-shaven and wearing a smart black suit poked his head into the room.

"Excuse me sir," he said.

"Yes Mosto?" asked Lit.

"I was just wondering if the Midgardians would like some refreshment?" he asked, politely.

"Midgardians?" asked Becca.

"Midgardians.....people from Midgard. You know as in Asgardians are from Asgard," Lit explained patiently.

"Oh, right so you guys are like Svartalfheimians?" asked Matt.

"Er no, we're dwarves," said Lit, looking confused.

"Idiot," muttered Sven, under his breath.

He had followed them into the room and was sitting on a comfy looking sofa near the desk.

"What are these Muppets doing here anyway?" Sven asked, glaring in Matt's direction.

"Sven," said Lit warningly. "These are our guests behave

yourself."

"Whatever," said Sven, under his breath.

Lit glared at him and turned back to Alex. "I'm sure you would all like some refreshments, Mosto please bring cups for all. We need to toast the return of Thor's son," Lit said happily.

Mosto reached into a cupboard near the door and withdrew six silver tankards.

"Please sit everyone we need to discuss your mission," said Lit.

"Should you wish to accept it..." giggled Mosto, handing out the cups.

"Don't mind him, he's a bit of a Tom Cruise fan," sighed Lit, gesturing to them to take a seat on the flowery sofas, which were pushed up against the walls.

They all took a seat and looked into the empty cups Mosto had given to them. They looked at each other confused. Lit was slurping noisily from his. He burped and wiped some froth off his white beard.

"Ah that's better," he said, settling back into the leather armchair he had sat in.

He looked around at the others puzzled. "Drink up, drink up," he said, waving his hand in encouragement.

"Er my cups empty," said Pete, looking into his cup and back at Lit.

"Well just tell it what you want," said Lit. "Look," he held out his cup so they could all see and said. "Beer please."

The cup filled to the brim with frothy beer.

"Oh my god that is awesome," said Pete. "Beer," he said, into his cup.

Nothing happened.

"Hey mine's broken," said Pete, shaking it vigorously.

"No, you're underage...and you didn't say please. Manners maketh man so they say," said Lit, tutting.

"It knows my age? Well that sucks," Pete looked morosely into his cup.

"Beer please," said Alex, smugly.

Nothing happened though.

"Hey I'm of age I turned eighteen last week," he said, looking at Lit.

"The legal age here is twenty-one," said Lit, grinning and draining his second cup.

"Tea please," said Becca, politely into her cup.

It filled to the brim with hot steaming tea.

"Banana smoothie please as I can't have beer," Pete asked his cup.

When it filled to the top he sniffed it cautiously then took a sip. "Mm that's pretty good," he said, sitting back in his seat and relaxing.

"Gross," said Matt, "I hate bananas, that smell makes me want to puke."

Suddenly his cup filled to the brim with a yellow, foul smelling liquid with carrots floating on the top.

"Ew, what's that?" he asked, holding the cup away from him.

"Oh dear," said Lit. "The cups recognise any liquid. I believe you just asked for banana puke. Mosto another cup for our guest please."

Mosto ran to the cupboard and retrieved a fresh cup for Matt, whilst Sven sniggered in his chair. Matt took his cup and quickly asked for lemonade before he made any more mistakes.

The others all settled into their seats with their drinks, hot chocolate for Sasha with extra cream and marshmallows and coffee for Alex, he figured he needed the caffeine.

"Right then, down to business," said Lit, slurring slightly.

Great, thought Alex, a drunk dwarf that's all we need.

"Cassie just said you were looking for Dvalin, might I enquire why?" he asked, looking at them with bleary blue eyes.

"We're looking for a sword and Cassie said he might know where it is," said Alex, sipping his coffee and sighing. He really needed that.

"Ah a sword, is it? Well I'm sure Dvalin is your man, he specialises in sword making. He's made some splendid pieces over the years," said Lit.

"It's the sword of Tyrfing, have you heard of it?" asked Alex.

"Ah the sword of Tyrfing, then yes he most certainly does know where it is," said Lit.

"Brilliant can we ask him then? Is he here?" asked Becca, excitedly.

"You can ask him but he won't tell you," said Lit, finishing his third beer and burping.

"What? Why?" asked Alex, sitting forward.

"Well it's cursed you see and he feels a bit bad about what happened to the others who used it. He made a vow no one else would ever touch it so he hid it where no one could find it," said Lit.

"We have to get the sword, if we don't then Hel will escape and will destroy Earth. We need it to close the portal," said

Alex, in despair.

"Alex, er didn't you hear the bit about it being cursed?" asked Matt.

"What type of curse?" asked Becca, worried.

"Well I know it always kills someone whenever it's drawn. I've seen it happen many a time," said Lit, shaking his head sadly.

"Great so I'm going to turn into a sword killing maniac," said Alex, jumping to his feet.

"Okay, so this is impossible, let's just go back home and see what happens," said Pete.

"Let's not panic, the Norns weave the web as they see fit. What will be will be. The best you can do is find Dvalin and ask him. If you explained your quest and how serious the situation is he might help," said Lit.

"Where can we find him then? Is he here?" asked Becca.

"No, he lives in Ostleheim," said Lit.

"Ostleheim, where's that?" asked Sasha.

"It's where the master craft dwarves live. They like to keep themselves to themselves. They get a bit touchy about dwarves copying their ideas, so they don't have a lot of contact with anyone else," said Lit.

"So, can we walk there? Is it far?" asked Alex.

"Yes, you could walk there, our tunnels will take you anywhere you need to go in Svartalfheim. You might want to take the Express rather than walking though, it will be much quicker," said Lit, cheerily.

"The Express?" asked Alex warily.

If it were anything like the hole in the ground method of travelling Cassie shared with them, he would prefer to walk.

"The train of course. Sven can take you. He won't mind," said Lit, smiling.

Sven glared at Lit. "Why can't Half go?" he asked moodily.

"I need Half here to supervise Freyja's dinner set. You know how particular she can be. Come on Sven, it will be an adventure," said Lit, patting him on the shoulder.

Sven wasn't at all excited at the prospect of an adventure but the Grandmaster had spoken and he would have to obey.

"Come on then," sighed Sven resigned. He would have to text Lia to cancel their date that night. She was going to be really mad at him.

Sven grinned at Matt. If he had to go he was going to enjoy himself with this Midgardian though. Suddenly a loud ringing tone pierced the air.

"Oh, that's me, please excuse me," said Lit, reaching into his pocket and drawing out a mobile phone.

"Phones work down here?" asked Matt, surprised. "We must be a hundred feet underground."

"Three miles to be exact sir," said Mosto, gathering their empty cups. "Coverage is very good though the Wi-Fi can be a hit and miss."

"You have Wi-Fi?" Matt stood up and walked to Lit's table. Sure enough there was a computer on his desk.

"Why don't we just email this Dvalin guy? That would be quicker?" he asked.

Sven sniggered. "Dvalin still lives in the dark ages, you'll see what I mean when you meet him."

Lit hung up the phone and turned to face them, he looked very concerned.

"Right best you get moving quickly, that was Cassie. It's

getting a bit hairy at the henge and the containment unit is having trouble. They just had a serious breach and some beserker spirits have got through the barrier. Dangerous creatures, they will cause all sorts of havoc," said Lit.

"Who ya gonna call?" Matt laughed.

"Matt this is serious; our families could be in trouble. Come on guys let's go, the sooner we get the sword the sooner Alex can seal the breach," said Becca, hurrying towards the door.

"She's right come on let's get going," said Alex. "Lit thank you for your help."

"No problem dear boy, come and visit me when this is all over. We can have a nice game of Tafl," he said, smiling at Alex and shaking his hand.

"Sven, please escort our guests to Ostleheim and help them any way you can," said Lit.

Sven nodded miserably and led the way out of the room. The others shook Lit's hand and followed Sven through the door. Just as Pete was about to leave the room, Lit reached up and put his hand on Pete's arm.

"Peter.....the cup please?" asked Lit, holding out his hand.

"Oh, can't I keep it as a souvenir?" asked Pete, hopefully.

"No," said Lit, gesturing for Pete to hand over the cup.

Pete handed it over begrudgingly.

"Nice try," sniggered Matt.

"I could have made a fortune on EBay," said Pete, shrugging.

"So how are we getting there?" asked Alex, as he caught up with Sven.

"We need to catch the Express train, there should be one

along soon, they are quite regular," said Sven, as he led them down a dimly lit tunnel.

They followed Sven for about thirty minutes as he led them down one tunnel and then another. Soon Alex was completely lost. Matt tapped Sven on the shoulder.

"Are we nearly there yet?" he asked.

He didn't want to admit it in front of the girls but his legs were starting to ache. Sven laughed and led them around another bend. Matt sighed, resigned, but then grinned with relief as he saw a train platform.

"Here we are, is everyone here?" asked Sven, counting them. "Oh, you managed to keep up then?" he asked Matt, sarcastically. "Now when it arrives the train will slow down; the doors will open and you'll need to step on quickly. Mind the gap, I don't want to lose anyone. Well except him," said Sven, nodding in Matt's direction and grinning wickedly.

They waited for a few minutes and then Alex could make out a rumbling in the distance.

"Here we go, are you all ready?" asked Sven.

He moved to the edge of the platform as a silver sleek modern looking train arrived.

"Oh, it's a proper train," said Sasha, as it slowed down.

"Of course it's a proper train, what were you expecting?" asked Sven, confused.

"Er I just wasn't expecting something quite so modern," she replied.

"Don't tell me, you thought it would be a quaint little steam train....or perhaps rickety old mine cars?" asked Sven.

Sasha shrugged.

"This isn't Harry Potter land," he said, in a huff.

The doors to the train hissed open smoothly and they all bundled on quickly, not wanting to be left behind.

"Right take a seat, it's going to be a long ride," said Sven. "There are refreshments in the fridge over there if you're hungry or thirsty," he said, gesturing to the back of the carriage.

Alex took a quick look around, the carriage looked very luxurious with several rows of comfy looking seats. They were the only passengers so there was plenty of room. He headed straight to the fridge. He was starving as usual and he helped himself to several packets of sandwiches and crisps.

"So how long will it take?" he asked Sven, with a mouth full of ham sandwich.

He sat down next to Becca and sank into the deep plush cushions. He took another large bite of his sandwich and grinned at her.

"Pig," she mouthed at him, smiling.

"That's right," he said. 'Ham!"

"About five hours, best you make yourselves comfy and get some rest. Knowing Dvalin he really won't make it easy on you. He's one of the traditionalists, even if he will tell you where the sword is, he won't do something for nothing and he's motivated by one thing only," said Sven.

"Oh, I'm sure Sasha would be willing," said Matt, digging her in the ribs with his elbow and grinning.

"Matt shut up," she punched his arm and went to move seats.

"You can sit with me sweetheart, I'm much better company than that human," said Sven winking and patting the empty seat next to him.

She sat back down quickly; there was something really creepy about that dwarf.

"Gold motivates him, gold and precious gems. He can't get enough of them. We believe he's the richest dwarf in Svartalfheim. He is certainly one of the oldest. Him and Lit, they go back centuries," said Sven.

"They're good friends then?" asked Becca, as she dipped her hand into Alex's crisp packet.

"Not exactly. Dvalin has never got over the fact Lit is immortal. He can't handle the fact his hoard of treasure won't be his forever and he's losing his looks. He's ancient and fading fast. Makes him a bit difficult to deal with. Oh, and for goodness sake don't call him grumpy whatever you do. He might be old and miserable but he still has a few tricks up his sleeve. You really don't want to get on his bad side," said Sven, settling into his seat and closing his eyes.

Becca reached over to dip into Alex's crisp packet again and he grabbed her hand.

"Oi get your own," he said, drawing her hand up to his mouth.

He smiled and brushed his lips over her knuckles.

"You okay there?" he asked. "It's been an even weirder day than yesterday," he sighed. "I keep thinking I'm going to wake up from a bad dream."

"I know and I don't think it's going to get any better," said Becca, resting her head on his shoulder.

Alex smiled to himself; he laid his head back and closed his eyes. At least one good thing had come out of all this. He was still holding Becca's hand and he ran his thumb over her wrist. He saw her smile from the corner of his eye and he held her hand firmly not wanting to ever let her go. The motion of the train made Alex sleepy and he soon slipped into a deep sleep with Becca's head on his shoulder. However, he woke with a sudden start when the mark on his chest started to tingle and burn. He rubbed it with his hand and stood up cautiously, trying not to wake Becca. Something wasn't right, his gut instinct was telling him to get out of there quickly.

Suddenly a loud popping noise filled the carriage and the lights went out plunging them into darkness. The only light came from irregular flashes from outside the windows. Alex scanned the carriage quickly and could just make out a dark figure crouched low in the corner. A pair of eyes gleamed in the darkness and Alex heard a deep chuckle. His chest was throbbing painfully and he felt as though the mark would burn a hole in his shirt. As he looked around he could see the others had all woken up and had leapt from their seats. They were all looking around trying to make sense of what was happening. Alex positioned himself in front of Becca protectively and she held onto his arm frightened.

The figure launched itself from the corner of the carriage and made contact with Matt with its foot. There was a meaty thwack as it hit Matt in the stomach, knocking him backwards into Pete. They fell in a heap on the floor. The figure stood, a scarf covered its face hiding its identity. It was the height of a child and was dressed head to toe in black.

Through the flashes of light, Alex saw Sasha dart forward and strike out her leg towards the figure. There was a crack and the attacker's head snapped back as she made contact with her foot. He recovered quickly and struck out a fist at Sasha. She moved swiftly to the side and whacked him on the head again with her elbow. He fell over onto his back, rolled over in one smooth motion and stood again ready to strike with his fists in the air. The eyes were directed at Alex and he stood poised ready to strike. However, before he made a move crackles of electricity filled the air and snaked along the metal rails. Sparks rained down and lit the carriage with an eerie glow. Matt looked at Alex; static electricity was pulsing from his chest, fingers and even his eyes, conducting on everything that was metal in the carriage.

"Alex," he shouted.

Alex's full concentration was on the figure in front of him. A blast of energy emanated from his chest and blew the figure off his feet. It slammed into the connecting door of the carriage and slunk to the floor, unconscious and smoking.

"Oh my god," cried Sasha, sinking to the floor and shaking.

Alex stood still; electricity was still sparking off him. He was mesmerised by what he had just done and the power he had felt.

"Alex, Alex....are you okay? Can you hear me?" asked Matt, worried.

He reached out and touched Alex's arm. A shock of electricity stung his hand and he leapt back with a yelp. Alex shook his head and the electricity sunk back into his skin.

"Matt, I'm sorry are you okay man?" he asked, worried.

He reached out to touch Matt and Matt backed away out of his reach.

"No way dude, back off, that really hurt. You need to ground yourself or something," said Matt.

"I've no idea how that happened. Who is that, is he breathing, is he okay?" asked Alex, pointing at the figure slumped on the floor.

Sven pushed his way through the group and knelt by the figure. He poked him with his hand and the figure moaned. "He's alive, quick find something to tie him up with, we need to ask him some questions."

Sasha reached into her bag and pulled out a silk scarf.

"Here, this should do it," she said, handing the scarf to Sven.

"Sash what the hell was all that fruit ninja stuff? That was awesome," asked Matt, as he rubbed his stomach where he had been kicked.

"Self defence classes, my parents insisted," said Sasha, grinning.

"Someone help me," said Sven, frustrated. "He could wake up."

Matt held the attacker's hands together and Sven tied them together with the scarf. When he was secure Sven removed the scarf, which was covering his face.

"Hmm a Flostheim dwarf, interesting," Sven muttered.

"A what?" asked Alex kneeling down next to Sven to get a better look.

The dwarf looked young and had a moon shaped scar on both cheeks.

"He's from the Flostheim dwarf clan, they're notorious assassins. I reckon he was after you Alex," said Sven.

"Christ, we're dealing with ninja dwarves now," said Matt, kicking the dwarf's leg none too gently. "Seriously this is crazy. Why would anyone want Alex dead?"

"Someone who doesn't want Alex to succeed in his quest to find the sword and seal the portal," said Sven, who was shaking the dwarf by the shoulder.

"Come on sunshine wake up. Let's see what you have to say for yourself."

The dwarf groaned and opened his eyes. Alex could see the panic in his eyes as the dwarf realised his predicament and struggled against the bindings.

"Let me go, you'll regret this," he hissed, between his teeth still struggling.

"Who hired you punk?" Sven poked him hard in the ribs with his foot.

"You know I won't tell you that," he sneered. "I'm a professional. I would rather die than betray my master."

"Professional? You just got your ass kicked by a girl," laughed Matt. "Come on speak up or we'll string you up like a piñata and knock it out of you," he said.

The dwarf glared at them all and shouted loudly, "Master avenge me."

He closed his eyes and started to shake. His face began to turn grey and he screamed in pain. His face was turning into stone. The grey spread quickly down his neck and cracks started to appear. In no time at all the dwarf had turned completely into stone.

"Okay that was disturbing," said Pete, looking over Matt's shoulder. "What happened?"

"UV tablet. The assassins implant them in their teeth for a quick death," said Sven, kicking the stone dwarf in disgust.

"Sven get away," said Sasha, shaken.

"Sorry what do you mean a UV tablet?" asked Becca.

"Ultra violet contained within a tablet. It's pure poison to our kind and turns us into stone. It's the reason why we live underground, sunlight kills us," explained Sven.

"I thought that was vampires," said Matt.

"Vampires don't exist silly boy," said Sven, shaking his head.

"Of course, how stupid of me. There are gods, witches, dwarves and monsters but no vampires, I got it," said Matt, pulling Sven away. "Sven cut it out," he said.

Sven was rifling through the dead dwarf's pockets.

"I'm just checking to see if he has any ID on him," said Sven. "He will have family out there who will want to know what happened to him."

"Save your pity, he was an assassin. I'm pretty sure he wouldn't have minded too much about killing Alex," said Matt. "Who would have sent him though? I mean, is word out now about who Alex is?"

"Not that I'm aware of. We have tried to keep it quiet so far. Once the dwarves know the portal is breached we'll have a panic on our hands. Most of their business comes from your world. If it's destroyed it will really impact their income. The unemployment rate will go through the roof. We'll have loans being called in, house repossessions, probably rioting, it will be chaos," said Sven, mentally calculating what this could cost him personally.

"Well someone has let the cat out of the bag. We should report this to Alan maybe he has some ideas," said Sasha, as she unbound her scarf from the stone dwarf.

"Sasha that's gross leave it, he's dead," said Becca, wrinkling her nose in distaste.

"It's Hermes and really expensive. It'll be alright after a rinse," she said, giving it a shake.

"Guys I think we should look around. How do we know he wasn't alone?" said Alex, scanning the carriage.

"Oh, they always travel alone, it's some sort of code of theirs. They trust no one and have just one master or mistress," said Sven.

"Hey there's a clue," said Becca excitedly.

"What's that Daphne?" Pete asked sarcastically.

"Before he turned to stone he said, 'avenge me master,' he must be working for a man or he would have said mistress," she replied.

"She's right, good spot. It doesn't really help us to narrow it down much though," said Sven.

"I bet whoever took Alex as a baby is involved in all of this. Someone really wants you out of the picture," said Becca, looking at Alex with a worried expression on her face.

"Well they can come and get me. I'm ready for them. This built in self defence mechanism works really well," said Alex, puffing out his chest and grinning.

He went over to the fridge to grab a can of drink. He was feeling a bit drained and needed an energy boost. He wasn't going to share that with his friends though, they would just fuss. He took out his phone to check the signal and sighed when he saw a Facebook message from Cassie asking how he was.

"My signal is really weak, has anyone got anything better? We really need to let Alan know the score," he said, sitting down and opening his drink.

"Phones won't work on the train," said Sven. "We're going to be out of contact for a while, there's no coverage in Ostleheim. As I said earlier, they're a bit old school and set in their ways down there."

"We'd better get some rest, we still have some way to go," said Sasha. "Sven, can you go scout around and check the train just in case?" she asked him, sweetly.

"For you my love anything," said Sven, grinning.

He made his way down the carriage and tripped over Matt's leg, which was blocking the aisle.

"Oh, sorry mate, how careless of me," said Matt, smirking.

Sven growled at him and made a rude gesture with his hand.

"Sven, I saw that," warned Sasha, laughing.

Alex leant his head back and turned to look at Becca. She had dark shadows under her eyes and she looked really tired.

"You okay?" he asked, reaching over to hold her hand.

A spark lit up as his fingers touched her and she jumped in her seat pulling back her hand quickly.

"Ow, you're still charged up," she said, rubbing her hand.

"Well I always thought there was a spark between us." he joked. "Hang on."

He twisted in his seat and poked Matt on the arm.

"All gone, we're good," Alex smiled and reached for her hand again.

He twisted his fingers through hers and rested their hands in his lap.

"And what if it hadn't gone eh? I'm not your personal conductor," complained Matt, poking his head through the seats. "So, it's okay to fry Matt now is it? Cheers dude, I'll remember that."

"Chill out, I was pretty certain it was gone," said Alex, laughing.

"Well test that theory on Pete next time thank you."

Matt sat back grumpily and closed his eyes.

Four hours later Alex woke when Becca shook his shoulder.

"Hey gorgeous, I was just thinking about you," he said, opening his eyes lazily and grinning up at her.

She blushed fiercely and hung her head so her hair covered her face.

"Sven said we're nearly there, we need to get ready to get off," she said.

Matt looked over at the stone dwarf. "Hey do you reckon he would fit in my backpack? He would look wicked in my front garden. My mum loves gnomes," he said.

"Seriously Matt? Have some respect," barked Sven. "Never call a dwarf a gnome. Gnomes are a menace to society."

The train slowed down and an announcement confirmed they had reached Ostleheim. When the doors hissed open they all jumped off and looked around. They were in a very dark tunnel with rough-cut stonewalls. Fire torches flickered and gave a little light. There was just enough to enable them to see where they were going. They followed the torches to the end of the platform to some stairs, which led downwards.

"Follow me," said Sven. "Pete, you bring up the rear. Keep close together, these Ostleheim dwarves are sensitive fellows and don't take kindly to visitors. If you see anyone just keep your head down and don't make eye contact. Let me do all the talking," said Sven, as he walked down the steep steps.

Alex clasped Becca's hand and Matt reached for Sasha's.

"Ever feel like you're the third wheel on a double date?" grumbled Pete, as he fell into line behind the others.

"Well you're not holding my hand you pervert," said Sven, over his shoulder.

"This isn't much of a date," giggled Sasha.

"How about I take you to the movies when we get home princess?" asked Matt, as he guided her carefully down the stairs.

"Yeah sure, why not?" said Sasha, grinning at Matt.

"Great idea, Becca are you up for that?" asked Alex, hopefully.

"Sure, that would be nice, if we ever make it out of here," she said, squeezing his hand gently.

A normal night at the movies seemed a long way away at the moment. Becca sensed him tense and whispered. "It's going to be okay you know. We just need to get this sword, get it to the henge and then we can get back to normal. Well whatever normal is going to be for a demi god," she smiled at him but he couldn't see her face.

It was getting darker and darker the deeper they went down the stairs. Soon there was no light at all and they had to feel their way down. They clung to each other and the rough sides of the rock walls.

"There's light just down there, we're nearly there," Sven called up to the others.

Continuing down the steps, Alex could see a glow emanating from the bottom of a closed door. Sven knocked on the door and they all waited. A small wooden shutter within the door swung open and an old grizzled dwarf with long messy grey hair, wearing round metal glasses poked his head through.

"State your business," he said, abruptly.

"Hello we have travelled from Manhattanheim to see Dvalin. We have some business with him," said Sven, importantly.

"Right, you need to answer this riddle to gain entry to Ostelheim," the dwarf said, in a matter of fact tone. "How can you get one by adding two to eleven?"

"Damn I'm rubbish at riddles," Alex said, rubbing his hand through his hair frustrated.

"Alex use your Ironman zapper on the door," whispered Matt, in his ear.

"It doesn't happen when I want it to. It just, I dunno, happens. Anyway, we can't just blast our way in there, that's not a great start, is it?" Alex hissed back.

"It's a clock, if you add two hours to eleven o'clock you get one o'clock," said Sasha, walking up to the door.

They all looked at her with their mouths open. Alex was impressed, she was actually a lot smarter than he'd originally thought.

"Correct answer, now answer your next one please. What.."

"Seriously? Come on let us in, we answered your riddle," Alex shouted at the dwarf, frustrated.

"Well the rules state one riddle per person who wants to gain entry...oh my..." he said, looking at Alex.

Alex's eyes flashed and sparked as he glared at the dwarf.

"Let us pass," Alex growled, menacingly.

"Oh, sir I didn't know it was you. Of course, of course please do enter." The dwarf disappeared and the door creaked open.

They had to bend down to enter, this was a door built for

dwarves after all. They entered a small round cavern with a low ceiling and Alex and Matt had to bend over to avoid hitting their heads. The cavern had several exits, which were lit with flickering torches.

"Welcome to Ostleheim, I hope you have a pleasant stay," he said, bowing low to Alex.

"My name is Rodri and if there is anything I can do to assist you please do ask," he said, groveling by Alex's feet.

Like Sven, Rodri was covered in gemstones; he even had them sewn into the front of his grey trousers and waistcoat. He was rather large around the waist and reminded Alex of a Christmas bauble. Alex tapped him on the shoulder embarrassed to have someone grovel before him.

"Er you know who I am?" he asked.

"Well at a good guess I would say you're one of the almighty Thor's sons. Only his children have eyes that do that," he said.

"Do what?" asked Alex, confused.

"Alex, you have lightning coming out of your eyes, it's really freaky. It happens when you get angry," said Matt.

"Great so now I'm the Incredible Hulk? Don't make me angry or I'll electrocute you," said Alex, exasperated.

Crackles of static electricity filled the air and everyone's hair started to stand up on end.

"Alex, calm down, it's okay," said Becca, moving towards him.

"Don't touch me, I'll hurt you," he cried, terrified he would shock her again.

He had absolutely no control over what was happening to his body and he was scared.

"Chill man, take some deep breaths," said Matt, worried.

Alex took some deep breaths and the static in the air calmed down. Sven patted down his hair and turned to Rodri.

"Could you direct us to Dvalin now please? We're in a bit of a rush," he said.

"You just need to take the tunnel on the left over there, he lives at the end. Though I warn you, I don't think he'll see you. He hasn't come out for years. Sends all visitors away and refuses to work on anything. He's still obsessed with trying to open the Gulldyrr. Been at it for years. I think it's driven him a bit mad if I'm honest," he said.

"The Gulldyrr?" asked Becca.

"Yes, it's a door which leads to Thor's greatest treasures. We're not sure what they are exactly but Thor said no one must enter the chamber and he locked it with a charm. Dvalin is obsessed with breaking it and owning the treasure," said Rodri.

"But that's stealing," said Sasha, shocked.

"Yes, but Dvalin suffers from gold fever. Several dwarves have it. You can probably tell already we like precious objects, jewels, gold etc," said Rodri, gesturing to the gems sewn into his clothes and wound into his long shaggy beard.

"Dvalin is obsessed with being the richest dwarf ever. He already has a cavern filled with gold, diamonds, rubies, and emeralds. You name it he has it. He wants more though and he won't stop until he has Thor's treasure as well."

"Does Thor know about this?" asked Sasha.

"Yes, he thinks it's hilarious. He's convinced Dvalin will never succeed as he has protected it so well," said Rodri.

"Well we need to at least try and talk to him. We've come

this far," said Becca, moving off towards the left tunnel.

"Guys we're wasting our time; don't you think we should just head home now? It's obvious he's not going help us," said Pete.

"No Becca is right we need to at least try. Let's start thinking of a plan B though, I think we're going to need it," said Alex, following Becca and Sven down the dark tunnel.

There was a strange musty smell and Alex could see pools of water on the floor where it had dripped through the ceiling. Sven had been right when he said Ostleheim was old school, this place looked ancient.

Chapter Eight

"Sven, Rodri said I must be one of Thor's sons because of my eyes. How many children does he have?" asked Alex, as they walked down the tunnel.

"Three, you have a step sister, Thrud and two step brothers, Magni and Modi. I'm sure they'll be thrilled to meet you soon," said Sven, grinning.

"Yeah sure," Alex replied, distracted.

In the space of a few days he had discovered he had a whole family. He somehow didn't think he would be having family film night with them anytime soon though. It was going to take him some time to adjust to his change in circumstances. He thought about his foster family and smiled to himself. They were going to be surprised to learn they had the son of a god living in their spare bedroom.

After walking for ten minutes they came to a dead end. Alex looked around but all he could see were the rough damp walls surrounding them.

"We must have gone wrong," he said, turning around to head back the way they had come.

"Stand back everyone," said Sven, moving towards the rock face.

He placed his palm on the rock and muttered under his breath. "Syna dyrr."

The rock face glowed yellow and a wooden door was revealed. Sven looked very pleased with himself.

"Dwarf trick," he said winking.

He knocked on the door several times. "Dvalin are you home?" he called through the door.

There was no answer. "Dvalin can you hear me? It's Sven from Mahattanheim. I've brought some friends who need to speak to you," he said.

"Bog off," growled the reply from behind the door.

"Dvalin, thank Odin you're there, can we speak to you? It's very urgent," said Sven, through the key hole.

"I said bog off, I'm busy," said Dvalin.

"Hmm nice fellow, now what?" asked Pete.

"Shut up boy," snapped Sven. "Dvalin, we really do need to talk to you. I have one of Thor's sons with me, he is on a quest to save Midgard, it really is vital we talk," Sven said, desperately.

"Stop pestering me, I can't concentrate, I think I nearly had it then," complained Dvalin.

"The Gulldyrr is that what you're working on?" asked Sasha, pushing Sven out of the way. "Hey we can help you open it if you let us in," she said, through the keyhole.

The door suddenly flung open and an ancient looking dwarf with jet-black shoulder length hair glared up at them. His face was deeply lined and his blue eyes looked rheumy. Unlike the other dwarves, he wore no gems in his hair, which was obviously dyed. His clothes were very plain, just brown trousers tucked into old black boots and a grubby grey shirt.

"No, it's mine, all mine, go away or you'll be sorry," he shouted at them, before slamming the door in their faces.

They all looked at each other dismayed.

"Alex, I think it's time to turbo charge. Come on do your angry thing, he might change his mind when you blast open his door," said Matt, pushing Alex forward towards the thick heavy door.

"Dvalin," Alex called out. "We don't want your treasure but if you tell us what we need to know we'll try and help you open the door. I swear we don't want anything from you other than your knowledge."

The door creaked open slightly and Dvalin poked just his head out. "You swear, do you? Would you swear on the lives of your friends here?" he asked, pointing at them all. "If you break your oath I'll turn them all into stone."

"Look I swear, just let us in and we can talk about this. We've walked for miles and we would really like to sit down."

Alex felt fine but the others were looking tired and in need of a rest.

"Come on Dvalin, these Midgardians are our guests, you owe them hospitality, it's our way," said Sven, pushing through their legs and placing a foot in the doorway so Dvalin couldn't shut it again.

Dvalin growled, opened the door wider and waved them in.

"Fine but if you take anything or mess my house up I will turn you into stone," he grumbled.

His house was just one small room. There was a bed tucked into one corner, two little sofas, a wooden table and a small kitchenette. It was a complete mess, there were cobwebs hanging from the ceiling and papers were stacked on every surface and strewn all over the floor. Dirty plates and cups were stacked up on the table and filled the small sink and there was a horrible smoky smell from the flaming torches on the walls.

"Dvalin, you can't live like this surely?" asked Sven. "It's unhygienic."

"Mind your own business," muttered Dvalin, gathering

papers from a small brown sofa and off some chairs and dumping them onto the floor.

"Well sit down then and tell me what you want quickly, I'm busy," he said grumpily, standing by the sink with his arms crossed.

"Lit said you may know the location of the Tyrfing sword," said Sven, sitting down on one of the rickety old wooden chairs.

"No," Dvalin said, abruptly.

He had turned very pale and shook his head.

"No, I can't tell you that," he added, still shaking his head vigorously.

"Dvalin it's very important. The survival of Midgard depends on Alex finding the sword and using it to seal the portal to Hel's realm," said Sven. "There's a prophecy that foretells that if he doesn't do this Hel will be released and will destroy everything in Midgard. She has always sought vengeance; you know what she's like. She will release every beast and soul in Helheim and it will be the end of Midgard as we know it," said Sven, desperately. "Think about the impact on Svartalfheim, we'll be ruined."

"It's impossible, you have no idea what you're asking of me," said Dvalin, trembling. "My brother and I cursed the sword when we created it and I've regretted it all my life. The lives it has taken, brave men, men who didn't deserve to die. I can't reveal it to you, it's too dangerous. I swore an oath it would never be used again, oh the shame, the shame of it..."

Dvalin was crying now, tears were streaming down his wrinkled old face and he sniffed noisily. Sasha dug into her bag and pulled out some tissues and handed him one.

"Here, please don't upset yourself. Tell us about this curse. There must be a way to break it surely? There is always some sort of get out clause surely?" she asked, dabbing at his tears with a tissue.

"Not this curse, we made it ever binding, it was our revenge you see. My brother and I were tricked and captured by a Midgard King. He forced us to forge a sword that had a golden hilt, that would never break or rust, would cut through stone and would never miss its mark. He tortured us for weeks until we gave in and made the sword. We cursed it though so whenever it was wielded someone would die and it would also kill the person who drew it. If you take the sword you will die. There isn't anything I can do to reverse the curse, it was bound with dragon's blood. Those curses are binding for eternity," he wept.

"So, if Alex uses the sword to seal the henge he will die?" asked Becca, shocked.

"Not straight away but it will happen. The sword always takes its revenge. How and when is up to the sword," said Dvalin, sniffing loudly again and blowing his nose.

"We have no choice, without the sword we will all die," said Sven, wringing his hands.

"No Midgard will die, we can seal off Svartalfheim," said Dvalin. "This hasn't got anything to do with us."

"But who will we trade with? They're a good source of gold. The giants in Jotunheim are not interested in our goods. The natural balance will be destroyed, we will be doomed," cried Sven, angrily.

Alex stood up from the small sofa he had crammed himself into and went to stand in front of Dvalin.

"Look it's my risk, my choice. Once I seal the henge you can have the sword back and hide it again. I need to do this, please tell me where it is," he said.

"Look if you tell us where it is we'll take a look at this Gulldyrr or whatever it is and help you figure out how to open it. You'll be the richest dwarf ever," said Sasha, trying to persuade him.

Dvalin's eyes gleamed with greed for a moment but then he shook his head.

"It's no use, it's impossible. I've tried every combination and nothing works," he said, miserably.

"Let us take a look anyway, you never know, a fresh set of eyes and all that. What is this Gulldyrr anyway?" asked Sasha.

"It's a door leading to Thor's greatest treasure. He got a Volva to charm it so no one would steal it from him. Charms can be broken though they're not like curses. I want that treasure, I deserve it," he said, petulantly.

"I can't believe you want to steal from Thor, that's just not right," said Sasha, sternly.

"He deserves it, meddling god. If it weren't for him, that little twit Lit would be dead by now. Arrogant, self-conceited piece of...."

"Hang on," interrupted Becca. "You want the treasure because Thor made Lit immortal when he kicked him into Baldur's funeral pyre?"

"What is this treasure anyway?" asked Pete.

"No one knows for sure. It must be good though, Thor is very rich. There must be a pile of gold as big as a mountain," said Dvalin his eyes glazing over. "There is something I want more than the gold though. There is a rumour there's a potion in there, which can protect dwarves from sunlight. I want that. To be able to go outside like Lit. He has no idea how lucky he is," said Dvalin bitterly. "I'm getting old now, I can't have much more time left. Just to go outside during the day and to see the sun, that would be special."

Another tear trickled down Dvalin's cheek. "It's impossible though. I'm out of ideas."

Dvalin sat on the floor, put his head in his hands and started rocking back and forth. Alex looked around at the others and shrugged.

"Dvalin, if we help you open the door will you tell me where the sword is?" he asked, bending down and touching him gently on the shoulder.

Dvalin sniffed and hiccupped.

"You can try, but it's no good," he said, twisting the laces on his boots.

"Where is it? Please tell me it's somewhere near here, my legs are killing me," said Matt, getting to his feet and stretching.

"It's not far, I moved to this house so I could be closer to it. Follow me and I'll show you." Dvalin said, perking up a little.

They all followed Dvalin out of his house and he stopped about fifteen paces away. He put his hand on the rock wall and a narrow tunnel appeared. He disappeared into the gloom and they followed in single file. Alex could make out a light ahead and the tunnel opened up into a large cavern. Directly opposite there was a large door, which glowed yellow. A skull face was embossed into the surface and protruding from the door about half way up were what looked like giant finger bones, laid out in a line like a piano.

"Is that door gold?" asked Pete, as he entered the cavern.

They all moved closer to get a better look.

"Yes, solid gold. I planned on removing it when I broke the charm," said Dvalin, his eyes filled with greed again.

"You don't do things by half, do you?" asked Sasha, disapprovingly.

Dvalin just shrugged.

"Ew, that's creepy," said Becca, as she inspected the gold door. "Are those bones? They're massive."

"Yes, they're the finger bones of some Jotun giants who annoyed Thor," said Dvalin.

"What did they do?" asked Becca, fascinated.

"They stole his hammer Mjolnir. Thor had to dress up as a woman and pretend to be a potential bride for the King of the Jotnar to trick them into giving it back to him. He said he wanted to see the famous hammer before he agreed to the marriage. It worked, Thor got Mjonir back and he killed all the giants in sight. He chopped off their hands and arranged for some dwarves to create this door. I think it's a bit of a warning to others," said Dvalin, lost in thought.

"And you want to steal off him? Not wise my friend, not wise," said Matt, touching one of the bones.

A deep note reverberated around the cavern and they jumped back.

"Alex please remind me not to annoy your dad," said Pete.

The door had really shocked him, it was all very macabre.

"Okay, so what's the score with the door then?" asked Alex, pushing another bone down.

A higher note sounded and echoed around them.

"Alex, stop it," Sasha hissed.

"The door is sealed with a music charm. You need to play the right piece of music and then it will open. I've tried everything though. Every piece of music known to dwarf, man, elf, giant, you name it I've tried it," said Dvalin, sounding depressed.

"Chopsticks?" asked Matt.

They all turned to look at him with raised eyebrows. "What? It's the only piece of music I know. I gave up piano lessons after learning that one," he grinned.

"Trust me I've tried everything. I even played them all backwards just in case. Whatever this music is, it doesn't exist in the Nine Worlds," said Dvalin, staring at the door morosely.

"Crikey, that must have taken some time," said Matt, playing a few notes of chopsticks.

Sasha batted his hand away.

"Oh, only about three hundred years," said Dvalin sighing.

"You're three hundred years old?" asked Becca, amazed.

"I'm older than that. I can't say for sure, I gave up counting," he said, pondering.

"But I thought dwarves were mortal?" asked Becca.

"We are, we just age better than you humans. Must be because we live underground, no sun damage you see," he said. "So, do you have any ideas or not?" he asked.

"Well if you have tried every single piece of music played before, how about trying something that has never been played before. A new piece of music." Sasha suggested.

"How would that work? If it's never been played before how would the Volva who sealed the door seal it?" asked Dvalin, confused.

"Think about it. It wouldn't be as easy as being a piece of music in existence. Volvas can see into the future, right?" she said, warming to her idea.

"Yes," said Dvalin, still confused.

"Well let's say this Volva looked into the future and sealed the door with a piece of music that hasn't been created yet but will be in the future," said Sasha, excitedly.

"You could be onto something there," said Dvalin, jumping up and down on the balls of his feet and clapping his hands together.

Sven just looked at them all bored.

"Okay genius and how do we find a piece of music that hasn't been written yet?" asked Pete. "This is impossible, we're wasting our time here. Look dwarf just tell us where the sword is and we can get on with saving the world. Or better idea let's just leave this and go home. I bet Alan has sorted this all out by now," he said, frustrated.

"No, you swore to help me open the door and then I'll help you. I think I have an idea," said Dvalin, tapping his chin.

"Alex, we're wasting time. Come on zap him a few times, then he'll talk," said Pete, walking up to Dvalin and grabbing him by his arm.

"Pete cut it out. I'm not into torturing dwarves. We agreed to help so let's do this. The quicker we get this sorted, the quicker we can get the sword. What's your idea Dvalin?" asked Alex. "If it involves contacting the Volva who created the charm then count me out," he said, pushing Pete out of the way.

"The Volva who created the charm is dead so that's not an option. No, I was thinking you need to find Fossegrimen, we call him Grim for short. He creates new pieces of music all the time and he's a big favourite of the Volvas. He's quite good looking apparently," said Dvalin, bursting with excitement.

The more he thought about Sasha's idea the more he thought it could work. "That must be it, that must be. Quickly you need to go and find him," he said, bouncing up and down.

He's got a lot of energy for someone so old they couldn't remember, thought Alex grinning.

"Okay and how do we do that, do you know where this Grim, lives?" asked Alex.

"Not exactly but I know he hangs out where there are waterfalls, so that's your best bet," said Dvalin.

"Can you narrow that down? There are millions of waterfalls, we can't visit them all," said Alex, pacing around frustrated.

He could feel static electricity start to build up in his fingers tips so he took a few deep breaths to calm down.

"There's only one person who could say for sure," said Dvalin, grinning from ear to ear.

"Please not a Volva. I've really had my fill of them already," moaned Alex.

"Sorry yes a Volva, it's the only way. They always track him, I think they're a bit obsessed with him," said Dvalin, laughing.

"There's no way we're going back to Cassie, she's crazy," said Alex.

"I think scary would be a more accurate description," said Matt.

"We don't need to bother Cassie, we have our own local Volva here in Ostleheim. Come on let's go summon her," said

Dvalin, hurrying off down the tunnel.

They followed him back to his house and watched as he scurried around gathering random bits and pieces from all over the room.

"So how do you summon a Volva?" asked Becca, watching him root around a small cupboard and bring out a bottle of what looked like eyeballs.

"Very carefully," said Dvalin, clearing a table and placing his items in a row.

"If I get this wrong, she'll be really mad at me. Goodness knows what she will do to us. She can be a bit mean sometimes. The last time she was summoned, the dwarf who did it used the wrong feather and she came through naked. She was livid, she made a portal and sent him to Midgard," said Dvalin.

"Well that's not so bad, is it?" asked Becca.

"It was daytime and he turned to stone. All because he used the wrong feather. So careless.," said Dvalin, tutting.

He double-checked all of the items on the table carefully.

"Right that should do it," he said. "A phoenix feather, a mermaid scale, a tear of a virgin, they're hard to find these days I can tell you," he said, tutting and pouring one drop from a small jam jar. "One goat eyeball and a hint of dragon's breath."

"Dragon's breath, how do you get that?" asked Alex, peering over Dvalin's shoulder.

"Carefully, very, very carefully," said Dvalin. "I nearly lost my beard getting this last lot. The dragon coughed just as I got near and he singed me. It was very painful, I had nightmares for weeks," he said, gathering all of the items together and placing them in a small bowl.

"Right everyone stand back, you don't want her landing on you," he said, waving everyone back.

They all moved back as far as they could against the stone walls and watched Dvalin as he muttered what sounded like a spell over the bowl. The flaming torches on the wall flickered and a mini tornado whipped up in the centre of the room sending all of the loose papers flying around in the air. The wind picked up and Alex had to shield his eyes from the debris flying around the room. Suddenly there was a loud sucking noise, followed by a big bang, then all became still and there was just the sound of paper fluttering to the floor. Alex opened his eyes and in the centre of the room stood a haggard old woman dressed all in black. Her eyes were completely jet black, no white showed at all. Her skin looked like it was rotting and hanging off her bones. She scanned the room and hissed.

"Dvalin is that you? What do you want? I was waiting for my shopping to arrive. This had better be good you scoundrel," she said, glaring at him.

"Hello Maggie, you're looking well," said Dvalin, coughing and raising his eyebrows at her.

"What? Oh Odin," she said, looking at her gnarled hands.

She swept them over her face and she suddenly transformed into a slim young girl with long luxuriant chestnut coloured hair and bright blue eyes.

"Ah that's better. Sorry about that folks, I didn't have time to prepare before I was so rudely interrupted," she said, glaring at Dvalin again. "Oh well, hello there," she said eyeing up Alex and sidling over to him.

She scanned him up and down and literally undressed him with her eyes.

"You must be Thor's new son, quite the piece of gossip at the moment. Yes, yes very handsome, oh and I can sense the power in you. You're going to be very strong when you learn how to control it."

"Fat chance," said Pete, sniggering.

Her head snapped around to him. Her eyes were black fathomless pits and she snarled at him.

"Don't interrupt me you rude boy," she said, gliding over to him.

Her feet were hovering two inches off the ground.

"Well, well, what have we here?" she asked, sniffing the air around Pete. "I can smell him on you, oh yes I will never forget that smell," she cackled.

She turned to face the others and her eyes were normal again. She walked in front of all of them sniffing the air carefully.

"Hmm interesting," she said.

They stood still, petrified, no one dared to say anything but they all wanted to ask her about what she could smell on Pete.

Alex turned to him and mouthed, "what?" but Pete just shrugged his shoulders.

"Maggie dear we need your help," said Dvalin, breaking the uncomfortable silence. She turned to face him smiling broadly showing off perfect white teeth.

"Of course I will help Thor's son, what is it?" she asked.

"We need to find Grim, do you know where he is?" asked Dvalin.

Maggie sighed and her eyes glowed.

"Of course I know, as if I would let that young hottie slip away. Why do you want him?" she asked, narrowing her eyes suspiciously at the girls.

"I would like him to create some music for me, something original for a birthday gift and these fine youngsters agreed to talk to him about it for me. You know, me not being able to go outside and all," said Dvalin, studying a feather intently, which he had plucked off the table.

"Ah, a birthday gift, is it? Who for?" she asked.

"Why the Grandmaster of course. I want it to be a surprise so please don't tell anyone," said Dvalin.

Alex looked at him with raised eyebrows and Dvalin shrugged.

"Liar," she hissed, as she flew over to Dvalin and leaned over him. "Now why would you lie to me?"

"I'm not, I'm not," he squeaked, backing away.

"Are you still trying to open that door?" she laughed.

"I might be but that's none of your business," he said haughtily.

"You're a fool, but you make me laugh so I'll help you. Grim was hanging out under the Seidrfossen falls yesterday," she said, moving back to Alex's side and running her hand down his arm.

He shivered with distaste and moved away.

"Ah the one in Norway?" asked Dvalin, excited.

"Yes. Now I need to go home or I'll miss my delivery," she snapped.

"I don't suppose you could do us one more favour?" asked Dvalin. "We're in a bit of a rush, if you could open a portal to the falls that would really help," he said, looking at her pleadingly.

"Oh, is that all? Can you do this? Can you do that? What am I your slave? What do I get out of all of this?" asked Maggie.

Her eyes had started to turn black again and she spun around to face Alex.

"Tell you what," she said, eyeing him up again. "If this handsome young god takes me on a date I'll do it."

"You what?" cried Alex, in a panic.

"Why what's the matter with me? Do you think I'm ugly? Am I not good enough for you?" asked Maggie, looking very hurt.

"No, no of course not. Er I just don't think my girlfriend would be too happy about that," said Alex, moving to Becca's side and reaching for her hand.

"Girlfriend? Her?" screeched Maggie, her eyes blacking up fully.

She stood over Becca menacingly. She was a good head taller than her when she was hovering off the ground.

"Okay, okay, I'll do it," said Alex, stepping in front of Becca protectively and holding his hands up.

"Take us to the falls first, give me a few days and then I'll sort a date out. Dinner, the movies, whatever you want," he said, desperately.

"Lovely, okay but you have to swear an oath first, I don't want you backing out of this," she said, smiling and stroking a finger down his chest.

She brushed over his mark and a tiny spark made her jump back.

"Yeah right whatever," he said, moving out of her reach

again. "I swear to take you on a date sometime in the future," he said.

That future could be a long time from now he thought to himself and he grinned.

"Right okay then, let's get you to the falls so you can get your music for Dvalin's 'Grandmaster'," she said, sarcastically.

She moved over to the table waved her hand and it moved to one side making more space in the centre of the room.

"I'll get you as close as I can. Portals can be a bit hit and miss near water. If I try and get you too close you could end up in the water. Gather together really closely in a circle and give my love to Grim," she said, winking.

"Wait hang on, what about Dvalin and Sven, I take it you guys can't come?" asked Alex.

"No, we can't go outside, especially not in the day. We'll wait for you here. I'm sure we have lots to catch up on," said Dvalin, looking around for Sven.

He was sitting comfortably on a sofa playing Candy Crush on his phone and did not acknowledge the others at all.

"Go on you had best get going, you don't have much time," said Dvalin.

They gathered together into a tight circle and wrapped their arms around each other. Maggie drew a circle around them with a stick of chalk she pulled from her pocket.

"Chalk? Cassie took all night creating some sort of potion for the portal she created for us," said Alex, confused.

"We all have our different methods," said Maggie, closing her eyes.

She started to chant repeatedly. "Hyrr, logr, mold, lopt. Hyrr, logr, mold, lopt...."

The chalk began to glow a bright white and flames licked up around them. Sasha squealed and moved in closer. Alex could feel an intense heat rise up his back and he felt as though he were on fire. Then suddenly he felt icy cold, as though someone had poured a bucket of icy water over him and then he fell through a hole in the floor.

Chapter Nine

"Not again," cried Matt, falling down uncontrollably.

The wind rushed passed Alex's face and he struggled to breathe. He tightened his grip on Becca and Sasha; he didn't want to let them go. There was a sudden flash of light and they landed on a soft surface. Alex felt himself being sucked into a pillowy softness and then he felt himself bouncing up and down a few times. Looking down, he could see the earth rippling and undulating under them. It was like they were on a big bouncy castle.

Once their fall had been broken the earth became firm again and they got to their feet unsteadily.

"Oh my god I'm going to puke," said Matt, bending over at the waist and taking some deep breaths.

"That's like the freakiest fairground ride ever," he said, straightening up.

Alex flattened his hair, which was standing on end and looked around at the group.

"Everyone okay?" he asked.

Pete was patting the back of his legs where his trousers were smoking.

"That witch burnt me, look, there's a hole in my jeans," he said angrily, turning around so they could see the scorch marks.

"Well she did say to get in close, you'll live," said Alex, laughing.

He looked around and took in their surroundings. "Where are we? There's no waterfall here," he said, confused.

They were standing in a green valley with mountains

rearing up on each side. Tall trees covered the slopes and the sun glistened on a river in the distance. There were no houses in sight and no signs of life anywhere.

"Oh wow, this is beautiful," said Becca, looking around in appreciation.

"Stunning," agreed Sasha. "It's so peaceful."

It was nice to be out in the light again. It had felt like they had been underground for days.

"Listen," said Becca, cocking her head to the side.

Alex stood still and listened. He could hear the rumbling noise of a waterfall in the distance.

"Over there," he said, pointing to the river, which was curling through the valley.

"If we follow the river, we'll come to the waterfall. It sounds like it's over that way."

They started to walk towards the river, casting looks about them as they made their way through thick lush green grass.

"It doesn't look like anyone lives here. Look, there are no houses, sheep, cows, goats, nothing," said Pete, looking down the valley into the distance.

"Pete what was that witch talking about when she said she could smell him on you? That was really weird," asked Sasha.

Alex had forgotten about that and listened closely.

"Dunno, weird old bag. Maybe she could smell my dad, he wears really strong aftershave," he joked. "I'm more interested in where Alex is going to take the lovely Maggie on their date," he said, changing the subject quickly.

"Man, there is no way I'm taking that crazy old woman on a date," said Alex, pushing Pete away from him playfully.

"But you promised Alex. You need to be careful. If Cassie

finds out, then you'll be in trouble."

Pete skipped out of the way as Alex swung a punch in his direction.

"Well I figured I would be dead anyway. As soon as I draw that sword then from the sounds of it I've more or less signed my death warrant," he said, plucking off the head of a stray piece of corn and crushing it between his fingers.

The enormity of his situation struck him and he started to feel angry. He had never asked for this, it was so unfair he thought to himself. A rumble of thunder sounded in the distance and echoed between the mountains. Alex looked up to the sky and saw dark clouds gathering covering up the sun. A flash of lightning lit up the clouds and it started to rain. The others had stopped in their tracks and were staring at Alex horrified.

"Alex that's not going to happen. Look we'll figure it out. There must be some way to break that curse. You are a god, it probably won't even apply to you," said Matt, draping an arm around Alex's shoulders.

"I'm only a demigod and I'm not immortal, look what happened to Baldur, he died," said Alex, shrugging off Matt's arm.

"He's not really dead, he's just stuck in Helheim, with the niece from Hell," said Sasha.

"He might as well be dead. It's okay I'll join him for a few beers it's cool. We all have to go sometime. I might as well do it saving the world. Total hero and all that. You can build statues and worship me. It will be awesome," he said, sounding braver than he felt.

He wasn't feeling very confident and he felt sick every time he thought about the sword. He was hoping there would be some sort of get out clause. There must be some perks to being a demi god and a son of Thor. His granddad was Odin for goodness sake he thought to himself smiling. He was pretty sure Odin wouldn't let his new-found grandson die without a fight.

Becca came over to his side and slipped her hand in his.

"We won't let anything happen to you I promise," she said squeezing his hand gently. "Anyway, you promised me a date first remember, the movies?"

"How could I forget," said Alex, bending over and kissing the top of her head.

She looked up into his eyes and placed her other hand on his chest and tilted her head up.

"Come on you two, we'll never get there," called back Sasha. "And Alex do something about the rain will you, I'm getting soaked," she moaned.

Alex grinned and quickly kissed Becca on the forehead and pulled her after him. The sky lightened with his mood and the rain stopped almost immediately.

"Just you wait until we get five minutes alone," he growled, softly.

"Only five minutes? Really Alex I'm disappointed," she said, bumping into his arm.

"Oh my god, come on let's go in this direction, we'll catch them up later," said Alex, as he tried to drag her over to a copse of trees.

Becca pulled him back.

"We'll have plenty of time for that after we've saved the world," she laughed blushing furiously.

Every cell of her body wanted Alex to drag her into the trees but they had a task to do and had to focus.

"But we might not make it. Who says this Grim has the right music? He might not give us anything then we'll never get the sword and it will be the end of the world. This could be our last chance, come on," he pleaded.

"No way we're running out of time come on," she said, pulling him towards the river. "Thinking about time, it's been ages since we last spoke to Alan. He must be going out of his mind."

Alex dug his phone from his pocket. "Damn, no signal," he said, holding his phone up into the air and twisting around in all directions. "You're right he must be going crazy. On the positive side, I can't see any weird stuff happening, no wandering spirits, no monsters so I guess the henge is still holding up."

"That's true but I doubt we have a lot of time. Come on stop dawdling," said Becca.

She started to jog to catch up with the others who were nearing the stream and Alex increased his pace.

"It's sounding closer already, come on guys, I reckon it's around that bend up there," said Matt, pointing up the river to where the valley narrowed about a mile upstream.

They followed the riverbed, scrambling over large boulders and pushing their way through tall grass. Eventually they came to a bend in the river and they made their way carefully around the corner. The sides of the mountains converged and just the water separated the thick trees on either side of the river. They stepped carefully between the trees, slipping on the muddy ground. When they came around the bend the trees opened up and revealed a lake completely surrounded by the tall mountains. At the furthest end of the lake a waterfall cascaded over a ridge protruding from the side of the mountain. The water plunged into the blue water of the lake sending up a fine mist and creating a glistening rainbow.

"Oh wow, this is amazing," said Becca, shading her eyes.

The sun was sparkling off the waterfall and the lake, making it hard to see.

"How do we get over there? There's no path and the sides are too steep to climb," asked Pete, looking around.

"I hate to say it but I think we're going to have to swim," said Alex, looking at the water.

It looked really cold.

"No way man, that water will be freezing, we'll get hypothermia," said Pete, backing away.

"Well unless you can see a boat we don't have much choice. Tell you what I'll go on my own. I don't feel the cold too much," said Alex, stripping off his t-shirt.

Becca looked at Sasha and grinned. He really had a body to die for. She couldn't tear her eyes away when he started to unbutton his trousers. Becca's heart was thumping and her stomach turned over. A shout made her tear her eyes away.

"Hey look there's a boat over here under these trees," called Matt, from back where they had just come from.

Alex hadn't noticed he had disappeared.

"Cool problem solved," said Alex, buttoning up his trousers and slipping his t-shirt back on.

"Oh, for god's sake," muttered Becca, under her breath.

They pushed their way through a large bush near the edge of the water where Matt was rustling around. Sure enough there was a small rowing boat tied up to a tree.

"Okay, who can row?" asked Becca, helping Matt pull away some branches, which were covering the boat.

They all looked at each other blankly.

"Don't look at me, I've never been in a boat before," said Alex, holding out his hands.

"Me neither," said Matt. "It can't be that hard though. Come on jump in, we should be able to squeeze in."

Matt held the boat steady and the girls stepped in gingerly and sat on a small seat at the back of the boat. Alex got in next and sat on the seat in the middle and inserted an oar into the oar support. Pete crouched at the front and held out a hand to Matt who sat beside Alex and inserted the other oar. Matt pushed off the bank with the oar and the boat drifted into the lake.

"Okay together now," said Matt, dipping his oar into the water.

Alex pulled on his oar too but pulled harder than Matt and they ended up going in a circle.

"Guys we're not getting anywhere," said Becca, looking around. "Try pulling at the same time."

"We are, what's going on?" asked Alex, frustrated.

He could feel static electricity build up in his fingertips and he made a mental note to keep calm. Electricity and water did not mix.

"Just one of you row," suggested Sasha.

Matt and Alex looked at each other and shrugged. It was worth a go. Alex sat back and Matt grabbed both oars and started to row. At last they started to make progress and they slowly made their way across the lake towards the waterfall.

"So how do we find this Grim then?" asked Pete, peering towards the waterfall.

Matt started to back paddle with the oars, the spray from the waterfall was starting to get them wet.

"Listen what's that?" asked Sasha.

The sound of a violin echoed across the lake. It was the most beautiful sound Alex had ever heard and he was mesmerised by it.

"Look over there," said Becca, pointing to the rocks on the left-hand side of the waterfall.

Alex looked over and could see a naked man with long flowing blonde hair half sitting in the water and half on the rocks playing a violin.

"That must be him," whispered Becca excitedly, gripping Sasha on the knee.

The man was truly stunning. The most beautiful man she had ever seen with a strong jaw and chiseled cheekbones. He was even better looking than Alex she thought and that was saying something. He was completely engrossed in his music and did not see them.

Sasha nudged Becca and mouthed, "oh my god."

The girls giggled and the boys shifted around in their seats and glared at them. The boat wobbled alarmingly and the girls shrieked and clung onto the sides. The violin suddenly stopped and there was a loud splash. When they looked back the man had disappeared.

"Damn it, where did he go?" asked Alex, looking over the edge of the boat into the water.

"Why hello my lovelies what brings you here?" asked Grim.

He was resting his elbows on the back of the boat and

talking to Sasha and Becca. They jumped and looked behind them making the boat wobble again.

"Oh, er hello. I don't suppose your name is Grim, is it?" asked Sasha gazing into his eyes.

They were a bright blue and glowed. He took her breath away and she blushed bright red.

"Charming," he purred, looking at both of them appreciatively. "Yes, I am he. It's been a long time since a human young lady graced my presence. Please let me play you a little something I've been working on," he said, in a low voice.

He slid under the water and the girls looked at each other and giggled again.

"Really?" asked Alex, moodily.

"Shh, look there he is," whispered Becca, pointing to a rock near the edge of the waterfall.

Grim pulled himself out of the water; he flicked his head so the water from his hair fanned out around him showering droplets everywhere.

"I'm going to puke," Matt whispered, to Alex grimacing.

Alex growled in response and looked back at Becca and Sasha. They were practically drooling and their eyes were popping out of their heads.

"I call this one 'Lovers on the Lake'," said Grim, winking at the girls.

They sighed, leant forward with their elbows on their knees and their hands on their chins and waited.

Grim started to play the violin and the most beautiful music Alex had ever heard echoed across the lake. He was completely entranced for the entire song. By the end of it they were all leaning forward with their elbows on their knees cupping their chins with their hands with dreamy looks on their faces. The final note echoed between the mountains and then all was still except for the sound of the waterfall splashing into the lake.

Grim opened his eyes, placed the violin in his lap and looked directly at the girls.

"Did you like that my beauties?" he asked, softly.

"Oh my god yes, that was the most beautiful music I've ever heard," gushed Sasha.

Grim slipped under the water and emerged behind the boat again.

"I am so pleased you liked it, I made that up just for you two."

He smiled seductively and reached into the boat to stroke a strand of Sasha's hair. He then ran his hand down Becca's arm.

"How about I do another one, then perhaps you could do something for me?" he asked, raising his eyebrows suggestively.

"Er excuse me," said Alex, cutting in loudly and glaring at Grim. "We're a bit pushed for time, so if it's all the same to you we'll have to listen to another song another time. Becca perhaps you could explain to Grim why we're here," he said, looking at Becca.

Alex figured Grim would be far more receptive if one of the girls asked him.

"Becca, what a lovely name," Grim crooned. "Please go ahead how can I help you?" he asked smiling.

His teeth were perfect and Becca wanted to lean forward and kiss his red lips. She shook her head.

"Ah right, well you see we have a bit of a predicament," she stuttered, shyly.

She was finding it hard to form words whilst he was gazing into her eyes.

"We need to find the sword of Tyrfing so Alex here can close a breach to Hel but Dvalin, the dwarf won't tell us where it is unless we help him unlock a door to a great treasure which is protected by a charm and we think if you created a piece of new music that might be the key to unlocking the door," she said, breathlessly.

"My, my now that is a predicament. What happens if my music doesn't work then?" asked Grim, smiling lazily and playing with a strand of Becca's hair.

"It will be the end of the world as we know it," said Sasha. "Hel will be free to roam the Nine Worlds and will release all of the spirits and whatever else she has locked up down there."

"Hmm yes that could be a bit of a problem. Okay here's the deal. I'll create a piece of music for you to unlock your door, but there is a price. I can only write music for others in return for a lamb."

"What? Are you serious? A lamb, why?" asked Alex, surprised.

"Yes, a lamb. Those are my normal terms, though typically people come and ask me to teach them how to play music, not create music," he said, lying on his back and floating. "The second part of the deal is the young ladies will stay here with me whilst you boys fetch it for me," he said, looking at Alex slyly.

"We're in the middle of nowhere, where do we get a lamb

from? I doubt there's a sheep shop anywhere near here and we're running out of time."

Alex's eyes felt itchy and he guessed arcs of electricity were gathering. He took a deep breath and closed his eyes.

"Look we really need help here. We have been going around in circles and not getting anywhere. Is there anything else we can get you or do for you which is actually possible quickly?" he asked.

"Well I'm sure the young ladies here have plenty they can give me," said Grim, grinning.

"No," shouted Alex and Matt at the same time. " Leave them out of this," said Alex.

"A lamb it is then," smirked Grim.

"Okay any top tips on where we could get it?" asked, Alex pushing his hand through his hair and making it stand on end.

"There are farms along the valley, they would be your best bet."

"We didn't see anything for miles, what are we meant to do row the whole length of the river, seriously? We just about rowed across this lake, we'll never get anywhere," asked Alex, exasperated.

"And don't suggest a portal, we're not going there again. I would rather walk," said Matt, worried.

Twice was already enough for him. There was something about dropping into a black abyss, which made him feel not quite in control of his life.

"Well I could lend you Gorvir, she would be faster than your boat but you'll get a bit wet," said Grim.

"Gor...who?" asked Alex.

"Gorvir, my pet," said Grim, grinning.

"Oh right, cool, okay. Where is she then?" asked Alex, looking around.

"Right now, she is under your boat. I'm standing on her," said Grim.

"What?" Sasha squealed and looked over the edge of the boat making it rock.

The water was very clear and she could see a long, thick scaly body stretched right under the boat. Alex peered over the side too and sighed. His visions of galloping to the nearest farm on a horse quickly disappearing.

"What is that?" he asked, pointing under the boat.

"That is Gorvir, one of the daughters of Jormungand, she helps me travel between waterfalls. Quite handy really and she keeps the Volva's in check when they get a bit frisky. Hang on I'll have a word with her."

Grim dipped below the surface and Alex turned to the girls.

"Is this guy for real?" he asked.

They shrugged their shoulders and leant over the boat to look for Grim. After a few minutes his head broke the surface and next to him appeared what looked like a cross between a dragon and a snake. Gorvir was huge, droplets of water cascaded from her scales, which were a deep blue colour. She had dark purple horns circling her head and yellow eyes. She opened her mouth wide and revealed two huge fangs. Everyone in the boat reared back in panic and it rocked alarmingly.

"Don't worry," said Grim, steadying the boat with his muscular arms. "She's just a bit sleepy I woke her up, she's yawning."

"Crikey, I thought we were dinner then," said Pete, pushing Alex and Matt back onto their seats.

"She's good to go and is happy to help," said Grim cheerily, stroking Gorvir's head.

"Okay so how does this work then?" asked Alex, eyeing up the dragon snake suspiciously.

"Well this is where you'll get a bit wet which is why I suggested the young ladies stay with me. We don't want them getting chilly," said Grim, winking at the girls.

They were both staring at him with big grins plastered on their faces.

"There is no way they're staying here with you alone," said Alex, glaring at Grim.

"Hey you and Matt go. I'll keep an eye on things here," said Pete. "I can't swim very well anyway, and there is no way I'm getting in the water with that thing," he said, pointing at Gorvir.

"You would do well not to insult her boy," said Grim, menacingly.

"Alex, we'll be fine, you go. It will be quicker that way," said Becca quickly, before Pete said anything else insulting. "Nothing will happen, we'll just wait here and we'll have Pete. Honestly it will be fine," she said.

"Okay let's do this. Matt, are you with me?" asked Alex, patting Matt on the back.

Matt grinned. "I get to ride a snake along a river, too right I'm up for this....hang on though, it is safe isn't it?" he asked Grim. "Does she need to eat first?"

Grim chuckled. "No, she's good. You'll have to slip into the water and hold onto her and she'll pull you along."

Alex dipped his hand into the water and shivered, the water was icy cold.

"We'll get hyperthermia you must be kidding," he said.

"If I'm not mistaken you're the new demigod all the Volva's are excited about. You can command the water around you to be warm. Gorvir may be a little uncomfortable as she likes the cold but you two will be fine," explained Grim.

"Hang on. Sorry but I've no idea how to do that. Are you saying I just tell the water to be warm and it will just happen?" asked Alex. "Awesome."

Grim sighed and rolled his eyes. "It's a bit more than that, you need to feel as one with the water and think of it as being warm. Give it a try."

Alex shrugged and dipped his hand into the water again. It was icy and his fingers soon became numb. He was trying to concentrate but didn't really have a clue what he was meant to do.

"Come on, try harder, just believe the water's warm," said Grim, impatiently.

"It's not working this is ridiculous," said Alex.

He took his hand out of the water and shook it to get some feeling back into his fingers. They were completely numb.

"Okay let's do this the hard way," said Grim, moving swiftly to Alex's side of the boat.

He reached up and grabbed Alex by the arms and threw him into the water. Alex fell head first into the icy lake. He felt as though pins and needles were piercing his entire body. He kicked his legs and broke the surface gasping for air.

"Come on show us what you've got or you'll die from the

cold really soon," said Grim, swimming out of his reach.

Alex trod water and pictured himself in a warm bubble. Gradually he started to feel his legs again. It was either starting to work or his bladder had released he thought to himself. The warmth spread slowly up his body and fanned out around him.

"There you go, that's it." Grim said, smiling. "Your turn," he said to Matt, grabbing him quickly by the back of his shirt and pulling him into the water.

"Dude that was not cool," said Matt, spluttering and shaking the water from his eyes. "Oh, it's like a bath in here...nice," said Matt, swimming closer to Alex.

Gorvir had slipped under the surface and emerged directly underneath them.

"Right grab a horn on each side and let her pull you," said Grim, moving back to the boat.

It had started to drift away. Gorvir broke the surface of the water and Alex grabbed hold of one of the purple horns behind her head and clung on tightly. Matt grabbed another horn on the other side and Gorvir surged forward towards the mouth of the river. Alex looked back at the boat and saw the three of them wave. He would have waved back but he was terrified of letting go. As Gorvir took them around the bend he saw Grim pulling himself into the boat. He was really glad Pete had stayed behind; there was no way he trusted Grim with the girls.

Gorvir was weaving from side to side, her powerful body pushing them quickly through the water. Alex just about managed to keep his head above the water. He was concentrating hard on keeping them warm and began to experiment with the temperature. When it got too warm Gorvir started to slow down so he tried to keep it tepid. Alex started to relax and looked around trying to find signs of a farm.

After several miles, Matt pointed to the left bank. "Look there's smoke behind those trees," he spluttered, through a mouth full of water.

Alex looked over and could see the smoke; it was worth investigating he thought to himself.

"How do we stop this thing?" he shouted to Matt.

"No idea," shouted Matt, back laughing.

He was really beginning to enjoy the ride.

"Whoa Gorvir, whoa there girl," shouted Alex, pulling back on her horn as hard as he could.

Matt started to laugh hysterically. "She's not a horse you moron."

It did the trick though and Gorvir immediately slowed down and drifted to a stop near the bank.

"Stay there, good girl," said Alex, patting her on the head.

Gorvir reared up into the air and hissed angrily. Alex swore under his breath and quickly swam to the shore trying to get out of her reach as quickly as possible. He scrambled up the muddy bank on his hands and knees.

"Yeah, real cool man, patronise the thirty-foot serpent," said Matt, staggering up the bank. When he reached the top, he flopped onto his back and looked up at the sky.

"No one at home is ever going to believe the day we're having. They'll think we're on drugs," he said, grinning.

"Yeah I know what you mean. I keep thinking I'm going to wake up and discover it's all a dream, no make that a nightmare," said Alex, flopping down next to Matt.

"Ha, then you'll have to start all over again with Becca. You guys seem to be getting pretty close," said Matt, winking at Alex.

"Speak for yourself, I saw you holding Sasha's hand down those stairs," said Alex, laughing.

"I was being a gentleman. Anyway, we'll both be out of luck unless we get a move on and get back to them. I think they were both a bit taken with Grim," said Matt, grumpily. "I bet he's on steroids, no one has arms that muscly or a six pack that good," he said, standing up.

He reached out a hand to Alex and pulled him to his feet. Alex squeezed the bottom of his shirt and looked around. They had passed the copse of trees where he had seen the smoke and they headed back in that direction. Alex looked towards the river. Gorvir was trailing them slowly. When they reached the edge of the copse they could see a large house through the trees.

"The chimney is smoking so there must be someone at home," said Matt, hiding behind a tree. "Now what? Do you have a plan, because I don't?" he asked.

"Well it looks like a farmhouse, look there are barns over there. Let's get closer and listen for any animals," said Alex, peering through the trees.

They moved closer using the trees as cover. Alex stopped on the edge of the copse and held up his hand to stop Matt.

"There, listen," he whispered.

Matt stopped and strained his ears. He could hear the sound of an animal bleating. He looked at Alex and gave him a thumbs up. They looked around to make sure there were no people around and then hurried out of the trees and ran to the side of the barn where the sound of the bleating was coming from.

"I don't know about this Alex. We can't steal a sheep, that's just wrong, my mum will kill me if she finds out," said Matt, looking worried.

"I know but Grim said it had to be a lamb. He was quite particular about it," said Alex, rubbing his hand through his hair. "I was thinking we steal it but then send the owner the money when all of this is done and then everyone's happy."

"Okay that's all very well but have you ever killed a lamb before?" asked Matt, peering around the corner of the barn.

"No, I wasn't going to kill it, he just said a lamb. We can just grab one and give it to Grim alive. He can kill his own dinner thank you," said Alex, grinning.

They both peered into the barn and saw three lambs in a pen towards the back of the barn. They were munching on hay and staring at them. The largest bleated loudly making them jump.

"Come on let's take that little one," he said, pointing to the smallest lamb in the pen.

"Look there's a rope over there, we can use that," whispered Alex, pointing to a coiled rope on the floor in the corner closest to them.

They looked around and it all seemed quiet so they entered the barn.

"I don't think 'sheep rustler' is going to look too good on our CVs," said Matt, in a low voice as he picked up the rope from the floor.

He tiptoed to the pen and the large lamb bleated loudly

again. He jumped back in fright knocking over a bucket, which clattered, loudly to the floor. He looked at the door quickly to see if anyone had heard the noise.

"How do you keep them quiet?" he asked, looking at Alex.

"Gee I dunno, let me take a quick look at my sheep handbook which is in my back pocket. Come on hurry up with that rope someone might come," said Alex, pushing Matt towards the pen.

Matt made a loop with the rope, realising the knot tying skills he learned in Scouts was time well spent after all. He slipped the loop over the neck of the smallest lamb who had come over to investigate. It nuzzled his hand looking for food.

"Quick open the door," he said, leading the lamb to the entrance of the pen.

Alex undid the bolt and Matt led the lamb out. The others jostled to follow him and bleated loudly when Alex pushed them back in.

"Come on quickly," he whispered, loudly.

They checked no one was around and quickly ran towards the trees. The lamb bounded along beside them quite happy to be out in the open. When they reached the riverbank they realised they had a problem.

"Okay Einstein, this was your plan. How do we get a live lamb back to the waterfall on a snake?" asked Matt, stroking the lambs back to keep it calm.

"Yep I didn't think that far. Do you think Gorvir will eat it?" asked Alex, looking up and down the river trying to spot the serpent.

"Probably, but better the lamb than us. Can you hold it in one arm and hold onto the horn do you think?"

"Yeah because that'll work. I don't see this lamb coming quietly. We'll have to kill it after all," said Alex, eyeing the lamb dubiously.

It bleated loudly and backed away from Alex as though it understood.

"No way, you can't kill Bob," said Matt, standing in front of the lamb protectively.

"Bob? You named the lamb Bob? Matt, you can't name an animal who is about to become someone's dinner," said Alex.

"I was kind of hoping Grim would change his mind. Look Bob is really cute, look at those eyes," said Matt, holding the lamb's head.

"Bob's a girl you moron. Come on there's Gorvir," said Alex, pointing downstream towards the thick scaly body which was weaving its way through the water.

"Okay I have an idea, let's tie its legs together and I'll carry it around my neck," said Alex.

Matt flipped the lamb onto its back and tried to tie its legs together but it kicked and struggled and bleated loudly in protest. Alex knelt down and helped and eventually they managed to tie the feet together but they were covered in scratches and bruises when they were finished.

"Lift her up and put her legs over my head," said Alex.

"That sounds so wrong, rather you than me," said Matt, laughing.

He lifted the lamb up and draped its body over Alex's shoulders. The lamb bleated indignantly and Gorvir reared up out of the water to take a look.

"There, there Gorvir, it's just a little friend for you to play with later, you might even get to nibble on a leg if you're good," said Alex, slipping down the bank carefully and sliding into the water.

The lamb started to struggle and bleat but Alex held onto its legs firmly and started to think about warm water surrounding him in a bubble. Immediately the water began to warm up. He was really getting the hang of this and he started to wonder what else he was capable of. He looked over at Matt; he had slipped into the water too and was holding firmly onto Gorvir's horn. Gorvir slunk into the water and Alex gripped on tight with one hand and held onto the lamb's legs with the other. He chuckled to himself and Matt looked over.

"What?" asked Matt.

"Could you imagine if someone is watching this and videos us? We would be on YouTube, 'huge serpent, two boys and a lamb swimming along the river. You just couldn't make it up," he said, laughing.

Gorvir made good time heading back and before too long they were back in the lake. The boat was tied to a rock and the girls were sunbathing on a large rock listening to Grim play the violin. There was a fire smoldering and the smell of cooked fish wafted across the lake. Alex's stomach grumbled loudly, he was starving. Grim looked up when he heard Gorvir splash.

"Ah you're back. Come let me see quickly," he said, looking at the lamb dangling around Alex's shoulders.

"We brought you the most succulent lamb we could find," said Alex, struggling to swim over to the rocks with the lamb wriggling around on his shoulders.

"It certainly looks a handful," laughed Grim, swimming over to help Alex.

He plucked the lamb off Alex's neck with one hand, untied its feet and looked closely into its eyes.

"I don't believe it," said Grim, turning white. "Mia, is that you?" he asked the lamb.

He waved his hand over the lamb's face and sang a haunting melody. Suddenly the lamb started to transform into a woman.

"Mia, my love, it's you," he cried, grasping Mia around the waist and swinging her high into the air.

She was very plain looking and had mousy brown long hair. She was also naked. Grim drew her down into the water when he saw the boys ogling her.

"Grim, you found me," she cried, wrapping her arms tightly around him. "I can't believe you broke the spell."

"Mia, Mia," he crooned into her neck. "My true love, my one and only, at last."

"Er can someone explain what's going on?" asked Alex. "I'm really confused."

Grim looked up, tears were shining in his eyes and he looked like he was glowing.

"You found her. I can't thank you enough. I am indebted to you forever."

"Found who? Who is she?" asked Matt.

"Sorry, this is Mia, my fiancé. Her mother didn't approve of our relationship. She made some terrible accusations about me being a womaniser," he said, rolling his eyes.

Matt looked at Alex and raised his eyebrows.

"My mother told me if I ever saw him again she would turn me into a lamb and hide me where he would never find me. She said if I wanted to be a lamb heading to the slaughter then I could be one, literally. I couldn't stop seeing Grim though. She caught us and placed a spell on me to turn me into a lamb."

"I've been looking for her for years, I can't leave the water for too long so I have had to rely on people visiting me. When they ask for music or music lessons I ask them to find me a lamb. Always in the hope they will return Mia to me."

"My love we will have to hide. If my mother ever discovers you found me she will take me away again. I'm not being turned into a lamb again, it was disgusting," she said, shuddering.

"Don't worry my love, I'll take care of you. She'll never separate us ever again."

Grim kissed Mia passionately and Alex and Matt looked at each other and grinned when they saw the girls faces. They recovered quickly when they saw the boys laughing at them and sat back down on the rocks.

Alex sat down next to Becca. She handed him a large piece of cooked fish and he ate it hungrily. He heard a splash and looked over at the lake.

"Thanks Gorvir," he shouted and waved.

The serpent raised her head from the water, gazed intently at Alex and bowed her head majestically before slipping beneath the surface.

"You okay?" asked Becca.

"Yep, you? I take it Grim behaved himself? Where's Pete?" said Alex, looking around for Pete.

"I'm here," called Pete, from the boat.

He had been lying in the bottom soaking up the sun. "All good here, no funny business," he said, shading his eyes from the sun.

"So, Grim, sorry to interrupt but how about that piece of music? We fulfilled our part of the deal," said Alex, wiping his greasy fingers on his trousers.

"Yes, you certainly did," he said, gazing intently into Mia's eyes. "Here you go. I composed it whilst you were gone," he said, conjuring a sheet of music on thick creamy vellum with a wave of his hand.

It floated over to where Alex was sitting and he plucked it out of the air.

"Er is that it?" asked Alex "Just one side, isn't that a bit short?"

"What were you expecting a whole symphony? That will do the job trust me," said Grim, winking, his arms still wrapped tightly around Mia.

"Okay that's, er, great then, thanks."

Alex gave the sheet of music to Sasha to put in her bag.

"One last problem guys," said Pete, sitting up in the boat. "How do we get back to Dvalin? I don't think this boat will get us there somehow."

"You'll need a portal," said Grim. "I expect Maggie will be here soon. She visits quite often. I think she's quite a fan of my music."

"Yeah right, it's all about the music I'm sure," said Matt, laughing.

Mia raised her eyebrows at Grim and he kissed her passionately again.

They sat on the smooth, grey rocks waiting for Maggie and Grim played on his violin with Mia tucked up close to his side. The haunting melody echoed across the lake making Alex feel despondent. He was still very far from completing his task and fulfilling the prophecy, he just couldn't see the end in sight. He looked around at the others; they were all lying back in the sun listening to Grim's music. Alex couldn't relax though, he just wanted to get back to Dvalin and finally get the sword so this could all be over. He could feel his frustration building and his fingers started to tingle. He looked at his hands and little sparks of electricity were jumping off the tips of his fingers. He concentrated on his hands trying to channel the energy. The feeling immediately intensified and suddenly a ball of white light shot from the palm of his hand and struck a tree, which was overhanging the waterfall. It burst into flames immediately.

"What the? Alex!" shouted Becca, jumping up suddenly and backing away from him. "What are you doing?"

"Sorry I was just practicing," he said, sheepishly.

"Practice in your own back yard," said Grim, sternly.

He waved his hand and a stream of water shot up from the lake and doused the tree extinguishing the flames. Alex stood looking guiltily at the smoking blackened tree stump.

"Hello hot stuff. You need to learn to control yourself," said Maggie, appearing on a ledge, which was hidden from sight behind the waterfall.

"Hello Maggie, looking as gorgeous as ever," said Grim, standing up and going over to help her off the ledge.

He carried her in his arms over to the rocks where the others were standing.

"It doesn't hurt to flatter a Volva," he whispered, to Alex winking.

Alex sighed and Mia huffed. Grim quickly pulled her up

next to him.

"Mia? Is that you?" asked Maggie, squinting in the sunlight.

Mia nodded cautiously. "Maggie, please don't tell my mother, I beg you," she pleaded.

"Hmm fine, I never did like your mother, batty old crone," said Maggie, haughtily.

"Maggie, they need to get back to Dvalin, can you help them?" asked Grim, desperate to change the conversation.

"Yes, I expected they would need a lift back. It will cost you though," she said looking at Alex and grinning.

Luckily, she was in her transformed human state and actually looked quite pretty.

"Okay, now what?" he asked, dreading what she was going to ask for.

"Let's just say you'll owe me a favour sometime and when I ask for it you can't refuse," she said, gazing at him intently.

"Fine, providing it doesn't involve hurting anyone I agree," said Alex, resigned.

Maggie laughed and clapped her hands together excitedly. "Perfect, come on then gather close, let's get you back to Dvalin."

They found a flat grey boulder and gathered together closely into a circle. Pete squeezed himself into the middle. "What? I'm not being burned up again," he said.

Alex pulled Becca and Sasha in tight with his arms and Maggie drew a circle around them with her chalk muttering under her breath.

"You must come back for our wedding," called Grim, puling Mia close to his side.

Becca and Sasha looked at each other and shrugged. The

boys grinned and gave Grim a thumbs up. Then suddenly they were falling through the hole and before they knew it they were bouncing up and down on Dvalin's floor.

Chapter Ten

When the floor stopped undulating and heaving beneath them Alex stood up and saw Dvalin and Sven pressed up against the sides of the room looking horrified.

"I suppose Maggie thought that would be funny," said Dvalin, looking at the mess in his room.

The bed, sofa, table and chairs had overturned and there were papers floating up in the air.

"We got it," cried Sasha, jumping up to her feet and digging the sheet of music out of her bag.

Dvalin snatched it out of her hand greedily and scanned the page of notes.

"This will work, will it?" he asked, looking around at them. "It's not very long."

He turned the page over to see if there was more.

"Grim seemed to think so, come on let's try it now," said Alex, moving to the door.

They all hurried down the tunnel back to the Gyrrdorr chamber and stood in front of the golden door. Dvalin studied the music closely and tried a few notes. After a few attempts he managed to play it without making any mistakes. They stood holding their breath wondering what would happen. When the last note finished reverberating around the chamber there was a loud clicking sound and the door sprung open.

"It worked, it worked," cried Dvalin excitedly, bouncing up and down on the balls of his feet.

He grabbed a flaming torch from its sconce in the wall and ran inside the room. The others followed quickly behind.

Dvalin stopped and looked around the square shaped stone room confused. It was empty. Both the perfectly smooth dark grey stone walls and floor were bare.

"What?" he cried, sweeping the torch around the room. "Where is it? What's going on?"

He looked around frantically but there was nothing there.

"How about a hidden door?" asked Sven, studying the walls.

Dvalin and Sven moved around the chamber patting the rock and muttering door opening spells.

"Perhaps someone got here first and took the treasure," said Sasha.

"Impossible," cried Dvalin. "There must be something here. It's another enchantment."

"Dvalin, look we're running out of time. We opened the door, that was our agreement. You need to tell us where the sword is," said Alex.

Dvalin swung around to face him. There was a dangerous look in his eyes and he growled, "No, you need to stay and help me figure this out, then I'll tell you."

"Oh, come on this is ridiculous." Alex shouted.

Suddenly the door behind them slammed shut. The sound of it echoed around the room making everyone jump.

"What the?" cried Matt. "What's going on?"

He went over to the door and pushed but it was shut firmly. He looked over at Alex and shrugged. "There's no handle this side, I can't open it."

Suddenly, a squealing, grinding noise echoed around the room.

"What's that?" asked Becca, frightened.

She moved to Alex's side and gripped his arm tightly.

"I have a really bad feeling about this," said Sven, looking up.

Everyone else turned their heads up to see what he was looking at. The ceiling was moving down slowly, grinding against the stonewalls and making a loud crunching sound.

"Oh, come on," cried Pete. "This stuff only happens in the movies," he said, pushing at the door with Matt with his shoulder.

There was no way it was going to budge.

"Dvalin do something," shouted Alex. "There must be a way out."

Dvalin looked at Sven. "We should have brought a Volva with us," he said. "She could have created a portal out of here."

"You should have thought about that before you got us in this mess," snapped Sven.

"Come on think. If you were hiding your greatest treasure what would you do?" he said, thinking furiously.

"Guys hurry, this ceiling is coming down really fast," said Matt, throwing himself at the door with his shoulder.

Dvalin scurried around still pushing at the walls.

"Wait," said Becca, crouching on the floor. "You've already tried the walls, what about the floor?"

Dvalin fell to his knees and starting to swipe his hands across the floor muttering spells. Sven did the same. The ceiling brushed the top of Alex's hair and he crouched down pulling Becca to his side.

"God Becca, I'm so sorry I got you into this," he said, brushing her cheek with his hand.

He could see she was terrified.

"It's not your fault, we're in this together remember?" she smiled at him weakly and he pulled her closer and crushed his lips against hers.

"Here," cried Sven.

They all scrambled over to him bent double. The floor just in front of Sven was glowing yellow in a circle. Dvalin placed his hands on the circle and it grew brighter lighting up all of their pale faces.

The dwarves chanted together repeatedly. "Syna dyrr, Syna dyrr, Syna dyrr..."

The circle glowed even brighter so they couldn't look at it and then suddenly the light disappeared to reveal a hole in the floor and what looked like a slide leading off into the blackness.

"Quickly everyone down here," said Dvalin, pulling Sasha's arm.

"You sure about this?" asked Pete, peering into the hole with a worried expression on his face.

"Well you can stay here if you like but I don't want to become mincemeat," said Sasha, pushing herself down the hole feet first.

The ceiling was pressing down quickly and scraped the top of Alex's head again, he moved Becca forward towards the hole.

"Go, I'll be right behind you," he said, pushing her back.

She slithered towards the edge of the hole on her bottom and sat at the edge with her feet hanging down. She took a deep breath reached back squeezed Alex's hand and then pushed herself off the side. Matt quickly followed and then the others until it was just Alex left. By this time, he was flat on his stomach and the ceiling was pushing against his back. He used his elbows to shuffle forward and looked down the hole.

Here goes nothing, he thought to himself. He used the rough edge of the hole to shift his body forward but he was stuck, he couldn't move. The ceiling was pressing too tightly against his back pushing him into the floor. He began to panic and pulled harder with his arms, he wiggled to and fro and finally managed to squeeze through. He fell down the hole head first, his shoes hitting the ceiling as it crashed down with a bang over the top of the hole.

Alex slid down, flying around corners and hitting the sides uncontrollably. It was pitch black and it felt like the hole was going on forever. He tried to hold out his hands to slow himself down but he just seemed to go faster and faster. Suddenly he went flying out of the hole and landed in a heap on a stone floor.

"Ouch," he cried, rolling over several times.

An arm grabbed him by the shirt stopping him roll any further. He looked around and saw his leg was hanging over a deep chasm. He rolled back away from the edge and carefully sat up. He looked at his hand as it was stinging. A large gash bled from the palm.

"Damn it," he said, wiping at the blood with the bottom of his t-shirt. "That was close, I nearly went over the edge," he said, shakily.

"Here let me see," said Becca, reaching out and taking his hand. "It's really deep, I think you're going to need stitches."

"Well that'll have to wait, I doubt there are any hospitals

near here," he said, looking around.

Dvalin held up the torch which he was still holding and from the dim light Alex could see they were in a circular stone cavern and were standing on a narrow ledge at the edge of a massive chasm.

"We need more light," said Alex, peering into the gloom.

"There's another torch over here," said Matt, pointing to the wall beside the hole they had fallen through.

Dvalin held his flame to the torch and it burst into life. A smaller flame ran along the wall lighting another torch, which then lit another torch further along the wall. The line of fire continued around the circular cavern until the cavern was ablaze with a hundred flaming torches. The additional light revealed a stone pillar rearing out of a black abyss and on top of the pillar there was a large wooden chest bound with iron bars.

"There," shouted Dvalin, pointing to the chest.

The sound echoed around the chamber.

"That's all very well but how do we get over there?" asked Pete, looking over the edge.

He couldn't see any bottom to the pit. It was pitch black.

"Okay what would Indiana Jones do?" asked Matt.

"Use his whip and unless I'm mistaken none of us has one of those," said Pete, sarcastically.

"In the Last Crusades he stepped out onto what looked like an invisible pathway," said Sasha, throwing gravel into the pit.

The gravel just fell down into the hole. It was so deep they couldn't hear it hitting the bottom.

"No, oh well it was worth a try," she said, grinning.

Dvalin and Sven were conferring together quietly and turning out their pockets looking to see what they had on them. Alex saw them nodding enthusiastically.

"Hey I hope you guys have a plan because you do realise we're stuck here," he called over.

"We're going to build a bridge," announced Dvalin, proudly.

"Right, what with thin air?" sneered Pete.

"No with rocks dummy," explained Sven.

"Er there are no loose rocks lying around, you might want to rethink that one," said Alex.

"We're surrounded with rock, we just need to mine it. It may have escaped your notice but dwarves are very good miners," said Sven, indignantly.

"Okay what are you going to mine with then, your bare hands?" asked Alex, looking thoroughly confused.

"Sven here has a portable pick with him," said Dvalin, pushing Sven forward.

Sven held a tiny pick in his hand.

"Well that will get you a few pebbles. Did you get it out of a Christmas cracker?" laughed Matt.

Sven grinned waved his hand over the pick and it unfolded itself over and over until it became a full-size pick.

"I've got a better idea," said Alex, grinning. "You want rocks? I'll get you rocks. Stand back everyone."

He held out his hands to the rock face behind them and concentrated on summoning energy. From deep within he could feel a surge of power racing through his veins. His hands started to spark and he released a ball of energy and threw it at the rock. There was a huge explosion and large chunks of rock fell from the wall. Everyone started to cough and splutter. They were covered in rock dust.

"Alex that was really dangerous, look at us," said Sasha, shaking her hair out.

Bits of grit flew everywhere.

"That was cool," said Matt, in awe.

The dwarves looked at each other and grinned. They scurried over to the pile of rocks which had been blasted out of the wall and began hauling them over to the edge of the chasm. Sven pulled out a bottle from his pocket.

"Rock cement," he explained, holding it up to show them. "A dab of this binds the largest rocks together in seconds."

Dvalin and Sven got to work fixing the rocks together from the edge. The glue set immediately and held the rocks firm as they worked away from the edge creating a bridge of sorts. They worked quickly together, completely in their element and in no time at all a bridge snaked across the chasm and they jumped across to reach the chest.

"Come on over, it's safe," said Dvalin, trying to encourage the others to come over.

"We have come this far, let's open the chest together," he said, rubbing his hands together in excitement.

Becca looked warily at the bridge, whilst it had held the dwarves weights she wasn't convinced it would hold them. Alex held Becca's hand for balance and he stepped onto the first rock gingerly. He figured if it would take his weight then they would be okay. He put his full weight on the rock and it held so he shuffled across slowly and eventually reached the other side.

"Come on guys it's fine," he shouted across.

They went across slowly one at a time. Dvalin was hopping up and down in excitement, desperate to open the chest and reveal the treasure. As soon as they were all over they crowded around the large wooden chest curious to see what Thor had placed in there. Alex was just hoping it held what Dvalin wanted. Whilst it was a large chest, it wasn't quite the mountain of gold and silver he was expecting. The chest had a large silver padlock securing it and Sven was on his knees trying to pick it. There was a loud click and the padlock fell open.

"Ha, master lock pick extraordinaire," he crowed.

Dvalin lifted up the lid and a golden glow lit up the chamber blinding them.

"What is it?" whispered Becca, squinting in the dazzling light.

Dvalin looked into the chest and then looked around at them. "It's hair," he said, confused. "It's a load of hair. This can't be right we're not in the right place."

He looked distraught.

"What?" asked Alex, looking into the chest.

Dvalin was right there was a huge pile of glowing golden hair.

"Is there anything else in there?" he asked, picking up handfuls of the hair and taking it out of the chest.

Dvalin climbed into the box and felt around with his hands. "There's something here," he cried.

He brought out a small wooden box, which had an elephant, engraved on the lid. He opened it carefully and peeked inside.

"Come on what's in there?" asked Sven, impatiently.

"Shoes," said Dvalin, confused. "Four little baby shoes, oh and there are three little teeth and three locks of hair. But where is the daylight elixir? This is just rubbish," he cried, throwing the box back into the chest. "It must be here. It's a precious treasure. Where is the gold, the silver, the gems? We must be in the wrong chamber," he cried.

"Dvalin think, would it be precious to Thor?" asked Sasha. "It may be great treasure to you but why would Thor want it? He doesn't need money or daylight elixir," she said, patting him on the back sympathetically.

"She's right. The rumours weren't true," said Sven.

Dvalin sat in the box and big tears rolled down his cheeks. "All this time," he said, sobbing. "I've wasted all this time for this."

"What's with the hair anyway?" asked Matt, fingering strands of the golden hair.

It was silky and very thick and continued to glow and light up their faces.

"Well at a fair guess I would say it's Sif's hair," said Sven. "She had the most beautiful hair of all the gods and Thor loved it. He was always talking about it and showing off about how he was married to the woman with the most beautiful hair in the Nine Worlds. Loki got fed up with his boasting and snuck into her bedchamber one night. He cut off all of her hair. When Thor found out he was furious and he nearly killed Loki. Loki loves playing his tricks but he went too far that time. To stop Thor from killing him he said he would fix it and would find her even better hair. He persuaded a group of dwarves to create a new headpiece for her. The sons of Ivaldi wove her new hair and she loved it so Loki got to keep his life.

I guess Thor preferred the real thing though and he thinks of it as his greatest treasure."

"Okay that's a bit creepy. What does he do, come and play with it?" asked Matt. "What's with the little shoes and teeth? Alex I'm not sure about your dad you know."

"Four baby shoes for four children, your two brothers, your sister and I guess one of those was meant for you Alex," said Sasha, looking into the box.

"Three first baby teeth, three locks of hair but not a fourth as you were gone," said Becca, looking into the box too.

"That's so sad," said Dvalin, weeping some more.

"Come on everyone get a grip, it doesn't mean anything," said Alex, annoyed at how emotional he felt. "We've more pressing matters on our hands," he said, irritably. "We really need to find the sword Dvalin. I think you'll agree that what you were looking for isn't here, it's over."

Dvalin hiccupped climbed out of the box and dried his face on a handful of golden hair.

"Okay, a deal's a deal. Niddhogg," he said, miserably. "I gave it to Niddhogg."

"And Niddhogg is who exactly?" asked Alex. "If it's another Volva then count me out."

"It's worse than that," said Sven, scuffing his feet on the stone floor. "Niddhogg is a dragon. The worst possible dragon you could ever hope to meet. He lives at the bottom of the Yggdrasil, the world ash tree and gnaws on the corpses of evil people. You know murderers, rapists, and those types. When he gets fed up with the taste of their badness he gnaws at the roots of the tree and tries to destroy it."

"He is pure evil," added Dvalin. "If he ever destroys the

tree the whole Nine Worlds will collapse."

"Well that's just fantastic," said Alex, dumping the hair back into the chest.

He stood up straight with his hands on his hips. "You're basically telling me we have to find the most badass dragon in history and ask him for the sword which will save Earth, or Midgard, whatever you call it. Somehow, I don't think he is going to give it to me," he said, glaring at Dvalin.

"No, he won't give it to you, I guess you'll have to steal it," said Sven.

"Stealing again? I don't believe this," cried Matt. "My mum is going to kill me when she finds out."

"I think the evil dragon will do that for her," smirked Alex.

"I'm still registering dragons exist," said Pete.

"Really? After all we've been through today?" Sasha looked around at all of them. "I think we have a bigger problem anyway," she said, looking worried.

"What?" asked Alex, "What can be a bigger problem than stealing a sword off a dragon who eats people?"

"Getting out of here for a start," she replied.

They stood silently looking at each other. She had a good point. There were no exits they could see other than the hole they had fallen through. Even if they could have climbed up it the ceiling in the chamber above was blocking the entrance. Alex looked over the edge of the stone column. There may be an exit down there but it was so deep and they didn't have a rope. He looked over at the golden hair and thought of Rapunzel but realised it would never be long enough.

"I might be able to help there," said Sven, pulling a piece of chalk from his pocket.

"What's that?" asked Becca.

"Maggie's chalk, the one she uses to create portals," he said, looking around to see if there was enough room on the pillar.

"You stole a Volva's chalk?" asked Sasha, horrified.

"No, I found it on the floor, when you appeared in Dvalin's house. She must have dropped it and it fell through the portal with you," he said.

"Well why didn't you use it when we were about to be crushed to death?" asked Pete.

"I forgot I had it until we went through our pockets earlier," he said, defensively.

"Don't you need to have magical powers to use that?" asked Alex, skeptically.

"Guess we'll find out," said Sven, with a grin. "I remember the words she used, it was just earth, air, fire and water but in ancient Norse.

"Well it's worth a go, it's not like we have many options," said Sasha.

"Right gather around then, there should be enough room if we squeeze in tight," said Sven.

He drew a circle on the rough stone floor with the chalk and stood back to admire his work. He then stepped into the circle and reached up to put his hand around Sasha's waist." You need to get a bit closer come on," he said, grinning and winking.

Sasha sighed and moved his hand which had snaked down to her bottom. They all squeezed into the circle and waited for Sven to say the words. Alex was not convinced it would work and was frantically trying to think of another plan.

"Hyrr, logr, mold, lopt," said Sven, repeatedly.

Alex looked over his shoulder and could see the chalk starting to glow.

"It's working," he whispered, excitedly.

Suddenly there was a large pop and the floor fell away sending them tumbling down into the dark. They ended up in Dvalin's room and the floor bounced a few times to break their fall. Dvalin's furniture was lifted up into the air again and crashed down in a heap. Alex jumped to his feet and looked around at the mess.

"Don't worry, we'll help you clear up," he laughed.

He looked over at Dvalin, he was lying on the floor facing away from them.

"Dvalin are you okay?" asked Sven, bending down and shaking him gently on the shoulder.

"He's dead," he cried.

Becca joined him and gently rolled Dvalin onto his back and he groaned. They all sighed with relief.

"Dvalin are you okay? Can you hear me?" asked Sasha, holding his hand and rubbing it.

He felt icy cold.

"What happened?" he mumbled, trying to sit up.

Becca pushed him back down again.

"Hey take it easy, it looks like you passed out," she said.

"I feel terrible, my head is pounding and...."

He lifted his hand up to his nose and wiped away a trickle of blood. Sven looked horrified.

"This is serious. We need Maggie, she'll know what to do," he said, wringing his hands.

"Can you call her like Dvalin did?" asked Becca.

"No, I don't know that spell," he said, miserably.

"How about using the chalk to create another portal?" asked Alex, looking at Sven.

"I think that was the problem," said Sven, looking at the chalk in his hand. "He was fine until we used the portal. He's so old he probably couldn't cope with what it does to your body."

"Er, excuse me, what're you saying? Travelling through a portal damages your body?" asked Pete, poking Sven on the shoulder.

"Well you're passing through another dimension, sometimes there are side effects," said Sven, looking sheepish.

Pete grabbed Sven by the shoulders and lifted him up so he could look him in the eye. Sven's legs kicked helplessly in the air.

"Great and we're just being told that now? We have done this like four times. Is it going to scramble my brain or what?" asked Pete, angrily.

"No, no," squealed Sven, clawing at Pete's hands. "You're all young, you'll be fine. Put me down."

Pete dropped Sven to the floor and he landed on his feet with a thud.

"Do that again punk and you'll be sorry," snarled Sven, glowering and straightening his bejeweled waistcoat.

"Oh, gee I'm so scared, what are you going to do, nibble on my ankles?" laughed Pete, pushing Sven away.

Sven bunched his fists and Alex stood between the two of them.

"Cut it out you two, we have more serious problems," he said, looking at Dvalin worried.

He was very grey and his breathing had become wheezy as

though it were an effort. Suddenly there was a loud pop, a whoosh of air and Maggie appeared out of nowhere in the middle of the room.

"There you are you thief," she snarled at Sven, pointing a gnarled hand at him.

She was in her true form and looked hideous and terrifying. Her eyes were black pits and her skin was falling off her bones. Sven jumped back in fright and put his hands up.

"No, no Maggie, I found it I promise. You must have dropped it through the portal when you returned them and I kept it for safe keeping, I was going to give it back I promise," he whimpered.

"I can smell a liar," she growled. "Give it back now. You have no idea of the damage you could have done. You could have killed Alex and then we couldn't have gone on our date."

Alex gulped and stepped back a few paces.

"I'm sorry forgive me, I meant no harm. Please we need your help, Dvalin is sick, look."

Sven pointed to Dvalin who was lying propped up in Becca's arms. Blood was seeping from his eyes as well as his nose now.

"You want my help again?" she hissed. "I should just put you all out of your misery. When did this happen anyway?" she asked, pointing at Dvalin.

"Just now when we came through the portal from Thor's treasure chamber," said Sven. "Can you help him?"

"I knew you created a portal I could sense it. That's when I realised my chalk was missing," she said, glaring at Sven.

She had changed back into human form and didn't look quite so terrifying.

"So, you found Thor's treasure, did you? Where is it?" she asked, looking around greedily.

"It wasn't what Dvalin was after. There was no gold or jewels just Sif's hair, you know the hair Loki cut off all those years ago?" said Sven.

Maggie laughed. "Of course," she cackled. "Thor's great treasure. Her hair obsessed him. Wasn't there anything else though?"

"Just a few bits and pieces, nothing important though," said Alex, looking at his feet.

He looked up at her. "Dvalin told us where the sword is we were just about to figure out how to get it when this happened," he said, gesturing to Dvalin who was looking worse by the minute. "Can you help him?" he asked.

Maggie looked Dvalin over quickly and shook her head.

"He's too far gone, he won't have long now. He shouldn't be travelling through portals at his age. It's dangerous. Best you just make him comfortable and wait for him to croak it," she said bluntly. She stood up and looked at the group. "You're lucky he is the only one dying. You should never mess with a Volva's magic. I feel violated," she said, glaring at them.

"Surely there must be something we can do?" asked Sven.

Whilst he hadn't known Dvalin very long, he felt very guilty. The death of a dwarf hardly ever happened as they lived such long lives and this was his entire fault. He must have said the spell wrong.

"The only thing in the Nine Worlds that can save him is a golden apple but I can't see Iduna handing one over, she only gives them to the gods themselves," said Maggie.

"I'm a god, well half a god, would she give one to me do you think?" asked Alex.

"Possibly but you'll have to go to Asgard and you'll have to go alone. Only gods, demigods and Volvas may enter Asgard," said Maggie.

"No problem, it's worth a try," he said.

"Hang on guys. Are you forgetting something? The sword...saving the world and all that?" asked Pete.

"That's true Alex. I hate to say it but there are more lives at stake here. Dvalin has had a long life, perhaps it's time for him to go," said Sasha, quietly.

"Look, I'm thinking I'll need one of the golden apples myself," said Alex.

"If this sword really is cursed then I'm going to need all the help I can get. Perhaps the apple could heal me, or at least give me a few more years to live."

"That's true," said Sasha, looking at Alex sadly.

"Okay tell you what, let's get back above ground, call Alan and we can see what the score is. If we have time we owe it to Dvalin to at least try. It's our fault he's lying there," said Alex.

"Okay how do we get back up top though? I'm not going through another portal and risking my life," said Pete.

"I'll go on my own, you guys stay here and look after Dvalin," said Alex, determined.

"But it's dangerous, we have done it too many times already," said Becca, worried.

"He's a demigod, he'll be fine. His body is stronger than yours. Tell me Alex, have you ever been ill before?" asked Maggie, standing in front of him.

"No, now you mention it I can't remember ever being

sick," said Alex.

"What? Not even a cold, you must have had a cold?" asked Matt, amazed.

"No, I haven't. The only time I took time off school was when I bunked off to get out of a test," he said. "I haven't really thought about it before, I just thought I was healthy and looked after myself."

Becca came over to his side and touched his hand. "But you can get hurt, you cut your hand earlier remember. You're not entirely invincible."

Alex looked at the hand, which he had grazed when he fell out of the hole. There was nothing there, not even a scratch. He held it up and showed the others.

"Okay, now that's weird. Guess you're invincible dude," said Matt, coming over to take a closer look.

"That settles it," said Alex. "I'm going to Asgard to get a golden apple. Maggie, I don't suppose you could create a portal for me?" he asked, smiling at her hopefully.

"For you sweetheart...anything," she said, winking.

"I'll be back as soon as I can," he said, looking around at the others.

Becca touched his arm, stood on tiptoes and kissed him quickly on the lips. "Take care Alex and please be careful," she whispered to him.

He squeezed her shoulder and smiled.

"Maggie, can you send me home first so I can check on what's going on? I'll then need a lift to Asgard if everything is okay," he said.

"I can send you home but you'll have to call Heimdall to get to Asgard. Your friend Alan can show you how," said

Maggie, bumping into Becca and knocking her out of the way.

"Come on then handsome," said Maggie, bending down and drawing a circle around him with the chalk.

"If you see my mum, let her know I'm okay," shouted Matt, as Alex fell through the floor into a black void.

Chapter Eleven

Alex landed heavily on his feet and bounced up and down a few times on the rippling earth. He was getting the hang of portals now. He looked around and saw Alan, Nancy and a strange man lying flat on their backs next to the henge.

"What on earth?" cried Alan, rolling over and jumping to his feet.

"Alan," shouted Alex. "It's me, Alex."

Alan pushed his glasses up his nose and looked over. It was dusk and the light was fading fast.

"Alex? Thank Odin! Did you just come through a portal? One minute we were standing there talking about going to get a pint, the next the floor turns to jelly. It was most disconcerting I can tell you," said Alan, shaking Alex's hand vigorously.

"Yes, yes that was me. I've been to Svartalfheim, I met Lit and he sent me to find Dvalin but I needed to come back here first to check on things. Maggie created a portal for me and here I am. Is everything okay?" Alex asked, breathlessly.

"Slow down Alex," said Nancy, coming over to where he was standing. "Cassie called us and confirmed our suspicions about who you are, a demigod eh?"

Alex nodded and looked embarrassed.

"She said you went to Svartalfheim. Do you have the sword?" asked Nancy.

"The sword?" asked Alex. Nancy raised her eyebrows. "Oh, the sword," he exclaimed. "No, not yet but I know where it is. So much has happened, I don't know where to start. To be honest there's no time for that anyway. I need to get to

Asgard and find Iduna. I need a golden apple."

"Oh my goodness, are you sick?" asked Alan, looking at Alex worried.

"No, I'm fine, couldn't be better. It's Dvalin, he's dying and I need to get a golden apple for him to save his life."

"Dvalin," said Alan, excitedly. "I didn't think he would be still alive after all this time. No one has heard from him in years."

"Well he won't be soon unless I get an apple for him. He's in a really bad way and it's our fault. He had to go through a portal with us and it was too much for him. It was that or we did it wrong, I don't know. We didn't have a Volva with us so it was a bit of guess work."

"Alex that is so dangerous, you could've died," said Nancy, shocked.

"Is my son okay?" asked the strange man.

"Your son?"

"This is Magnus, Pete's father," explained Alan.

"Oh right, yeah he's fine. He's a bit worried about his health. We've been through a few portals you see and didn't know it was dangerous. No one said anything. That's why I'm on my own, they'll have to come back the long way," said Alex.

"But it's dangerous for you too Alex," said Alan.

"Well I figured I would be okay. I've never been ill in my life. Also, I cut myself down there and it healed in no time at all. I guess I've a few immortal genes in me," said Alex, grinning.

"Alex what about the sword, where is it?" asked Magnus.

"Oh, some dragon has it. Nid something or other, I can't

remember. I'll go get it after I have the golden apple. Well providing Hel isn't about to break loose here. It looks like you have everything under control," said Alex, looking around at the henge.

There were wisps of smoke seeping from a large crack in the central stone and it was drifting across the grass slowly but he couldn't see anything else sinister.

"Well we have had a few hairy moments but we think Baldur is getting a grip on things down there and the prayers our end seem to be working. Nothing has come through for a day now and there have been no noises," said Alan, glancing back at the henge.

"Great, I have time then. I need to get to Asgard quickly. Maggie said you would show me how to get there," said Alex.

"No Alex, you need to get the sword, the breach could happen at any time," said Magnus.

"But Dvalin.."

"Dvalin is an old dwarf, it's his time. You have a responsibility to seal the breach or we could all die. You need to look at the bigger picture Alex. I'm sure Dvalin will agree," said Magnus, sternly.

"No, I promised I would help him and I've a really strong feeling we need him. He cursed the sword and even though he said it couldn't be undone I'm sure he could find a way," said Alex.

"In any case I need a golden apple too. If Dvalin can't break the curse then I will need to prolong my life as best I can."

"This is wyrd," said Alan, nodding his head. "Alex it's your fate, the Norns are weaving a complicated web for you and this is an important part. I agree we need you to save Dvalin. Getting a golden apple is going to be difficult though. Iduna won't just hand one to you easily."

"I figured she would give one to me, you know me being a demigod and all," said Alex, puffing out his chest.

He was beginning to enjoy his new status.

"Yes, but she will expect you to eat it yourself. She won't be happy if she knows you gave it to a dwarf. It will upset the natural balance, it's already bad enough Lit is immortal," said Alan.

"Well I won't tell her if you won't. It will be our little secret," grinned Alex.

"Okay, but don't say I didn't warn you. The wrath of a god is certainly not something you should take lightly but if it's the only way to save Dvalin I guess we don't really have a choice," said Alan.

"Great now we have settled that, how do I get to Iduna? Maggie said I would need to call Heim someone or other," said Alex, excited at the thought of going to Asgard.

"Heimdall," said Nancy. "He is the guardian of Bifrost, the bridge which connects our world to Asgard."

"Ah he's been in the films. Big guy with a sword, he's blind but can see everything," said Alex, nodding his head.

Nancy muffled a laugh. "Alex the Avengers films portrayal of the gods is not entirely accurate. Alan has been dying to set them straight for ages but everyone would start to wonder where his intel came from."

"You'll see what she means when you get to Asgard. Heimdall will be here soon, he would have heard us talking about him," said Alan, looking up into the sky.

It was starting to get dark and Alex's stomach grumbled loudly.

"When did you last eat Alex?" asked Nancy.

"Ages ago, I'm starving," he said, rubbing his stomach.

Nancy swung a rucksack off her shoulder and dug inside. She pulled out a container filled with sandwiches.

"Here have these, I made them for us to have later but we can go to the pub once you're gone and our replacements arrive," she said, opening the container and handing it to Alex.

"Your replacements?" asked Alex, as he jammed half a sandwich into his mouth.

"Henge Guardians," said Nancy. "You saw them that first night when we held the ceremony. We've been taking it in turns to watch over the henge and say prayers in case anything else comes through. We've managed to exorcise the ones who did slip through and who possessed some of the locals. We returned the souls to Hel."

"Exorcise? How did you do that, get a priest to say a prayer?" asked Alex.

"We killed the hosts," said Magnus, bluntly. "They were too far gone. Their own souls had been taken over and couldn't return. It was the kindest thing to do."

Alex looked stunned, this was far more serious than he had expected. People had lost their lives. He suddenly lost his appetite and he handed the box of sandwiches back to Nancy.

"Look," said Alan, pointing up.

Alex looked up and saw a streak of white light flash across the dusky blue sky. The light was heading straight towards them and as it got closer Alex could make out the shape of a huge white horse with a flowing golden mane and a giant man sitting astride it. The horse swept down from the sky and skidded to a halt near the henge kicking up large clods of grass. The man kicked the horse in the sides and it trotted over towards Alex. When it was two paces away the man jumped down off the horse and grinned. He was incredibly tall and broad shouldered. He had long black hair pulled back at the nape of his neck and his teeth were pure gold. A huge horn and a long sword in a plain scabbard were attached to a thick leather belt around his waist.

"Nephew," he roared enveloping Alex in a big bear hug. "You're the talk of Asgard, quite the gossip," he said still grinning widely.

Alex stared at him in awe speechless. This giant of a man was his uncle!

"Heimdall, welcome old friend," said Alan, greeting him warmly. "It's been a long time."

"Indeed it has. Quite the situation you have yourself here," said Heimdall looking around at the henge. "Hello Nancy, Magnus," he said nodding in their direction. "That devil Loki must be behind it. Wherever there is trouble he'll be there, stirring it all up. He has always wanted to rescue Hel. Odin knows why, she's an ugly duckling if ever there was one," he said, laughing.

"We were beginning to think it was Loki," said Alan, reaching out to stroke the horse.

It lifted its head and snorted loudly. "Easy Gulltoppr," he said, soothingly.

"Oh, it's Loki alright. Thor is looking for him now. I've told him to call me when he finds him. This will be the most fun this millennium," said Heimdall, rubbing his hands together in anticipation.

Alex stood still feeling completely out of his comfort zone. He was standing in a field with a horse, which just flew out of the sky and a god, a real, full sized, giant of a god and to top it all off, this god was his uncle! It was quite a lot to take in and he had no idea what to say or do so he just stood there quietly.

"Heimdall we need a favour. Alex here needs to get a golden apple from Iduna," said Alan, looking at Alex and winking. "We need to make sure he has as much protection as possible for when he gets the sword which will close this portal."

"Protection?" asked Heimdall. "Protection from what?"

"The dragon Niddhogg," said Alex, speaking up.

Heimdall snorted and shook his head. "Niddhogg has the sword? Well good luck with that nephew."

"Is Niddhogg really that bad?" asked Alex.

Heimdall nodded slowly and Alex looked at the others. He started to panic when he saw the look of horror on Alan, Nancy and Magnus' faces.

"Imagine the worst tempered creature in existence, the one which would give even Odin nightmares, then times that by ten, well that's Niddhogg," said Heimdall, looking at Alex seriously. "He's so evil the only way we can control him is to feed him souls. Only the very worst souls will keep him quiet, the most evil, disgusting, terrifying souls imaginable. It's probably what makes him so foul tempered. Nothing can get past him and if he has your sword, there is no chance he will let you have it. He will snap you in two and suck out your soul before you know it."

Alex stood horrified with his mouth wide open.

"Okay that has totally just freaked me out. Dvalin didn't mention anything about that. I mean he said he was bad but I didn't think he would be that bad," said Alex, feeling sick to the bottom of his stomach.

"Dvalin, that old dwarf, is he still alive? Last I heard he was rooting around in Ostleheim trying to get into Thor's treasure room. He's been obsessed with it for years. Thinks there is some elixir in there which will enable him to go into the daylight," Heimdall laughed.

"It wasn't there," blurted out Alex.

Heimdall looked at him keenly. "I know," he said. "Thor told me ages ago. I was going to tell Dvalin but it's been quite a laugh watching him...what?" he asked, looking around at their incredulous faces. "We need something to keep us amused. Now that we can't mingle with humans we need something to keep us busy."

"Are you even allowed here?" asked Alex. "I thought all of the gods were banned from visiting."

"Only if I'm called. I wouldn't normally ride Gully across the sky like that, it tends to freak people out and they report me to NASA as some sort of alien spacecraft," snorted Heimdall. "I've been looking out for you though and waiting for you to call me. I figured you would want to meet your father at some point. That will have to wait until he has found Loki though. That rogue needs to be dealt with once and for all."

"Can you take me to Asgard though? I really need to see Iduna and get a golden apple," asked Alex.

"Right, yes, for 'protection'," said Heimdall. "You do know I can see and hear everything?"

Alex gulped and looked at Alan in a panic. Alan shrugged his shoulders.

"So, you know about Dvalin then? Why did you ask if he was alive if you know he is close to death?" asked Alex, confused.

"I was testing your honesty. You failed by the way. Only joking nephew," he laughed when he saw Alex's crestfallen face. "We all would have done the same. Saving a friend is a worthy cause and I will be happy to help. I'm not sure you'll persuade Iduna though. She's a bit distracted at the moment. Odin knows why, she's normally really easy going but she snapped my head off yesterday. Anyway, she might talk to you, you're the newest celebrity after all. Take my advice and keep out of Sif's way though. She's pretty mad at Thor for cheating on her with your mother."

"I'll go straight to Iduna, get an apple and will head straight back to Ostleheim," promised Alex.

"Come on then, you'll have to ride behind me," said Heimdall, jumping back into the saddle easily.

He reached down and grasped Alex's arm and pulled him up behind him.

"Alan, can you call Matt, Becca and Sasha's parents and tell them they're okay? They'll wait with Dvalin until I return. We'll then have to figure out how to get them back without using a portal," said Alex, settling in behind Heimdall on the large horse.

"Of course, leave it with me. We'll think of a way to get them back whilst you're gone," said Alan.

"Hold on tight nephew, this will be a bit bumpy," Heimdall called over his shoulder.

Alex grasped Heimdall's belt tightly and squeezed his thighs tight against the horse's sides. This was his first time on a horse and he held on for dear life. Heimdall kicked with his legs and Gulltoppr strode off across the field. After three strides, he bunched up his hind legs and launched himself into the sky. Alex swayed back and gripped harder. The ground fell away beneath them quickly as they soared into the night sky. Alex looked down and could barely make out the others waving up at him. He did not dare let go and wave back, he continued to hold on tightly to the belt. The wind rushed past his face and made his eyes water so much he couldn't see.

"Take a deep breath," Heimdall hollered over the wind.

Alex peered around Heimdall's chunky arm and could see a white glow just up ahead. As they got closer it looked like a swirling tunnel in the sky. He took a deep breath and closed his eyes as they galloped towards it. Suddenly Alex felt as though the life was being sucked out of him and then the feeling disappeared as quickly as it had come. He opened his eyes cautiously and looked around. Up ahead he could see a huge city in the distance perched on a mountain and surrounded by water. Gulltoppr started to descend towards the water to a large grey castle which was built onto the side of a cliff. He skidded to a stop right on the edge of the cliff making small rocks cascade down the slope.

"Home sweet home," laughed Heimdall, gesturing to Alex to get off the horse.

Jumping down off the back of Gulltoppr Alex looked out over the jagged cliff. A
huge bridge glowing with all the colours of the rainbow stretched out across the water, connecting the castle to the

huge city. He stood transfixed. It was a beautiful sight. The bridge was at least a mile long and was completely unsupported. It was as though it were hanging in thin air. On the far side of the bridge a huge wall made of sandy coloured stone surrounded a city bathed in marble and gold. The pointed tops of golden turrets rose majestically from the city walls and inside Alex could make out numerous large colonnaded marble buildings of all shapes and sizes. The city appeared to glow and pulse with life.

"It's amazing," said Alex, gazing across the bridge longingly.

"Well it should be, it is the home of gods after all," said Heimdall, resting his meaty hand on Alex's shoulder. "You had better get a move on nephew. You'll probably find Iduna in her orchard. It's just outside the wall over to the left after you cross Bifrost."

"Are you not coming?" asked Alex, surprised.

"No, I need to stay here and guard the bridge. If the Jotuns decide to pay a visit I need to warn everybody," he said, pointing to his horn.

"Right, okay, I'll go get the apple and will come back. I'll need a ride back to Dvalin," said Alex.

"I'm not a taxi service," said Heimdall, indignantly.

"Sorry no, I didn't mean that. How do I get back though?" asked Alex, embarrassed.

"Iduna will help," said Heimdall, taking Gulltoppr's reigns and leading him towards the castle. "I expect you to come and visit me soon though," he said, winking. "We have a lot to catch up on. Until we meet again nephew," he gave Alex a quick salute and walked off without a backward glance.

Alex walked over to the bridge and stepped on it tentatively. It was glowing so brightly he wished he had brought his sunglasses. As soon as Alex stepped down onto the bridge, the area under his foot lit up red. When his other foot pressed down, that lit up blue.

"Cool," Alex said to himself grinning.

He tested out all of the colours by leaping around the bridge like a child. He threw his head into the air, laughed out loud and then ran quickly across the bridge. The sky lit up with the colours of the rainbow. On the other side of the bridge a marble path led off to the left of the wall. Alex followed the path until he came to another wall, which had a silver metal gate set into it. Peeking through the gate he saw hundreds and hundreds of apple trees, their branches hanging low with ripe fruit. This must be Iduna's orchard thought Alex to himself but he couldn't see any gold apples on the tree though. He pushed on the gate and it opened smoothly.

"Hello," he called. "Is anyone there?"

He stepped inside the orchard and listened carefully. He could hear the sound of muffled crying in the distance and he made his way through the trees toward the sound. As he approached a large old gnarled apple tree in the middle of the orchard he saw a woman sitting on the floor with her back against the tree. Her hands were covering her face and she was weeping quietly

"Hello...are you okay?" asked Alex, tentatively.

Startled, she hastily wiped her eyes on the corner of her gown and looked up at Alex, with eyes which were red rimmed and puffy.

"Who are you? she asked. "What are you doing here?"

"Er I'm Alex...you may have heard of me recently," he said.

She stood up in one graceful movement and Alex stared at her transfixed. Her long cream gown was almost translucent. It clung to her body in soft folds and left very little to the imagination. Iduna laughed and it was the most beautiful sound he had ever heard, it was like tinkling bells. He looked up from her body and met her eyes, they were a clear blue with flecks of gold.

"Alex, dear nephew welcome," she said, smiling holding out both hands to him.

Her face lit up and Alex went bright red. Despite her tear stained face she was the most beautiful woman he had ever seen. Her hair was long, silky and bright gold and her skin was perfect and creamy. She had a perfect red rosebud mouth and a perfectly shaped nose.

"Nephew?" he stuttered confused.

"Well nephew by marriage, my husband is Bragi, one of Odin's sons. He's not here right now, Odin knows where he is, he goes off you see, long trips to 'find himself'," she said. "Just when I need him too, it's so typical," she collapsed on the grass and her shoulders heaved as she let out a large sob.

Alex fell to his knees beside her and patted her shoulder awkwardly. Her skin felt like silk and she didn't have a blemish on her. He brushed a strand of her long golden hair back from her face so he could see her.

"Why are you so upset? I can try and find him for you if you like," he said, desperate to stop her crying.

"It's not him I really want, it's my daughter, she's in terrible danger but she's not responding to my emails or text messages. I can't leave here and fetch her, I don't know what to do," she sobbed.

"Why can't you leave?" asked Alex, gently.

Iduna hiccupped and Alex's heart melted. Even with snot running down her nose she was stunning.

"I can't leave the golden apples unguarded, I'm trapped here forever. If I leave they could be stolen or they could rot. The gods will start to get old and they will eventually die. I can't be responsible for that, it happened before and it was terrible, I have to stay here....but my daughter..." she held her face in her hands and rocked back and forth weeping.

"Please let me help, I'll fetch her for you. Why is she in danger?" he asked.

"She's at a boarding school in Midgard. She needed to experience life rather than be stuck here with me all day. But I got word Hadron was after her again. I have already moved her schools once to get away from him but he followed her, damn, creepy good for nothing elf," she said, angrily.

"Elf?" asked Alex, confused.

"He's from Alfheim, the land of the Light Elves. They're cunning creatures, he has bewitched her and he wants her to marry him, he is obsessed with her but she's only seventeen, it's ridiculous," she said.

"Calm down, please don't upset yourself. I'll find her and will bring her back here for you. I just need one thing in return," he said.

"A golden apple," Iduna guessed. "That's the only reason people come and see me. Not for a chat and a nice cup of tea, no they always want something."

Iduna stood up quickly, wiped her face and started to walk off between the trees. Alex hurried after her and caught her arm.

"Listen I'm sorry, it's true. I initially came to see you for a golden apple. I've heard they can heal and will give strength. My friend Dvalin is dying and I need him to reverse a curse on a sword I need to find or I will die when I use it to close the portal to Hel. I'm guessing you've heard of the prophecy? One of your apples is the only way to save him," said Alex, desperately.

"I can't give a golden apple to anyone other than a god. They do more than give you health and strength; they will help to keep you immortal. We can't have everyone running around with immortality, there is already a population problem," she said, sniffing.

"But it's just one dwarf, they live for ages anyway. If I don't help him then I will die, surely you wouldn't wish that on your new-found nephew?" he coaxed, using his best smile.

Iduna laughed and kissed him on the cheek and he went bright red again.

"Okay, okay you got me, go fetch my daughter and I'll give you two golden apples, one for your friend Dvalin and one for yourself. You'll need to keep it a secret though. I don't want to find a queue of dwarves outside my garden thank you, begging me for apples," she said, sternly.

"I will don't worry and I promise next time I come to visit it won't be for an apple, we can have a nice cup of tea and chat,'" said Alex grinning.

"I wasn't serious about that, I hate tea. A nice glass of mead would be good though," she smiled.

"Great, mead it is then," he said.

"I need to warn you though, you'll have your work cut out

trying to get Lexi to come back home, she can be a stubborn madam and she doesn't like it here much. I tried to get all of the Midgard toys, computer, phone, television but she prefers to hang out down there."

Iduna sighed and walked towards a small little thatched cottage nestled between the trees. Alex followed her and entered through the wooden door. As soon as his eyes adjusted to the dark he looked around and gasped. This was no small cottage, it was like entering a Tardis. They were standing in a long-tiled hall, which had an enormous stone fireplace at the far end. It burst into flame when Iduna clapped her hands. Alex looked up and saw intricate stained-glass domes set into the ceiling. Light shone through them and lit up the black and white tiled floor in an array of colours.

"Wow, this is pretty spectacular," he said, gazing around in awe.

Large statues depicting Norse gods and goddesses lined the sides of the hall and thick tapestries hung from the walls. He felt like he was standing in a grand castle.

"It's home," she said casually, moving off to the left and entering a room.

Alex went to follow her but was drawn to a marble statue of a huge man with a flowing full beard. In his right hand, he held a large hammer.

"Okay that's weird," muttered Alex, to himself.

He looked into a long mirror, which was hanging off the wall opposite and shrugged. He couldn't see any family resemblance. He heard Iduna cough and he hurried into the room she had entered. She was standing by a desk by a long window and was looking through the drawers. He went over to join her at the desk and noticed her computer screen.

"You play Minecraft?" he asked, surprised.

"Doesn't everyone?" she raised her eyebrows and smiled. "I played it initially to engage with Lexi, she was obsessed with it, I couldn't get a word out of her. I figured if you can't beat them, join them. I confess I'm a bit addicted myself now. Look I built that town myself, pretty cool eh?" she grinned.

"That's awesome, but you could use andersite to finish off that side there, that would look nice," said Alex, critically.

Iduna laughed. "Oh no, not another one, I thought Lexi was bad," she said, shaking her head.

"Hey it's fun, educational too, designing, learning life saving skills...."

"Yes, because everyone needs to learn how to protect themselves from zombies and creepers," she laughed.

"Well you need to learn you need fire, shelter and food to survive," he said, defensively.

"And children could read that in a book or could just watch a Bear Grylls programme," she said, laughing again.

"Hey, I've just had a thought, we use golden apples in Minecraft for health," said Alex.

"I know, that made me laugh when I saw those. Shame I don't get to control them though. I would only give them to my friends," she winked at Alex and he could feel his face flushing again.

"Here, these are the details of the school she is staying in," she said, handing him a piece of paper.

"What does she look like? How will I recognise her?" he asked, looking at the paper.

"Oh, you won't be able to miss her," she said, smiling to

herself.

"Okay, so how do I get there? I don't suppose you have any buses passing through here?"

"Just click your heels three times and say 'there's no place like home'," said Iduna.

"Yeah hilarious, seriously how do I get there?"

"You can use my door. It will open to wherever you ask it to," she said.

"Cool that sounds easier than a portal."

"Portals are primitive Volva toys, dangerous too. I've heard of people going through them and never making it out the other end."

Alex looked stunned. He knew they were dangerous but not that dangerous. He made a mental note to firstly never use a portal again and secondly to never trust a Volva.

"Are you ready?" asked Iduna.

She was standing in front of the glass door and the sun shone through highlighting the translucency of her gown. Alex was pretty sure she wasn't wearing any underwear and if her long hair had not been draped over her shoulders she would have revealed everything to him. He quickly looked away and coughed. If Lexi was anything like her mother he was in for a treat, he thought to himself smiling.

"Sure, now is good, sooner the better," he said.

"Come here then and take this," she handed Alex a pink crystal which she had taken from the desk. "You will need this to get back. Keep it safe. Now look through the glass door."

Alex stood beside her and looked through the glass. He could see the apple trees, their branches swaying in a gentle breeze.

"Read out the school's address and step through the door. To return draw a doorway with the crystal and call my name. The doorway will find me."

"Right I've got it," he said, placing the crystal safely in his pocket.

He looked at the address on the paper, he was going back to America again, the Rocky Mountains this time. He read out the address clearly and the glass started to shimmer and glow.

"Go, now quickly," Iduna gave him a gentle push and he stumbled forward through the glass.

Chapter Twelve

Alex held his hands up to protect his face but there was nothing there. When he opened his eyes, he was standing in what looked like a library. There were rows and rows of books and he could hear the soft murmur of voices and rustling papers.

Walking to the end of the aisle he peeked around the corner. It was definitely a library. There were students seated at desks talking softly to each other. Alex looked around quickly to see if there was anyone resembling Iduna but no one stood out to him. He shrugged and made his way out of the library onto a large green. There were students standing around in groups and sitting on the grass. It was a beautiful sunny day and Alex had to shield his eyes from the glare to see properly. There was a particularly large group sitting on the far side of the green and Alex strolled over to them to ask them if they had seen Lexi. He had no idea what her surname was and was hoping there wasn't more than one Lexi in the school. It would be an awkward conversation if he met the wrong one.

*

Lexi strolled out of the canteen and made her way to the green. She had grabbed a salad for lunch and was looking forward to relaxing in the sun and catching up with her blog. It had been a particularly boring morning with double statistics and physics and she felt mentally drained. She looked around to find a secluded spot in the shade when she felt a tap on her shoulder.

"Hey gorgeous," said a low voice.

She swung around and sighed. Hadron again. She was hoping to avoid him this lunch, he was getting a bit intense these days and she was starting to get irritated.

"Hey, I'm shattered, if you don't mind I just need to sit alone for a bit to catch up," she said, turning away from him and walking towards a tree.

He grabbed her arm and swung her around to face him again. His grey eyes flashed dangerously.

"Now, now, none of that my sweet. You spend more time on your blog than you do with me," he complained, running a finger along her cheek. "Come on let's sit over there under the tree. I've bought you lunch, look roast chicken, your favourite," he said, smiling revealing a perfect set of pearly white even teeth.

"Hadron, roast chicken is your favourite, I've bought a salad, that's just fine," she said, letting him lead her over to a large leafy tree where no one was sitting.

She sank to the grass and looked up at him and he dropped to his knees in front of her, took her face in both hands and kissed her passionately on the mouth.

"Hadron, cut it out," she cried, pushing him away.

"What?" he asked, confused. "You've never complained before," he said, smiling mischievously at her.

"Everyone's looking at us," she said, looking around embarrassed.

There was only one person looking and that person looked frozen to the spot. He stood there staring at them and Lexi squirmed beneath Hadron's hands.

She had fallen in love with Hadron at first sight at her old school. He was stunningly attractive; tall, slim, silver grey eyes, hair so blonde it was almost white. He had been the perfect gentleman, taking her on dates, treating her like a complete princess. Then things started to change; he became possessive and wouldn't allow her to hang out with her friends. She hadn't really noticed at first, she had been so besotted with him. Then her mother started to interfere and told her she was being brainwashed by him. She hadn't listened though and continued to see him until her mother had made her change schools. It was fruitless though; he had followed her and acted as though nothing had happened. Lexi had been secretly glad at first. She had not known anyone at this school and she had missed him when they were apart. However, he never left her alone for a minute and it was becoming tiresome now. She really wanted to start making friends and hanging out with other people. All Hadron kept talking about these days were their wedding plans. She shook her head at the absurdity of it, she was only seventeen. She had a very long life ahead of her and had no plans to settle down and get married any time soon.

Suddenly a dark shadow fell over her and she looked up. The sight took her breath away. Looking down on her was the most beautiful boy she had ever seen in her life and that was saying something. Hadron was handsome; all elves were but this boy looking down on her made her heart stop. He was tall, broad shouldered and the sun glowed behind him lighting up his blonde tousled hair.

"Is this guy bothering you?" he asked, glaring at Hadron.

Hadron leapt to his feet and looked Alex up and down disdainfully.

"No, I am not bothering her," he snarled, in Alex's face.

"You're the one bothering her, now turn around and crawl back into the hole you slithered out of."

He went to push Alex back by the chest but Alex stepped back a pace.

"Dude don't touch me or you'll regret it," said Alex, taking another step back again.

"Is this guy serious?" Hadron asked Lexi.

"Hadron leave him alone, come on let's eat lunch," she said, standing up quickly and putting her hand on Hadron's arm.

"No, this punk needs to apologise," said Hadron, stepping forwards quickly and pushing Alex in the chest.

There was a brilliant white flash and Hadron went flying back ten paces.

"Dude I told you not to touch me. Are you okay? I think your hair might be on fire," said Alex, in a panic.

He looked around quickly to see if anyone had noticed but it didn't look as though anyone had. Hadron lay on his back and groaned. He raised his hand shakily to his head. The smell of burning hair brought him to his senses and he jumped up quickly yelping, patting at his hair with his hands.

"What the hell was that?" Hadron cried, glaring at Alex.

Lexi looked from one to the other completely confused.

"Look I warned you not to touch me," snarled Alex. "I take it you're the little elf who has been bugging Lexi. Leave her alone, it looks to me as though she doesn't want you around anymore."

Alex went to stand by Lexi's side.

"Who are you?" she asked, looking up at him.

"Alex...you may have heard of me recently?" he said

arrogantly, hoping to impress her.

"Er no and where do you get off zapping my boyfriend like that?" she asked, moving to Hadron and brushing his singed hair back. "You got a Taser up your shirt or something? That was dangerous," she said, her eyes flashing with anger.

"No Lexi, let me explain but not here and not with him. Let's get a coffee and I'll tell you everything, it's quite a story," he said, pleadingly.

"I have no idea who you are or how you know my name, I'm not going anywhere with you," she said.

"I suggest you get out of here you psycho before I kill you," Hadron's eyes turned to liquid silver and he grasped hold of Lexi's arm possessively.

"Hadron you're hurting me, let me go," she said, squirming and trying to pull her arm away.

"No, we're getting out of here. It's time you came home with me and stopped all of this nonsense," he said, glaring at her.

"What nonsense? You mean school, having friends, having a normal life? No Hadron, I need some space, leave me alone for a bit," she cried, still trying to get loose from his tight grip.

She expected there would be bruises on her arm.

"Lexi we're getting married, don't be ridiculous. We might as well do it now, then we can enjoy married life in peace away from all these distractions," he said, sweeping his arm around to encompass the school and students.

"No Hadron, we're not getting married. I'm only seventeen for goodness sake," she shouted.

"But you just told him I'm your boyfriend, you love me

you know you do," he whined.

"That was when I thought you were hurt, then I realised you're just as obnoxious as ever. I'm serious Hadron leave me alone."

Lexi wrenched her arm free bent down grabbed her rucksack and stalked off towards the canteen. Hadron went to follow her but Alex stepped in the way.

"You'll be sorry for this," hissed Hadron.

"Somehow, I don't think I will," smirked Alex as he walked backwards towards Lexi.

He did not take his eyes off Hadron. It was obvious already this guy was dangerous. He turned around when there was a good distance between them and jogged to catch up with Lexi.

"Hey wait up, please, it's important," he called, to her back.

She stopped and turned around slowly. Her beauty stunned Alex. She was breathtakingly beautiful. Even more gorgeous than her mother, if that were even possible. She was tall, slim, her long blonde hair swept down her back in soft waves and her eyes were a clear sparkling blue. He yearned to draw her to him, touch her hair and kiss her full red lips. There was something about her, which was calling to him, and he felt an overwhelming urge to protect her.

"So, tell me Alex, who are you and how do you know my name?" she asked, looking at him intently.

"It's a long story," he sighed.

"Well I have no more classes today so we have plenty of time. Come on let's get some coffee," she said, entering the canteen.

Alex smiled to himself and followed her. He looked

around and noticed all of the guys in the canteen had stopped in their tracks and were staring at her. He didn't blame them; he could barely tear his eyes away from her face himself. They grabbed a coffee at the counter and sat at a table in the corner next to the window. Alex looked out and saw a large black bird eyeing him up. He rapped on the window and it cawed loudly and flew away.

"Hey don't do that, it's rude, he was just keeping an eye on me," she said, stirring sugar into her coffee.

"What? What do you mean?" he asked.

"Oh, it's Gramps checking up on me. He drops by every now and then to make sure I'm behaving myself," she said.

"Gramps? You're saying that bird is your grandfather?" asked Alex, confused.

"Odin, the all father, he's my Gramps and it's my guess that you're part of the club too. That lightning that came out of your chest was a bit of a giveaway. So, who's your pops then?" she asked, sipping her coffee and looking at him over the edge of her polystyrene cup.

"Thor apparently. I just found out a few days ago when all this crazy stuff started to happen," he said.

"Uncle Thor, cool, he's nice, you're lucky. You only found out a few days ago, how come?" she asked.

"I was taken away from my mother at birth. They think it was Loki but we don't know yet, apparently Thor, er my dad is looking into it. It's all a bit confusing. What I do know is when I turned eighteen a curse was triggered which would allow Hel to be freed from Helheim. My mum is a human you see and Thor shouldn't have been with her. As soon as I turned eighteen some weird stuff started to happen. There has been a breach at a henge near me and some spirits have come through. Nothing big yet and it's quiet at the moment but at any time Hel could break free."

Alex took a deep breath, this all sounded ridiculous saying it out loud.

"Anyway, there's a prophecy that the last-born son of Thor can close the breach if he finds the sword of Tyrfing and uses it to seal her in forever. So, in a nutshell I'm on a mission to find the sword. I know where it is but I need to help my friend first as he might be able to lift the curse which he placed on the sword which will probably kill me. I needed to get a golden apple to save my friend so he could save me when I used the sword. So, I went to Asgard, met your mother and...."

"Wait," Lexi interrupted his monologue. "You saw my mother? Hang on, she sent you here didn't she?" asked Lexi, suspicious.

"Yes, she's worried about you. You haven't returned her emails or her texts. When I saw her she was crying her heart out. She's worried the elf has bewitched you," said Alex.

"I'm not bewitched, that's ridiculous, she just wants to lock me up in that house of hers and never let me live," said Lexi, grumpily.

"Hey calm down, I really didn't get that impression. She loves you; she let you come to school so you could have a normal life. She's just worried he'll carry you off or something and marry you. You're young and have your whole life ahead of you, you need to live it, not be tied down to that guy...elf...whatever he is. Anyway, it's dangerous here at the moment. Take a break, go see your mum for a bit until I can sort out this portal, then it will be safe and you can make up your mind about what you want to do," he said.

"Come on Alex, you can't fool me. You just need to get me back to Asgard so you can get your precious apple," she said, looking at him with half closed eyes.

"I'm not going to lie to you, yes I need an apple, yes I need to get you home to get it, but I can't force you. If you want to go off with that elf and become his elf bride at seventeen be my guest. I'm pretty sure I can persuade your mum I tried. Personally, I think you need to get away and clear your head. You didn't look completely happy with big ears earlier."

"Big ears? He doesn't have big ears," she giggled.

"All elves have big ears, it's in all the books. His hair was probably hiding them," Alex grinned.

"Okay I admit they're a bit pointy," she giggled again and Alex felt his heart melt.

"So how come you're allowed to stay here? I thought Asgardians were banned from mixing with humans," asked Alex.

"True but Gramps has a soft spot for me. When I told him how bored I was he let me visit and he could see I loved it here. I mean you don't get Starbucks in Asgard."

"But the city looked beautiful from what I could see if it."

"That's the trouble, it's all so perfect and big, I got sick of it. I know I will have to go back but I can have some fun for a few years."

"Well it would really help if you could pay a quick visit now." Alex winked. "Doesn't have to be for long, just go show your mother you're okay and you have no intention of running off with elf boy."

"Oh yes and who says I don't want to run off with Hadron?" she asked, indignantly.

"Do you?"

"No"

"Well then."

"I can look after myself thank you, I don't need to go running back to mummy every time Hadron becomes a pain. I'll deal with him."

"Lexi it's more than that, look I'm running out of time. If I don't get the sword and seal the portal soon, Hel will break loose and she will destroy this world. No more Starbucks, no anything, just a wasteland. Please just come back with me now, the sooner we do this, the sooner you can reassure your mum and the quicker you can return," he pleaded.

"Okay, fine you win, I'll go. I could do with some time away from Hadron anyway. How are we getting back though, my mum normally comes to collect me?" she asked.

"With this apparently," said Alex plucking the pink crystal from his pocket.

"Great a crystal portal, cool. Let's go to my room, no one will see us there. It will look a bit strange if we disappear here," she laughed, her eyes twinkling.

Alex's stomach did a somersault at the thought of being alone with Lexi in her room and he stood up quickly crushing the cup in his hand.

"I'll have to sneak you in, guys aren't allowed in the building," she said, gathering her bag and tossing her coffee cup in the bin.

Alex held the door open for her and as she walked past he caught a whiff of her perfume. He closed his eyes savoring the moment.

"Alex, are you okay?" she asked, looking back at him.

"Er yeah all good," he grinned.

Lexi strode across the green towards her dormitory. There were not many people around as the students had returned to their afternoon classes. She looked back at Alex who was looking at her like a lovesick puppy and she smiled to herself. He was hot and she really liked the attention. She didn't think he had noticed all of the girls in the canteen drooling over him and the look of envy on their faces when she left with him. She was really looking forward to getting to know him a bit better and wondered if he had a girlfriend.

A loud cawing broke her out of her thoughts. She jumped and looked around quickly at the warning. She saw a black raven with one piercing black eye and one milky white eye sitting on the signpost to the science labs. It cawed again loudly and looked up into the sky. Lexi could hear the beat of wings and she looked up into the sky too and jumped back in fright. An enormous eagle as big as a car was swooping down towards her with its talons outstretched reaching for her. The raven cawed a final warning and took off into the air flying away from the eagle.

"Lexi look out," shouted Alex.

He sprinted towards her but it was too late, the eagle's talons grasped her around the waist and lifted her up into the air. She screamed and struggled, kicking her legs wildly but the eagle held on tightly.

"It's Hadron," she shouted desperately to Alex, as the eagle climbed higher into the sky.

Alex stood there helplessly as the eagle flew further away

into the distance with Lexi dangling in the air.

"Damn it," called a voice behind him.

Alex whipped around and saw a girl looking up into the sky, shielding her eyes from the sun. She was very petite, had short, black spiky hair and was dressed all in black.

"He's taken her, I knew he would try something like this, I should have seen it coming," she sighed and looked at Alex.

"I'm sorry, who are you?" he asked, confused.

"Lexi's roommate. I was meant to stop him from taking her by force. Iduna is going to kill me," she said.

"You know Iduna?" asked Alex.

"Yes, she hired me to keep an eye on her, she knew Hadron was up to no good. I'm meant to protect her. I saw her with you though and thought she would be okay for five minutes. How wrong could I be?" she said, accusingly.

Alex felt terrible; if he had reacted quicker he could have grabbed hold of her or used his electricity to fry the bird.

"I've never seen a bird that big," said Alex, scanning the sky to see if he could still see them.

They had completely disappeared.

"It was Hadron, he has the power to transform into an eagle. He would have taken her back to Alfheim, we need to follow them and get her back," she said, firmly.

"I don't believe this. There's no time. If I don't get the sword soon the portal will be completely breached. We're talking about the end of the world here," said Alex, exasperated.

"Look this is your fault. If you hadn't shown up I would have been more on the ball. Odin help us if Iduna finds out. If she loses her daughter she'll get depressed and the apples will die. It's happened before you know. The gods started to age and it was a nightmare."

"Okay, okay I get it. How do we get to Alf what did you call it?"

"Alfheim, the land of the Light Elves, that's where Hadron lives," she said, impatiently.

"I need an address to use this crystal door thingy Iduna gave me," he said, showing her the pink crystal.

"It's okay I'll create a portal," she said, reaching into her rucksack and pulling out a small bag.

"Hang on, you're a Volva?" he asked horrified.

This was the third he had met in a couple of days. What were the chances? He thought to himself miserably.

"Of course I am. Who did you think I was?" she asked, testily.

"No idea. Nothing is surprising me today; I'm just going along with it all. When I get to catch my breath, I'll have a think about it all and then I'll probably freak out."

"Come on stop rambling, we're wasting time," she grabbed his arm and drew him close to her.

Bending down and sprinkling what looked like salt crystals around both of them, she muttered a spell under her breath.

"Here I go again..." Alex groaned, as the ground fell away beneath them.

*

They landed in a clearing in the middle of a wood.

"This is as close as I dare get," she whispered. "They have really good hearing and he'll be on high alert. He knows I'll come and get her."

"Where are we?" Alex asked, looking around.

Trees surrounded them and Alex could hear the sound of water bubbling away close to them.

"We're in Alfheim, in the woods surrounding the Light Elves capital city. He must have taken her there. It's like a fortress and heavily guarded," she said, looking around cautiously.

They were not safe in these woods, all sorts of strange creatures lived in them and it made her very nervous.

"You sure about that? It's a bit obvious, isn't it?" asked Alex.

"He's arrogant, he wants us to find them. We're on his turf here, he has power and friends, this is not going to be easy," she warned.

"What's the plan then?"

"No idea, I was going to ask you the same question," she said, looking worried.

"Can't you just do some magic and whisk her away?" asked Alex.

"Oh, yes I hadn't thought of that, how rubbish of me. Come on idiot we're wasting time. He could have married her by now," she snapped at him.

"Calm down, I don't know what you Volva's can or can't do. I didn't even know you guys existed until a few days ago," said Alex, following her into the dense wood.

"I don't even know your name."

"Ellewen."

"I'm Alex."

"I know who you are son of Thor. Now keep up."

They pushed their way through a thick bush and followed what looked like an animal trail until they came to a small pond with a waterfall trickling into it.

"Wait up," Alex called. "I'm thirsty," he said, dropping to his knees and cupping his hand under the waterfall.

"No," shouted Ellewen kicking his hand with her foot.

"What the...?" cried Alex rubbing his hand.

"You can't drink from there. The sprites will claim you," she said.

"The sprites?"

"The water sprites that live here. If you drink the water they will drag you under and feed off you."

"Ew gross," Alex stepped back a pace and peered into the crystal-clear water. "I can't see anything," he said, looking back at Ellewen.

"Look now," she said.

He looked back into the water and saw a silver flash just beneath the surface and heard a tinkling, bubbling laugh.

"That was close, you need to be really careful here, not everything is as it seems. Come on we're getting closer and keep quiet."

Alex followed Ellewen and gave the pond a wide berth. He made a mental note to not eat or drink anything until he was back home. He looked around but couldn't see anything unusual, just moss-covered trees, grey rocks and spiky bushes.

After walking for an hour Ellewen quickly pulled him behind a large gnarled tree and put her finger to her lips. Alex could hear voices up ahead and he crouched down next to her.

"They have guards on the gates," she whispered.

"How will we get past them?" he whispered back.

"How good are your powers?"

"My powers?"

"You know what I mean, I can sense the energy in you from here. Can you control it enough yet to take them out?" she asked, quietly.

"I don't know, I might end up killing them. Did you see what I did to Hadron? I wasn't even trying then."

She nodded and pursed her lips thinking. "Okay, we don't need dead elves on our hands, that could start a war. I'll try a spell instead but I'm a bit rusty. I haven't practiced much recently."

"What type of spell? Can you turn them into frogs or something?" asked Alex.

Ellewen glared at him. "Frogs...really? You need a better imagination. I'll try a sleeping spell but we'll need to get a bit closer," she said.

They crept around the tree and crawled on their hands and knees through the bushes trying to make as little sound as possible. They stopped about twenty large paces away from two huge wrought iron gates, which were intricately carved with leaves and flowers. The gates were set into a tall grey wall, which stretched as far as the eye could see in both directions. Alex looked towards the top of the wall and could see two guard towers either side of the gates. He couldn't see anyone in the towers, they were too high up but he did see the sun glint off a spear in each tower and figured there was one guard in each. Two tall good-looking men wearing silver helmets with cheek pieces were standing by the gates with long spears in their hands. They were staring straight ahead on full alert.

Alex mouthed "four" to Ellewen and pointed up towards the guard towers. She nodded her head in understanding, closed her eyes and started singing a beautiful lullaby. Alex looked at her confused.

After a few moments, Alex stifled a large yawn and she nudged him on the arm.

"Put your hands over your ears," she hissed.

"Why?" he asked confused.

"The spell is affecting you too stupid," she whispered.

Alex did what she asked and she continued singing softly. Alex looked at the guards and they started to rub their eyes and yawn.

"It's working," Alex whispered, excitedly.

She carried on singing until the guards dropped their spears and sank to the floor closing their eyes.

"Were you seriously singing a lullaby?" asked Alex.

"Of course, it's the oldest spell in the book. Millions of parents sing them every night to get their children to sleep and have no idea they're using magic," she said, grinning.

"Hurry we won't have much time before someone finds them," she said, standing up slowly.

"Did you get the ones up there too?" asked Alex.

"I hope so, we'll find out in a minute," she said shrugging her shoulders.

"How long will they be asleep for?"

"A few hours. They'll feel great when they wake up, there will be no lasting damage," she grinned.

They approached the gates tentatively expecting to be stopped at any moment by the guards in the towers but there was silence and no one was in the area other than the sleeping guards on the floor. Alex pushed open one of the gates and they slipped inside quickly closing it behind them. Alex immediately looked for somewhere to hide so they could get their bearings and plan their next move.

He gestured to the guard tower on the left and Ellewen nodded in agreement. Alex cautiously opened the wooden door and peeked in. There was a small room with a guard lying asleep on a table. They crept into the room and edged around the sleeping guard towards a set of stairs leading upwards. Alex led the way and climbed the stairs until he reached the viewing platform. He immediately saw another guard slumped on the floor deep in sleep. Ellewen joined him and he made his way to the edge so he could look at the view. On one side there was the green, dense forest. On the other, a huge city lay sprawled before them. There was row upon row of houses nestled between cobbled streets and in the distance a large turreted castle sat proudly on a hill.

"There," said Ellewen, pointing to the castle. "He would have taken her there."

"How do you know? She could be anywhere?" asked Alex.

The city was massive; there was no way they could search for her here.

"He's the Prince of Alfheim and that's his home, the palace. It's the most protected place in the city. There will be guards everywhere. I won't be able to put them all to sleep," she said, worried.

"Okay I have an idea," said Alex, looking at the castle. "We just need to get there without being seen."

Ellewen reached out and pulled his ears upwards.

"Ouch, what are you doing?" he asked, rubbing his ears. They felt strange.

"Helping us blend in," she said, touching her own ears.

They grew longer in front of his eyes and became pointed.

"You gave me big ears?" he asked, aghast.

"I'm helping us to blend in. It's a good job you're so good looking; you could definitely pass for an elf. I might have more of a problem," she said, wistfully.

"What? You're good looking," he said, looking at her. "Well, you are in this form." She looked cute with pointy little ears but she wasn't very tall.

"What do you mean, in this form?" she asked, narrowing her eyes.

"You know, human form. Not all old and wrinkly," he said.

"Old and wrinkly? How rude! This is what I look like," she snapped.

"Oh, but the other Volvas I met were hideous. They changed their appearance to look beautiful. I assumed you were like that, sorry," he said, embarrassed.

"If you're talking about Cassie and Maggie, they're ancient. At least a thousand years old. Pretty sure I wouldn't look that great if I were that old," she said, laughing now.

"A thousand years old? Are they immortal too then?" asked Alex, surprised.

"No but they use spells to prolong their life. It's very dangerous though. Only the crazy ones do it," said Ellewen.

"So how old are you then?" asked Alex.

"Seventeen."

"Cool, well you certainly don't need any spells to make you pretty," he said, flattering her.

He felt far more comfortable in her presence now he knew she wasn't about to turn into a scary girl from a horror movie. She blushed and checked her ears to make sure they were not too big.

"Come on let's do this," she said, climbing down the stairs.

Alex grinned and followed her quickly, quietly thinking he was meeting some rather cute girls recently.

*

The streets around the guard tower were virtually empty and they made quick progress down the narrow-cobbled streets. However, they soon came to a large open square, which was a hive of activity. Numerous people were packed around market stalls haggling for the best price for all manner of goods. Alex looked around fascinated. All of the people were as tall as he was and were stunningly beautiful. All the men had long blonde hair, bronzed faces and large muscly bare arms. The women were tall and elegant and also had long blonde hair, which reached almost to their feet. Both men and women wore long silky gowns in shades of green and brown.

"Just look like you belong," muttered Ellewen, as she pushed into the crowd confidently.

She was at least two heads shorter than anyone in sight and drew a few curious glances, especially as she was dressed all in black. Alex hurried over to her side but a tall man pulled his arm making him stop.

"Come here, come here look at these beauties," the man called, virtually dragging Alex by the arm to his stall which was packed high with strange looking fruit.

Alex could feel a tingle of electricity shoot down his arm and the man jerked back.

"Oops static," said Alex, apologetically.

The man looked at him suspiciously.

"What are you wearing?" he asked, looking Alex up and down. "You look strange."

"Oh er, Midgard clothes, I'm at school there with the Prince," he lied. "I've just come for a visit, you know. I have to rush, he's expecting me," he said, backing away from the stall.

"Ah you're here for the wedding," the man said, grinning. "Should be quite the party tonight," he said, rubbing his hands together.

"Tonight?" asked Alex, in a panic. "I er, didn't think it was going to happen that soon," he added, when he saw the man narrowing his eyes.

"Yes, he won't want to waste any time, I hear she's a stunner." The man licked his lips and grinned. "Here give her one of these," he said, handing Alex a weird looking orange fruit. "Tell her there are plenty more of those on Anar's stall. I have the juiciest ones in Alfheim," he grinned.

Alex felt sick, he pushed past the man and caught up with Ellewen who had made it through to the other side of the square and was trying to look inconspicuous.

"We have to hurry, it's tonight," he hissed.

"What's tonight?" she asked, puzzled.

"He's going to marry her tonight, come on," he said, dragging her by the arm down a small street.

They jogged through the narrow streets gathering strange looks as they passed. Everyone else was walking serenely as if they had all the time in the world. After a small while the streets opened up onto a large open green park. It was heaving with people setting up tents and building cooking fires. Tall, slender, beautiful children ran around screaming with laughter, getting in people's way.

"Word must be out about the wedding. That was so

quick," said Ellewen, furrowing her brow. "It's as though they knew beforehand," she said, looking at Alex.

"What, you think Hadron had preplanned this?" asked Alex, startled.

"He must have. Just look how many people there are. They must have travelled from miles around," she said, angrily.

"We need to hurry," said Alex, quickly following the footpath which led straight through the park and up towards the palace.

The palace was raised on a slight hill and a tall golden fence surrounded it. The gate was guarded with heavily armed Light Elves who had tall silver shields. Each one had a long broad sword in his hand and looked ready for action at any moment. Alex motioned to Ellewen to walk around the fence to the left. They kept their distance and tried to look like they were on a casual walk. Once out of sight of the guards Alex and Ellewen approached the fence cautiously and peered through the golden bars.

"Okay, what's your plan?" asked Ellewen, looking around.

"Well I figured I could blast a hole in the outside wall using my powers, we run in, find Lexi and then get the hell out of here using the crystal," he said.

"Are you serious?" asked Ellewen, raising her eyebrows. "We just blast our way in, with no idea where she is? We would be caught in thirty seconds and killed. Those guards don't look like the sort to take prisoners."

"Well can you think of anything better?" he asked. "How about your sleeping spell?"

"I wouldn't be able to do it quickly enough before others see and come out of the palace," she said.

"The fairy in Sleeping Beauty managed it," said Alex.

"Yes, well I'm a Volva not a fairy thank you very much. Fairies have much more magic than we do," she said, tartly.

"Really?" asked Alex stunned. "Fairies are real?"

"No but it was worth it to see the look on your face," she giggled.

"Yeah very funny. Honestly with the day I'm having I would believe anything right now," he said. "Come on do you have a better plan because I don't?"

"Not really. I wonder where he's keeping her?" said Ellewen, looking at the palace.

It was very big and looked like Sleeping Beauty's castle with all of the turrets and flying flags.

"I would put money on one of the towers," said Alex.

"That is such a cliché, kidnapping a princess and holding her prisoner in a tower," Ellewen shook her head. "I reckon the dungeon, it would be the safest place."

"No, I don't think so. Think about it, he wants to marry her; he's not going to lock her up in a dungeon. He will be up in that tower whispering sweet nothings in her ear and she'll be soaking it all up," said Alex, bitterly.

"True, okay let's try the tallest tower first, it's closest to this side anyway," she said.

"Hang on, you're a witch, can't you just fly up on a broom stick and get in the window?" Ellewen glared at him and growled.

"Okay, okay point taken," he said laughing, holding his hands up in surrender.

"Okay, we need to get through these bars, they look pretty solid. Can you handle this?" asked Ellewen.

Alex nodded and held his hands out. He concentrated and could feel the energy start to surge through his body, pulsing though his veins. Suddenly a blast of pure energy erupted from his palms completely melting the bars in front of them. Alex looked at Ellewen and grinned at the look on her face. She was standing with her eyes wide open and her mouth opening and shutting like a fish.

"Oh my god that was totally Emperor Palpatine," she said, amazed.

Alex laughed, "Yep pretty cool eh? Come on before someone comes."

He stepped through the melted bars and ran to the side of the palace walls. Alex faced the stonewall and started to focus on his hands concentrating on channeling the power he could feel in the pit of his stomach. The more he tried this the easier it was becoming, though he was starting to feel a bit tired.

"Psst, here..." Ellewen called over to him.

She was standing further up the wall and held open an emerald crystal glass door.

"Okay that's easier," said Alex, running over quickly.

They looked through the door and could see what looked like a grand dining room. Chandeliers hung from the ceiling and there was a long table in the middle of the room, which was laid out for a feast for at least a hundred people. A raised dais covered in white flowers was at the far end of the room and it too was laid out for a dinner.

"Well I guess we know where the wedding dinner will be, quick someone's coming," said Alex, pushing Ellewen behind one of the thick purple curtains which were hanging beside the glass door.

They stood as still as they could and listened.

"Has the screaming stopped yet?" asked a voice from the far side of the room.

"Not yet, she will lose her voice soon. I don't know what all the fuss is about, I mean who wouldn't want to marry the prince? She's crazy," said another voice.

Alex could feel static electricity pulsing from his skin, he was furious and tried to calm down. Burning the curtains down would definitely give away their hiding place.

"Well it will be over soon, Reigna is brewing her something to keep her calm, she'll be compliant enough soon. Just so long as she can still speak and say I Do that's all that matters. As soon as the ring is on her finger the apples will be ours. Her mother will do anything for her daughter, even if it means immortality for the Light Elves. I can't wait to see the look on the Asgardians faces when they realise they're all going to die of old age," the person sniggered and Alex heard the sound of the door clicking shut.

They waited for a few moments and then poked their heads around the curtain. The room was empty.

"Did you hear that?" Ellewen hissed. "He only wants her to get to the golden apples, the pig. Just wait until I get my hands on him."

She was burning with fury.

"Save it for later, come on let's find Lexi," said Alex, making his way over to the main door.

He opened it a crack and listened. Off to the right he could make out the sound of someone shouting loudly and a large crash.

"Over there," he whispered, pointing to a spiral staircase,

which led up to what looked like a tower.

Ellewen pushed past him and started to climb the stairs quickly. They paused half way up when they heard an enormous scream and the sound of someone thrashing around and then there was silence. They looked at each other in panic and raced up the remaining stairs. At the top, there was a large wooden door.

"Finally, I didn't think it was going to work." Alex heard Hadron's muffled voice on the other side of the door.

Reigna get her dressed, the guests will be arriving soon. I'm going to get changed myself, my darling wife to be has ripped this tunic to shreds, the little vixen. Just wait until we're married then I'll show her how a lady should behave."

Alex looked at Ellewen in panic; there was nowhere to hide. The only escape was back down the stairs.

Ellewen waved her arms in a large circle and muttered, "lagr firar."

"What are you doing?" whispered Alex.

Just as the door opened Alex felt himself falling to the floor.

"What happened?" he asked, confused.

Everything looked strange. There was a massive feather on the floor, which was at least twice the size he was. He looked up and saw the door; it was huge, taller than a mountain. Standing in the doorframe was a giant. It was Hadron Alex realised in shock. He had turned into a giant.

"It's okay I made us small," Ellewen explained. "Quick, it won't last long. It was the only thing I could think of."

"Small?" asked Alex, horrified. "Ants are bigger than this, you're going to get us killed," he complained.

"Shush, they'll hear us. Come on," she grabbed his arm and tugged him into the room.

A giant foot landed right beside Alex making him jump to the side. Hadron left the room and a giant woman followed him. The woman spoke and the sound of her voice boomed and reverberated around Alex's head.

"Stay here miss, I'll just go and prepare your bath," she said.

The giant woman left the room and the door slammed shut with an enormous thud. The sound of a loud click confirmed they were locked in. Alex and Ellewen breathed a sigh of relief. Alex started to feel tingly and all of a sudden, he started to grow again.

"Ah that's better," he said, grinning at Ellewen.

"Quick look," she said, pointing to the bed.

Lexi was sitting on the edge of the bed and looked like she was in a trance. She was not moving and had not reacted at all to their sudden appearance.

"Lexi," cried Alex, rushing over to the bed. "Lexi, can you hear me?" he asked, shaking her shoulder gently.

Lexi blinked very slowly and looked at Alex. There was no comprehension at all in her eyes.

"They drugged her," said Ellewen. "Looks like she put up a good fight though."

There was shattered glass and broken bits of furniture strewn across the whole room. The curtains were torn down and there were large bruises on her wrists. Alex looked at her furious at the way she had been treated.

"Quick, I'll carry her, let's make a portal and get out of here," said Alex, bending down to scoop her up in his arms.

Ellewen drew the pouch from her bag and sprinkled the

salt in a circle on the wooden floor. She stood inside and Alex joined her carrying Lexi in his arms. She hardly weighed anything and Alex felt a buzz of excitement at holding her so closely to his chest. Ellewen said the portal spell and they waited for the ground to fall away. Nothing happened though.

"Say it again," said Alex, frantically.

He could hear heavy footsteps approaching the room. Ellewen recited the spell again but nothing happened. Then the door crashed open and Hadron stood on the threshold grinning widely.

"You took your time," he sneered.

"Ellewen," shouted Alex, desperately. "Get us out of here."

"It's no good, no magic will work in this room. I have had it protected," said Hadron, with a very pleased look on his face.

"But you used magic to make us small," said Alex, looking at Ellewen in confusion.

"That was outside the room. I have no power in here," she said, miserably.

"Now if you would be so kind as to put my bride down, she has a wedding to prepare for," Hadron snarled at Alex.

Alex laid Lexi back on the bed and concentrated on his power. He felt a surge go straight to his hands and he drew them back ready to strike at Hadron.

"Guards," Hadron called loudly.

Two guards burst into the room and covered Hadron with their shields.

"The shields are rubber Alex, your electricity trick won't work this time so put it away little boy," said Hadron, enjoying himself.

Alex roared in defiance and the energy burst from his chest with an intense blast. The guards were knocked back against the wall with the force of the blast and they lost consciousness.

"Okay I didn't see that happening," said Hadron, backing away from Alex.

Alex's face was a mask of pure hatred. The energy was pulsing from every fiber in his body. His eyes radiated power and he gathered it into his hands ready to strike Hadron.

"Alex stop," Lexi called weakly from the bed.

She was sitting up and rubbing her head. "Don't hurt him, it's not his fault."

"What do you mean it's not his fault? He kidnapped you, drugged you and was going to force you to marry him. I'm going to end this," shouted Alex, angrily.

"No, Alex please let him go. He's just doing what his father ordered him to, he has no choice," she pleaded, standing up shakily.

"What are you talking about Lexi?" asked Alex, confused.

The energy was pulsing in his hands and making them itch. He was dying to release the power.

"The king is making him do this, he wants the golden apples for the Light Elves. If

Hadron marries me it connects our families and my mother will be obliged to hand him a share," said Lexi.

"But it won't be a share will it Hadron?" Ellewen snarled. "He wants them all for the Light Elves and the Asgardian gods will die," she hissed.

"No, of course not," spluttered Hadron, his arms outstretched as though to fend them off.

"Liar," shouted Alex, releasing a blast of energy and striking the floor in front of Hadron.

Large chunks of the floor flew up and Hadron squealed and jumped back. Suddenly he started to transform. His nose became elongated and turned into a hooked beak. Brown feathers sprouted on his face and two giant wings grew from his back. In no time at all he had transformed into a giant eagle. An ear-splitting cry filled the air and Hadron beat his wings knocking them all to the floor. He struck out his beak towards Ellewen and ripped a large tear in her arm. She cried and scrambled back against the wall holding her arm. Alex jumped to his feet and concentrated on recharging his energy. Hadron hopped towards him and darted forwards trying to tear Alex's head off with his beak. Alex ducked out of the way and Hadron tore a hole in the floor instead. Alex felt the energy in his hand return and he threw a massive bolt towards Hadron but he missed and hit the door instead. Chips of wood flew everywhere and Alex threw himself in front of Lexi to protect her. A large splinter embedded itself in Alex's thigh and he cried out in pain and collapsed to the floor. Hadron cried out in triumph and lunged at Alex again with his beak, completely intent on ripping him to pieces. Lexi cried out and pushed herself in front of Alex. Hadron's beak stopped inches from her head. He reared back and shrieked loudly in protest.

"Hadron stop. Leave them alone and I will marry you now, no fuss, no fighting, just let them go," she shouted.

His eagle eyes gleamed and he quickly transformed back into his natural form.

"Finally, you see sense. Lexi darling, it didn't have to be this way," said Hadron, stroking her cheek with the tips of his fingers.

"You're not going to get away with this you big eared bird freak," shouted Alex, hobbling forward and shoving Lexi behind him again.

"I think you'll find I already have. You heard Lexi agree to marry me, a promise is as binding as a contract in this land," said Hadron, gloating.

"She's not from this land elf boy," Alex snarled back.

"Alex it's over, he will kill you both if I don't do this," said Lexi, bending down and helping Ellewen to her feet.

She was whimpering and holding her arm in pain.

"Alex just leave while you can. I'll be fine, tell my mother I'm sorry and I'll see her soon," said Lexi, with tears in her eyes.

Alex felt the rage build within him. A large crack of lightning lit up the room and a wind whipped around them.

"Alex what are you doing?" cried Lexi, shielding her face from the debris flying around the room.

She looked at him and he was standing firm. His hair was being whipped around by the wind and lightning flashed from his eyes. He held his hands out to his sides and a huge bolt of electricity burst from his chest and struck Hadron square on the chest. Hadron was thrown into the air and he crashed down against the wall unconscious. Alex collapsed to the floor completely spent. He had no energy at all and could he barely lift his hand.

"Alex, are you okay?" cried Lexi, falling to her knees next to him.

She tried to roll him over onto his back but he was too heavy.

"Here let me help," said Ellewen, crawling over on her knees.

They managed to roll Alex over together and he groaned. Every nerve in his body was tingling and he felt sick and dizzy.

"Did I kill him?" he asked, trying to look over towards Hadron.

Lexi looked over and could see Hadron's chest moving up and down steadily.

"He's breathing, he'll be okay...I think," she said. "Quick we need to get out of here before he wakes up," she said, helping Alex up into a sitting position.

He cried out in pain and she saw the large splinter of wood in his thigh.

"Let me see," said Ellewen, shuffling forwards. "We have to take it out or he won't heal," she said. "He has some immortal blood in him so he should heal quickly if we get the splinter out. Lexi, you'll have to do it, I won't be able to get a good enough grip with this arm," she said, lifting her arm up and wincing.

Blood was pouring from the deep wound and she looked as though she could faint at any moment.

"Okay, Alex I'll pull it out after three, okay?"

Alex nodded and then screamed loudly when she ripped the splinter from his leg.

"What happened to after three?" he gasped.

She grinned and tucked a stray lock of his hair back, which had fallen into his eyes.

"I figured it was like taking off a band aid, the quicker the better. Do you think you can stand?" she asked, positioning herself so she could help him up.

"Yeah, it's feeling better already," he said, looking at the wound through the rip in his trousers.

It had stopped bleeding and new skin was already starting to form over the tear in his skin.

"Help me up," he said.

He didn't really need help but he liked the way she had wrapped her arm around his waist. He staggered to his feet and they helped Ellewen up. She was looking very pale and was shaking.

"I need to get out of this room, then I can sort this out," she said, motioning to her arm.

They made their way over to the hole where the door used to be and stepped over the debris. As soon as they were over the threshold Ellewen started to mutter a spell over her arm and the bleeding stopped.

"You can heal yourself?" asked Alex, impressed.

"Not completely, this is the best I can do but at least I won't bleed to death," she said. "Alex where is the crystal we need to use it now?" she asked.

Alex felt in his pocket and took out the crystal. He could hear the guards behind them moaning in the room.

"Quick they're waking up," he whispered frantically. "What do I do with this?" he asked holding the crystal in the palm of his hand.

"Draw a door on that wall," said Ellewen, pushing Alex towards the wall next to the stairwell.

He scratched a door shape into the wall, stepped back and said, "Iduna."

They waited but nothing happened.

"Iduna" he said, louder.

They heard a crash from the room and looked at each other in panic.

"Give it here." Lexi snatched the crystal from Alex's hand and drew a doorknob.

Suddenly the edges of the door started to glow yellow and the doorknob protruded out of the door. Alex grabbed the knob, twisted it and pulled. The door opened and they could see an orchard on the other side of the door.

"Stop," cried Hadron, behind them.

Alex quickly pushed the girls through the door and looked back. Hadron was standing in the ruined doorway glaring at him. His hair was singed and the pupil of one eye looked like it had a lightning streak running through it.

"See you later elf boy," said Alex, as he jumped through the door.

"Oh, believe me, you will," Hadron growled, as the door slammed shut.

Chapter Thirteen

"Lexi, thank Odin. Are you okay my darling?" Iduna cried, running towards them as they stumbled through the door.

"Hi, I'm fine, I'm sorry I should have listened to you," Lexi cried, throwing herself into Iduna's arms.

"Alex, thank you," Iduna said, over Lexi's shoulder.

Lexi was crying uncontrollably, sobbing into her mother's hair.

"Ellewen's hurt, can you help her?" Alex asked, holding Ellewen's arm out for Iduna to see.

"Oh Ellewen," Iduna cried, coming over to her to take a closer look. "Come follow me."

She took Lexi by the hand and made her way through the orchard. In the middle of the orchard Alex could see a large apple tree, which seemed to be glowing. When he looked closer he could see the branches were heavy with golden fruit.

"The golden apples," he said, amazed at the sight.

Iduna reached up and picked three apples and handed one to Ellewen. "Here eat this, it will heal your arm," she said, kindly.

"I can't touch that," said Ellewen.

Iduna looked at her confused. No one had ever turned down the chance to eat a golden apple.

"I don't want immortality," explained Ellewen, backing away from the fruit.

"It won't make you immortal, it will just extend your life for a hundred years or so," said Iduna, still holding out the apple.

"No, I'm fine, honest, the bleeding has stopped I just need

to rest," said Ellewen.

"You seriously don't want to live for an extra hundred years are you mad?" asked Alex.

"My family are not immortal, neither is my boyfriend. I don't want to see them all grow old and die before me. It's not right, immortality may sound great but in reality, I would be alone in the end. I don't want that," she said.

Alex nodded suddenly realising the enormity of the change in his life.

"You have a boyfriend?" asked Lexi, sounding surprised.

"Er yes. Tom and I have been going out for over a year now," said Ellewen, blushing.

"I didn't know, Ellewen I'm sorry I didn't even know, I've been a terrible friend," said Lexi, distraught she had no idea what her best friend had been up to for the last year.

"Lexi it's fine, you've just been a bit engrossed with Hadron," said Ellewen. "Iduna she can't go back to school she's not safe there. He's determined to marry her to bind your houses."

"And to get access to the golden apples too, I know," said Iduna, pursing her lips.

"Heimdall came and told me. This is the very reason why I can't leave here. Lexi I'm sorry but you're going to have to stay here with me until I can talk to Odin. He should be able to get the Light Elves to behave themselves. He'll be furious when he finds out about all of this."

"I think he knows already," said Lexi. "He saw me being carried off by Hadron but I don't understand why he didn't stop him," said Lexi, confused.

"I didn't know that. I expect he wanted to see how far

Hadron would go. Your grandfather loves war and chaos Lexi, you know that, but he does love you in his own way. I'm sure he wouldn't have let them hurt you," said Iduna, stroking Lexi's long blonde hair.

"But he would have allowed him to marry me. He wants war, doesn't he? I bet he's bored again and wants an excuse to fight the Light Elves," said Lexi, miserably.

"It wouldn't surprise me but because of Alex that won't happen now," said Iduna, going over and hugging Alex.

He blushed to the roots of his hair and Iduna laughed.

"Lexi, it won't be long I'm sure, you'll be back at school before you know it. I just need to make sure Odin knows he can't go to war with the Light Elves and to get him to tell Hadron to leave you alone once and for all," said Iduna.

"Will he listen to you though?" asked Lexi.

"Oh, I can be very persuasive," said Iduna, tossing the golden apple she had in her hand up and down.

They all laughed.

"Hey cheer up Lexi, I'll visit if I can and will bring you a Starbucks coffee and anything else you can't do without," said Alex, grinning.

Lexi's face lit up. "You'll visit us?"

"Sure, I promised your mum before. I reckon she needs some help building her village," he said, winking at Iduna.

"Her what?" asked Lexi, raising her eyebrows.

"Minecraft," said Alex, and Iduna together laughing.

"Oh, Mum you're not still playing on that are you?" asked Lexi, embarrassed.

"What? It's addictive, come and see the new castle I built. You'll love it. It even has a dungeon," said Iduna, giggling like a schoolgirl.

"Guys I really need to get going, things to do, people to see, saving the world and all that," said Alex, reaching out for the apples from Iduna.

"Of course, Alex I can't thank you enough," said Iduna, her eyes sparkling with tears.

She handed over the apples and he tucked them into his trouser pockets.

"Ellewen are you staying here?" he asked.

"Yes, just for a bit. I need to get my strength back then I'll head back to school. There will be some clearing up to do. I'm not sure how many people saw Hadron whisk Lexi off into the air but there must have been some. I need to do some mind wiping," she said.

"Mind wiping? That's sounds dangerous," said Alex, worried.

"They'll be fine, I'll just make them remember a slightly different version to what happened. Like a normal sized eagle carrying off a bird or something like that," she laughed.

"Thanks for your help Ellewen, I couldn't have done it without you," said Alex, pulling her into a bear hug, but being careful of her arm.

"Hey no problem, now hurry up and get that sword or I won't be able to enjoy my final years of school or anything," she grinned, pushing him away.

"Lexi," he said, resting his hands on her shoulders and looking deeply into her blue eyes. "I'll come back when all of this is over I promise."

She stepped forward into his arms and kissed him on the cheek.

"Don't be a stranger eh?" she whispered in his ear.

He smiled at her, tucked a long strand of golden hair behind her ear and stepped back before he was tempted to kiss her on the mouth.

"Right so how do I get back to Dvalin? Portal, magic door, ruby red slippers?" he asked. "Personally, I think Dvalin would prefer the door. I've messed up his house twice already with the portals," he said, grinning.

"Use the crystal," said Lexi, handing it to him. "Your friends will be able to use it too, there is no danger using this."

"You Volva's really need to get some of these," said Alex, to Ellewen holding up the crystal so it caught the light.

"Oh, whatever Alex, get going, I'm tired and need to lie down," she said, shooing him away with her good arm.

"Come into the house. Alex, you can use the window we used before and save the crystal. It only has a finite life span so you need to use it wisely," said Iduna, leading the way to her house.

They all followed and once inside Lexi led Ellewen off to a bedroom so she could rest. They waved to Alex as they disappeared up the stairs and he waved back wondering when he would see them again. He followed Iduna into the study and stepped in front of the glass door.

"Okay now say Dvalin's name clearly and step through the window like you did before. Don't be a stranger, I got the impression you and Lexi....well you know.." she said, smiling.

Alex went bright red. "Oh no, it's not like that, we're friends," he stuttered, embarrassed.

"Sure, just friends," Iduna smiled, laughing.

Alex looked at the glass at his reflection and swallowed

nervously. He had the feeling he had got himself into a bit of a mess as he thought of seeing Becca again.

"Dvalin," he called out clearly.

The glass shimmered in front of him and he closed his eyes and stepped through the rippling waves.

Chapter Fourteen

"Alex, oh my god you scared the life out of me," cried Matt, as Alex appeared through the stone wall of Dvalin's house.

"Hey Matt," grinned Alex. "Man, you'll not believe what has happened to me. How's Dvalin?" he asked, looking around the room.

Becca and Sasha were sitting with Dvalin and Sven was sitting on the sofa with Pete.

"Not good, he hasn't woken up since you left and he's barely breathing," said Becca.

She stood up and went over to Alex to hug him. "You've been gone for ages, what took you so long?" she asked. "You smell of perfume," she said, stepping back and looking at him accusingly. "What have you been up to?"

Alex blushed and shrugged. "Er I'll explain later, looks like I came back in the nick of time. Here give him this."

Alex reached into his pocket and gave Becca one of the golden apples. She looked into his eyes but he looked away embarrassed. Whilst he hadn't done anything with Lexi, he couldn't deny he had strong feelings for her. The trouble was he also had feelings for Becca and his stomach churned at the angry look she had shot at him. She took the apple out of his hand and went over to Dvalin quickly.

"He can't eat that he's unconscious," said Sasha, looking at the apple.

It was glowing bright gold lighting up the room.

"Let's cut a bit off and place it in his mouth, the juice might work," said Becca, looking around for a knife.

"Here," said Sven, pulling a penknife from his pocket and

handing it to Becca.

She cut a small piece of the apple with the knife and placed it in Dvalin's mouth. A golden glow replaced his grey pallor and his eyes flickered open slowly.

"What happened?" he croaked.

"It's okay, you've been unwell, the portal was too much for you and you collapsed," explained Becca, as she gently rubbed his hand.

He was feeling much warmer already and started to have a healthy glow about him. Sasha helped him to sit up.

"What's that?" he asked, pointing at the apple in Becca's hand.

"One of Iduna's golden apples. Alex went to fetch one for you," Becca explained. "Maggie said it was the only way to save you, you were dying."

"But that means..." he said, his eyes lighting up.

"Yes Dvalin, you now have at least another hundred years to live," said Alex, grinning.

"I feel fantastic, this is amazing," he said, feeling his face with his hands. "I can't thank you enough," he said, jumping to his feet and skipping over to an old broken mirror on the wall.

He looked at his face and gasped. The old wrinkled lines had disappeared and his face was smooth. He looked like a dwarf in the prime of life. He looked around at them all and grinned, clapping his hands in excitement.

"What about the sword, did you get it?" he asked.

"No that's next on the to do list. I had to save your life first," said Alex.

"Oh Alex, you shouldn't have," said Dvalin, moved.

"Hey what are friends for eh?" said Alex, grasping Dvalin's hand.

"I hate to break up this beautiful moment but I would really like to get out of here now and Alex you really do need to get that sword. We've wasted enough time," said Pete, standing up.

"Relax, I went back home and everything's okay at the moment. Pete, I saw your dad, he was at the henge. It's all cool, there have been no more breaches, just some smoke coming out of the ground," he said.

"Did you see my mum?" asked Matt, hopefully.

"No, just Alan, Nancy and Pete's dad. I asked Alan to call all of your parents to let them know you're okay."

"Okay, so we have time. How do we get to where the sword is?" asked Pete. "We're not using a portal again."

"With this," said Alex, pulling the crystal from his pocket. "Iduna gave it to me, we can create a door with this to wherever the dragon's lair is."

"A crystal door," said Dvalin impressed. "I've heard of those but have never seen one. Iduna gave you this? She must really like you," said Dvalin, grinning and winking at Alex.

"What?" asked Becca, not liking the knowing look on Dvalin's face or Alex's nonchalant shrug.

"She knew I needed it for you guys. It won't last forever though, just a few trips but she said it was safer than using a portal, no side effects or anything," said Alex.

"You sure about that?" asked Pete, skeptically. "I was kind of hoping we could grab the train."

"You won't find a train to Niddhogg's lair," said Sven, seriously. "The only way we could get there is a portal or with

Alex's crystal door."

"Well we're definitely not using a portal so the crystal it is," said Pete. "How does it work?" he asked.

Alex went over to the wall of Dvalin's house and scratched a door in the rock. Before he drew the doorknob, he hesitated. "Guys, I think I should take you all home first and then go get the sword on my own. This is going to be really dangerous and I don't want anyone else getting hurt," said Alex, looking at his friends.

"No way, we're in this together. It was bad enough you had to go on your own to get the golden apple. Let's just stick together for now. I'm guessing you're going to need our help," said Matt, shaking his head.

"Okay just us though. Dvalin and Sven should stay here, they've done enough. I don't want them getting hurt. From what Heimdall said this dragon is pure evil," said Alex.

"Heimdall?" asked Becca, "As in Heimdall who guards the rainbow bridge?"

"Yep the very same. He gave me a lift to Asgard," he said grinning. "It was awesome, we rode through the sky on his horse and the bridge, you guys really have to see that, it's amazing," he said, his eyes shining.

"We can catch up later. We need to concentrate," said Sasha. "I hate to say it but I think Dvalin should come. He might be able to help with the curse."

"He's done enough already, he nearly died helping us. I can handle the sword. Iduna gave me a golden apple, I reckon that'll help," said Alex.

"Excuse me but I can decide for myself. I'm coming, I can't lift the curse but I might be able to help in another way.

I've been to Yggdrasil before remember?" said Dvalin.

Alex was standing right next to him and saw him shiver. "Matt's right we need to stick together until this is over," Dvalin continued.

"Okay our Scooby gang just got bigger," said Alex, turning back to the rock wall and drawing a door handle. "Are you ready for this guys?"

The door glowed yellow and Alex looked around at his friends. They all nodded and stepped forwards.

He said firmly, "Niddhogg," opened the door and stepped through into what looked like hell.

Chapter Fifteen

The heat was the first thing Alex noticed and then the smell. As soon as they stepped through the door they all gagged.

"Oh my god, what's that smell?" asked Matt, bending over double and retching.

"Death," said Dvalin, looking around nervously. "Remember, Niddhogg feeds off dead souls, it's the smell of death."

Alex looked around; they were standing in a small cave with a tunnel leading downwards. Alex peered into the tunnel and felt a blast of heat on his face. The smell was stronger down the tunnel and he gagged again.

"Okay guys we need a plan. We probably should've thought of that before we stepped through the door but what the hell, we're making this up as we go," said Alex, trying to be cheerful.

He felt sick to the core with nerves. He had no idea what lay ahead but judging from the heat and the smell it wouldn't be good. He had to put on a brave face for the others though, they all looked terrified. Pete was feeling the wall trying to find the door they had stepped through.

"Well the only way to go is through that tunnel, so I guess we start there," said Alex, pointing down the tunnel.

"Dvalin what happened when you gave Niddhogg the sword? Did you see him put it somewhere?" asked Sasha.

"It was a long time ago. I remember Maggie creating a portal for me. It didn't come here though," said Dvalin, looking around. "There was a lot of fire, the smell was the same, you don't forget that in a hurry. I remember he was in front of me, I asked him to keep the sword safe and to never let anyone touch it again. He could have eaten it for all I know."

"Do you think we could just ask him nicely for it back?" asked Pete, hopefully.

"Pete, he will eat you before you get within thirty paces of him," said Sven.

"Why didn't he eat Dvalin then?" asked Pete.

"He doesn't eat dwarves," said Sven. "We're far too good for him. He only eats the lowest of the low. You know people like Matt here," he said, nodding in Matt's direction and grinning.

"What not even as a snack? A little appetiser?" asked Matt.

"If you don't shut up punk I will feed you to him myself," snarled Sven.

"You started it Grumpy," said Matt, skipping out of the way as Sven aimed a punch at him.

"Cut it out you two. Come on let's focus, this is serious. We have no idea what we're doing," said Becca, exasperated.

"Let's just look down this tunnel, we'll have a better idea of what we're dealing with if we can see more," said, Alex leading the way.

The tunnel was only wide enough for them to go single file. Alex walked slowly, careful not to make too much noise. He had no idea what he would find at the end of the tunnel and his heart was beating really fast. The heat was becoming almost unbearable and Alex could make out a red glow up ahead. The tunnel led into a large cavern and steam was seeping through cracks in the rock walls. The smell of sulphur filled their noses making them choke.

"Now what?" Alex whispered, as the others gathered into the larger cavern.

"Over there," said Dvalin, pointing to what looked like another tunnel directly opposite them.

They crept forward, looking around, paranoid they were about to be discovered by the dragon. Alex could feel his shoes crunching beneath him and he slipped a few times on the loose ground. He looked down and stopped moving.

"Oh my god, whatever you do don't look down," he whispered.

They immediately all looked down and Becca shrieked. She grabbed hold of Alex's arm and held on tightly.

"Are they what I think they are?" she whispered.

"Bones," whispered Sven. "Human bones."

"There are so many, thousands," Matt said, shocked, "I thought you said he only ate really bad souls, why are there bones down here and why so many?"

"He eats the flesh too, I guess there have been a lot of bad people over the years. Niddgodd is thousands of years old," said Dvalin.

"Guys, we're really not prepared for this. We need to go back and rethink this," said Matt backing away.

"We can't go back now, we need to see what we're dealing with first," said Alex.

"Dude if I'm about to become a dragon's dinner I will haunt you forever," said Matt, following Alex towards the tunnel.

"Matt I'm pretty sure I'll be his afters if you're his dinner," Alex joked, weakly.

"If he eats Matt first he'll have indigestion and we can

make a quick getaway," Pete added, grinning.

Alex entered the second tunnel; the smell was even worse than before. He grabbed the bottom of his shirt and lifted it up to cover his mouth and nose. His eyes were streaming and he could barely see. As they reached the end of the tunnel, Alex held up his hand indicating they should stop. He went forward on his own slowly, sticking closely to the sides of the tunnel and trying to be invisible. At the edge of the tunnel he poked his head forward cautiously to look around. The sight was staggering. He was standing at the edge of an enormous cavern. Stalactites hung from the ceiling and were dripping with what looked like blood. A huge tree root filled the cavern and Alex could make out a large scaly green body wrapped around the root.

"Niddhogg," he whispered to himself.

Alex gestured to the others and they all came forward to take a look.

"Is he asleep?" Matt whispered, poking his head out of the tunnel cautiously.

"Well he's not moving," Alex whispered back.

As soon as he said it the green scaly mass shifted and a long tail swung out in an arc sweeping the floor. Alex and Matt jumped back and stood as still as they could. The tail curled back around the tree and Alex could hear the sound of crunching.

"Oh my god, he's eating," said Matt, pulling Alex back into the tunnel.

"We need to move from here quick," Dvalin whispered urgently.

"Why? He can't see us here," Matt replied.

"When I was here before when he had finished eating he spat the bones out into a hole. Judging from the bone yard we just crossed I'm assuming this was the hole. Quick over there," said Dvalin, pointing to another tunnel off to the left.

They hurried over to the dark open space casting worried glances in the direction of the dragon. Alex brought up the rear and just as he was about to enter the tunnel, a splatter of liquid fell from the stalactite overhead and landed on his neck. He stifled a cry and wiped his neck with his hand. The skin on his neck was bubbling and burning. He looked at his hand; it was covered in a thick red sticky substance. The skin on his hand was blistering; it burst open and started to bleed. Alex looked at the others horrified.

"Alex, are you okay?" cried Becca, pulling him into the safety of the tunnel.

"It's burning, aghh, it's agony," he moaned, through clenched teeth.

"Venom," said Dvalin, looking up at the ceiling. "The whole ceiling is coated in snake venom."

"Venom?" asked Matt, looking up. "Snakes have venom, that's a dragon. What's going on here?"

"Dragon...snake, Niddhogg is one and the same," said Dvalin, looking at Alex's wounds.

"Alex, did you eat a golden apple?" he asked.

"No, it's in my pocket," he said, through clenched teeth.

"Quickly eat it, it will help with the healing process," said Dvalin.

Alex reached into his pocket with his good hand and retrieved the apple. He took a large bite and his wounds immediately started to close over and heal. He sighed in relief and inspected the shiny new red skin on his hand. He tucked into the rest of the apple eating all of it even the core. It was the sweetest apple he had ever tasted.

"Dvalin, you could have mentioned the snake venom filled roof from hell before we just ran under it," hissed Pete. "Details, we like details please."

"Shush," whispered Sasha, urgently.

Niddhogg's body was moving again. His tail swept out, narrowly missing Alex's foot. It had a jagged spine on the end and looked lethal. The giant body writhed around the tree root and suddenly his head appeared between two thick roots. Everyone froze to the spot terrified to move. Niddhogg opened his mouth lifted his head and gave a massive belch. Venom flew from his sharp jagged teeth and covered the ceiling. As it dripped onto the roots there was a large hissing noise and smoke rose into the air. Niddhogg slithered from between the roots, sniffed the air and looked around with red gleaming eyes. He had long twisted black horns on his forehead and dark green jagged spikes along his back. They were barely breathing now, trying to press themselves as far back into the tunnel as they dared without making any movement or noise. Niddhogg stretched out his black talons and scraped long deep grooves into the jagged stone floor. He reared back his head and then darted forward spitting bones into the tunnel they had just vacated. He then retreated back to the gnarled tree root, wrapped himself around it and was still. All they could hear was a rhythmic gnawing sound.

"What's it doing?" Alex whispered, out of the side of his mouth.

He still didn't dare move even though Niddhogg was

facing away from them.

"Chewing the tree, those roots belong to the Yggdrasil tree. If he destroys the root the tree will die and he will be able to escape," said Dvalin.

"It will also mean the collapse of the Nine Worlds. The tree binds them altogether," said Sven.

"We really, really need to get out of here before he starts chewing on us," said Alex, looking around in panic.

"We still need the sword," Pete reminded him.

"I know but it could be anywhere, we can't exactly stroll around and look for it," Alex hissed back.

"Think guys. If you were a dragon and were given a sword to hide where would you put it?" asked Sasha, looking at the others.

"I would bury it in my pile of treasure," said Matt.

"Hmm something tells me this particular dragon isn't fussed about treasure," said Sasha, looking over at the dragon.

"Well he seems hell bent on wrecking that tree so my guess is it's sticking in the tree somewhere doing it some damage," said Becca.

"That's a pretty good idea actually," said Alex. "Everyone look at the tree root, can you see anything shiny sticking out of it?"

Alex craned his neck forward to get a better look at the tree. He drew his head back quickly as a large blob of venom splashed down in front of him.

"Even if we do see it, we won't be able to get it, what about the venom?" asked Becca, pointing to the floor in front of Alex.

"I must confess I'm more worried about the soul sucking

dragon than the venom," said Alex. "You guys can't do anything but I can. Look I'm healed already, no scar or anything," he said, holding out his hand.

No one could see any evidence of the burn at all.

"There, up there, look everybody," cried Sven, excitedly pointing to the top left-hand side of the tree root.

Alex looked and could see a silver glint shining in the wood.

"Great, it just had to be at the very top," he groaned.

"It's too far, he will never make it," said Matt. "Look how much venom is dripping from the roof. A blob of that on his head and he'll be floozed even if he does heal quickly."

"It's okay guys I've got this. You can see the drips forming, I just need to keep an eye on them before gravity takes over," said Alex, looking at the ceiling again.

"Okay, so that's the venom, what about Niddhogg? He will hear you surely," said Matt, worried.

"I can do ninja quiet, it's cool. Look it's not as though we have any choice," said Alex. "If anyone has any better plans please go ahead."

They all looked at each other and shook their heads. Before anyone could come up with any more reasons as to why this was a bad idea Alex ran out into the cavern, darting to one side as a large blob of venom splashed down again near his feet. He looked up and judging where the next one was likely to fall darted forward again. Just as he reached the base of the tree root a splash hit the floor and bounced up onto his leg. Hopping to a stop on his good leg he doubled over holding tightly to the skin just above the burn. The venom had burned through his trouser leg and the skin beneath was bubbling and blistering. Breathing in and out of his nose slowly, Alex concentrated on the intense pain which was firing up and down his leg. As soon as the pain receded he stood up again and placed his foot on the wood. There was a cracking sound like a branch snapping and Alex froze to the spot. Niddhogg continued to be still and Alex breathed a sigh of relief. He placed his other foot gingerly on the root and it held. Looking back at the others he could see their pale faces peering out of the gloom of the tunnel.

Alex looked up and quickly planned a rough route up to where he could see the shining object. The wood of the root was ancient and gnarled; there were plenty of handholds and gaps for his feet. Alex started to climb trying to be as quiet as possible. Luckily there was no venom above him so he made quick progress up the tree. Very soon he reached the top and could see a silver crosspiece protruding from the wood. It was the sword. Stretching up his fingers he touched the pommel and a surge of power streaked down his arm. He pulled back quickly and gave a thumbs up to his friends.

Alex climbed a little higher to get a better grip on the sword and grabbed the hilt firmly. He felt a strange buzzing sensation in his arm. It felt as though the sword was connecting with him and becoming an extension of his arm. Alex tensed and pulled hard but the sword remained lodged in the wood. He tried again but it didn't budge at all. Looking over at the others he gestured at the sword and motioned it was stuck. He saw them put their heads together and they looked as though they were discussing ideas. Alex continued to pull on the sword and tried wiggling it and hanging off it with his whole weight but it still wouldn't move. He looked over and Matt was waving at him. Matt was holding out his hands and looked as though he was trying to throw something invisible. Alex soon realised what he was trying to say, they thought he should use his electric energy to free the sword. He looked at them skeptically and shook his head. If he blasted the tree, not only would he damage it which would be bad news, it would likely wake the dragon and that would be even worse.

Alex saw them talking again and they looked like they were arguing. It was obvious to Alex no one had any other ideas. He looked at his hand and then the sword. If he tried to limit the amount of energy it might work he thought to himself. Alex adjusted himself so one hand gripped the sword. His other hand was firmly wedged into a crack in the wood and his feet were on either side. Looking over at his friends he grinned. This was an all or nothing move. Focusing all of his energy on his hand he tried to release a small amount of power. A surge of energy raced up his arm from his chest and suddenly there was a bright flash, a loud crack and Alex was thrown backwards through the air.

Landing heavily on his back and hitting his head hard on the stone floor, Alex felt all of the breath knocked out of him. He lay still in agony, it felt like he had broken several bones. He tried to lift his head but it felt heavy and fuzzy and everything looked blurred. There was a loud buzzing noise in his ears and he turned his head carefully to the side and blinked a few times. He started to get his focus back and could see his friends in the distance. They looked horrified. Matt was holding tightly onto Becca who was struggling to get to him. She looked like she was shouting but Alex couldn't make out what she was saying, the buzzing in his head was too loud. She really needs to keep quiet; Alex thought to himself fuzzily, she is going to wake the dragon. He felt completely out of it and desperately wanted to close his eyes and sleep. Rolling back his head back and looking up at the ceiling he could see two gleaming ruby red eyes staring back down on him, Niddhogg.

Alex's senses quickly returned but he couldn't move. Looking down at his body he saw a huge talon digging into his stomach, pinning him to the floor. The slightest bit of pressure and it would pierce him straight through. Alex could hear the others screaming now and looked over at them, fear etched all over his face.

Dvalin and Sven were jumping up and down and waving trying to get Niddhogg's attention. The dragon's eyes were fixated on Alex though. It cocked its head to one side and hissed loudly. A long thin tongue lashed out and struck Alex on the side of his face. He screamed as a searing pain shot through him. It felt as though his face were melting. Niddhogg moved back a step releasing Alex from his talon.

"Alex run," screamed Becca.

Alex could start to feel his legs again. He was healing quickly. Scrambling back on his elbows and legs he winced as an elbow brushed through a pool of venom. He kept his eyes fixed on Niddhogg who seemed to be looking at him puzzled.

"Alex the sword, the sword," shouted Pete, frantically.

Alex looked around on the floor and could see the sword lying at the feet of Niddhogg. He groaned and lifted himself into a crouching position. Crawling forward slowly and not breaking eye contact he reached for the sword. Suddenly a large talon crashed down over the sword and Niddhogg shook his head slowly.

"Niddhogg, it's me Dvalin," called Dvalin, from the entrance to the tunnel.

Niddhogg looked over.

"I gave you the sword, but I need it back please."

Niddhogg shook his head and hissed. Alex could just see the hilt of the sword under his talon and he shifted closer whilst Niddhogg was distracted with Dvalin.

"Please Niddhogg, the sword is mine I need it back. I know I told you to never let anyone have it but this is Thor's son. He is the owner of the sword; I want to give it to him. I demand you give it back," Dvalin shouted, bravely.

He was shaking from head to foot and there were beads of sweat on his forehead. Niddhogg shook his head again and whipped his tail in front on Dvalin. He shrieked and went further back into the tunnel out of reach. The tail crashed into a tall stalagmite and pieces of rock flew across the cavern.

Niddhogg had shifted his body and Alex could see more of the sword. He stood up slowly and focused on tapping into his energy source. He could feel it building in his chest, coursing through his blood and felt dizzy with the power. Niddhogg turned his head towards him and Alex released the power from his chest. Electricity burst from him striking Niddhogg's talon. The dragon reared back on his hind legs, releasing his grip on the sword. Alex darted forward, grabbed the sword and ran straight towards the tunnel. He splashed through pools of venom but the healing power of the apple was coursing through his blood and the wounds healed immediately.

Alex felt invincible and laughed out loud hysterically. Just as he was about to dart into the tunnel Niddhogg's tail whipped in front of him. It caught Alex in the chest and flung him back onto the hard rock floor. The dragon roared spitting venom all over the cavern and crashed back down on his feet again making the walls tremble. Several stalactites fell from the ceiling and crashed down near Alex.

"Alex," screamed Becca.

Niddhogg's head darted towards Alex and he held the sword up to his face. The dragon reared back and stepped away from the sword hissing loudly.

"Alex, quick run over here, he won't touch you whilst you have the sword,' Dvalin shouted.

Alex kept the sword held high pointing it in Niddhogg's direction and ran over to the others in the tunnel. They ran down it until they reached a dead end. Becca grasped Alex's hand.

"The crystal quick," she said.

He reached into his pocket and pulled out the crystal. His hands were shaking so badly he nearly dropped it. Alex hastily drew a door in the tunnel wall and scratched in a doorknob. The doorway started to glow yellow and Alex shouted "Lokson's henge."

He tore open the door and bright sunlight shone through.

"Quick," said Alex, pushing his friends forward towards the light. Sven jumped back in horror.

"No," he cried. "I can't go into the sun."

Alex cursed his stupidity. He hadn't thought this through; he had just been intent on getting out of there and finally ending this. He looked over at Dvalin who was holding his hand up to the light shining through the door.

"Look," Dvalin said amazed. "It must be the apple, I haven't turned to stone. I can go in the sun."

He grinned and jumped through the doorway.

"Wait," cried Sven, but it was too late he had already gone.

"Sven," said Alex, helplessly.

"It's okay, you go. Give me the crystal and I'll draw another door to my home," said Sven, holding out his hand for the crystal.

Alex hesitated for a moment. He had thought to use the crystal to get back to Asgard and Lexi but he couldn't leave Sven in this hellhole. He nodded and gave Sven the crystal. The light from the door was starting to dim and Sven pushed Alex towards it.

"Quickly it's closing," he shouted.

Alex squeezed Sven's shoulder. "Make it home safe, we'll see you soon when this is all over," he said stepping through the door into the light.

Chapter Sixteen

The sun blinded Alex after spending so long in the darkness. He shielded his eyes and saw Dvalin skipping around on the grass like a child.

"The sun, the sun," shouted Dvalin, in excitement. "This is amazing, it's so warm, so beautiful. I've waited so long for this."

He fell onto his back and held his arms out to his sides soaking up the warmth.

"Dvalin be careful, the sun can burn your skin, you'll need some sun cream to protect you, if you lie in it like that," said Sasha.

Dvalin jumped up and skipped around again, he was already starting to look a bit red.

"Alex," shouted a voice.

It was Alan. He came running over and grabbed Alex by the shoulders.

"You have it, my dear boy I knew you could do it. Quickly there is no time to waste it has started to happen, the breach is getting bigger, we can't contain it anymore," he said, pointing to the henge.

Alex looked towards the henge and could see smoke pouring from the central stone. The smell of sulphur and death filled the air and he gagged.

"Quickly, show me the sword," said Alan, holding his hand out for the sword.

"No don't touch it," Dvalin cried, thrusting himself between Alan and Alex. "It's cursed, you can't touch it."

"Sorry who are you?" asked Alan, looking confused.

"I'm Dvalin. I created and cursed the sword with my brother. Odin help me I had no idea at the time what would happen. We were just trying to get revenge," he said, miserably.

"But you're a dwarf, how can you be out in the sun?" asked Alan, amazed. "I have only ever met Lit. I didn't know there were others," he said.

"Iduna gave me a golden apple to save his life," said Alex. "It took years off him, you should've seen him before, he looked practically dead on his feet, old and wrinkly and..."

"Alex, do you mind?" said Dvalin, sternly. "I didn't look that bad, did I?"

"No, no of course not," backtracked Alex, embarrassed. "It's just that you have changed so much."

"He can be in the sun without turning to stone, that's amazing," said Alan. "The dwarves will all be queuing up at Iduna's orchard now," he said laughing.

"No, we need to keep this quiet. She shouldn't really have given me one for him, but I helped save her daughter and she was very grateful," said Alex.

"Her daughter?" asked Becca, suspiciously. "Was that her perfume I could smell on you?"

"Er, it was actually. I saved her from a Light Elf called Hadron. He kidnapped her and Ellewen and I rescued her."

"Ellewen? Another girl? Seriously Alex, what have you been up to?" asked Becca.

Her arms were folded and she glared at Alex.

"Ellewen's a Volva, look it's a long story I promise I'll tell you later. Let's just finish this then we can talk," said Alex, reaching out and brushing Becca's cheek with his hand.

Alan and Dvalin had their heads bent together deep in conversation.

"This is so amazing," said Alan excitedly. "You say you created this sword and you cursed it?" he asked Dvalin.

"Yes, whoever touches the sword will die and whatever the sword strikes will die. It will cut through anything, wood, rock, even diamonds," said Dvalin.

"But Alex, you're holding it?" said Alan, looking at Alex in shock.

"I should be okay, I ate a golden apple, I think it will protect me," he said, more confidently than he felt.

"For now," whispered Dvalin, under his breath sadly.

Alex didn't hear him and he held out the sword for Alan to see. The pattern of a snake's body was engraved deeply in the silver blade. It wrapped itself around the sword with the tail of the snake as the tip and the head as the pommel. There were two rubies for the snake's eyes, which reminded Alex of Niddhogg. He shivered and held the sword up to the sun. It looked as though the snake's body was moving as the metal caught the sun.

"It's beautiful," whispered Alan, in awe.

"It's death," said Dvalin, sternly. "As soon as Alex has used it to seal the portal he must destroy it. I should have done it before but I was so proud of my workmanship I couldn't bear to destroy it."

"Alan, quick something's happening," cried Nancy, running over to them.

She looked in a complete state, dark smudges were under her eyes and her hair was all over the place. It was obvious she hadn't slept for days.

"What do I do?" asked Alex, looking around at the others.

"We're not sure but try plunging the sword into the central stone and see what happens," said Nancy.

"But the prophecy," said Sasha, taking a crumpled piece of paper from her bag.

"It says when day becomes night and the sword of Tyrfing is wielded by the last-born son of Porr, Hel shall be cast down and will no longer be able to wreak havoc ever again," she said. "This isn't going to work, it's daytime. What does it mean, when day becomes night?" she asked, looking at Alan and Nancy.

They both looked at each other and shrugged. They had no idea.

Suddenly there was a huge cracking noise and the earth rippled and heaved upwards as though it were waves in the sea. They all staggered from side to side under the undulating ground before they were thrown to their knees. Acrid yellow smoke poured through cracks in the ground and Alex could hear the sound of beating wings, followed by a terrifying howl.

"What's that?" asked Becca, frightened.

She crawled over to Alex on her hands and knees and held onto his arm tightly.

"I don't know, but I've a horrible feeling we're about to find out," he said, gripping hold of the sword tightly.

"It must be Hraesvelg, the corpse eater," said Dvalin. "He's an eagle who is trapped down there, he eats the dead that can't enter Helheim but who aren't bad enough for Niddhogg to eat."

"Like politicians," Alan said, wryly. "I think he's trying to find a way out. Quick Alex use the sword and seal the portal."

Alex got to his feet and ran over to the edge of the henge. He had to jump over large crevices, which had appeared in the ground. They were belching out yellow smoke, which stank of sulphur and blood. Alex's eyes were stinging and watering and he wiped them with his sleeve. He was finding it hard to see. Looking up at the sky, he saw thick dark clouds had gathered above him. They completely blocked out the sun making it dark.

"When day becomes night," he shouted, to the others pointing to the sky. "This is it!"

His words were whipped away by a wind, which blasted in his face. The sound of beating wings was louder and the wind was so strong he could barely stand. Tucking his head down he forced his feet forwards towards the central monolith. Suddenly a loud howl split the air and Alex looked around in panic.

"It's Garm," shouted Alan, pointing towards the centre of the henge.

Alex looked to where Alan was pointing and stepped back in horror. An enormous dog's head had burst through the ground. Two giant paws with sharp jagged claws scrambled at the earth tearing it to pieces as it tried to pull its way free of the ground.

"Nice doggy," called Alex waving the sword in front of him and stepping back a few paces.

Garm barked and the ground shook. Alex stumbled backwards and planted his feet firmly into the ground. He stared at the giant dog in horror. The beast was massive, as big as an elephant at least. Blood was dripping from its muzzle and it stared back at Alex with five piercing golden yellow eyes.

Its dark fur was matted and soaked in what looked like blood. Alex stood still, terrified. He had no idea what to do with the beast. He waved the sword in front of him, thinking back to Niddhogg, it seemed to keep that beast at bay but he didn't really know what he was doing. All he knew was he had to get the sword into the central stone and this huge beast was standing in his way and looked ready to eat him.

Garm lifted his giant head and howled again. It was a terrifying sound, a sound that would wake the dead thought Alex. He started to focus on building up the energy in his chest however Garm bunched his legs back and leapt into the air straight at Alex's head. His jaws were open ready to rip into Alex and he could see body parts wedged between his teeth from his previous victims. Just as Garm's teeth were about to sink into Alex's head the beast jerked back and fell to the side. Blood and drool sprayed over Alex's face and the stench of death filled his nose. Garm jumped to his feet again but stumbled. Alex looked up confused. He could see Dvalin running around Garm, darting between his giant paws and wrapping what looked like a thin silk ribbon around his legs. Soon the beast was completely entangled and he fell to the floor with a mighty thud shaking the ground and bringing everyone to their knees again.

"Alex, quick, the sword," shouted Dvalin.

Alex strode forward towards the central monolith careful to give Garm a wide berth. He was thrashing around on the floor entangling himself further. His giant jaws snapped open and shut trying to tear into Alex.

As Alex reached the central stone of the henge, there was a large cracking noise and the ground opened up in front of him.

He lost his balance and started to slip into the crevice. He scrambled at the earth with his hands and tried to find purchase to stop himself falling any further. He still held the sword tightly in his hand. He felt as though it were an extension of his arm and bound to him. Before he could slide any further down the hole he thrust the sword into the hard earth and hung onto the golden pommel. He just about managed to get a foothold in the earth and just as he pushed himself up over the edge of the hole something brushed past him. The air around him split with a huge shriek. Alex looked behind his shoulder and saw a large bird like creature burst from the crevice. It had the head and wings of an eagle but it's body was black and scaly and it had a tail like a snake. It reared up into the sky, beating its wings fiercely. When it was airborne it circled around the henge screeching defiantly.

"What's that?" asked Alex, shouting.

"Hraesvelg is free, Hel is about to break lose," cried Alan.

The wind was whipping about him making his sparse grey hair fly around.

"Alex, use the sword, hurry before it's too late," he shouted.

Alex stood up shakily and gripped the sword tightly in his hand. He leapt over the crevice and landed with bent knees. A shrill cry filled his ears as Hraesvelg swooped down, his talons were outstretched ready to rip his head from his body. Alex ducked down at the last moment and rolled forwards. A sharp talon scraped a long line down his back shredding his shirt but the bird couldn't get a grip on Alex. Hraesvelg beat his wings and flew up into the air again to prepare for the next strike. Alex rose to his feet cautiously. Blood was pouring down his back and soaked into his trousers. He staggered forward still gripping the sword and looked up into the sky. Hraesvelg had completed a full circle and was heading straight back down towards him again. His sharp beak opened and he let out a cry, which shook the earth.

Alex ran the rest of the distance to the centre of the henge. He leapt up onto a hillock, which had formed in the earth and jumped down into the centre of the henge with the sword pointing downwards. Alex struck the central stone with all of his strength and the sword slipped into the granite as though it were butter. There was an almighty clap of thunder and a jagged bolt of lightning struck the sword embedded in the stone. The stone crumbled and the sword fell to the ground. White light lit up the clearing and a fierce wind blasted around Alex. Garm howled furiously, his legs tangled together useless. Hraesvelg screeched and as he neared the ground he stretched out his talons, his beady eyes fixated on Alex.

"It's not working," shouted Alan, over the noise. "Baldur, we entreat you, help us," he cried lifting his hands to the sky.

"Odin protect us," cried Nancy, joining Alan's side.

There was another massive clap of thunder and the ground shook and opened up under Garm. He disappeared into the ground howling in anger, his feet still tied together. There was another massive clap of thunder and a tornado rose up out of the centre of the henge just below Hraesvelg. The wind tore at his wings and flung him around and around in circles. Suddenly there was a loud sucking noise and the tornado sucked Hraesvelg back into the earth. The earth closed back up again with a shudder, the wind died down to a gentle breeze and then there was silence.

The thick black clouds which had covered the sun dispersed and the sun shone brightly warming Alex's face. He had felt chilled to the bone and his legs were shaking uncontrollably. He looked behind him at his friends. They were all standing looking around warily and wondering whether it had really worked. Birds started to sing and the breeze blew away the stench of the acrid smoke and blood.

As the smoke lifted it revealed the henge. It was completely intact and the ground was back to normal. Alex gave a large sigh of relief. He had done it. He dropped to his knees and rubbed his hands through his hair. It was sticky with dark red blood and he grimaced. As he looked up from his hands he saw a tall man step from behind the central stone. The man was dressed in a long black leather coat and his long dark hair was tied back. He looked very pale and his black eyes glinted dangerously.

"Hello nephew," he said, smirking. "You're meant to be dead. Magnus, long time no see dear friend. Would you care to explain why my nephew is still alive?" he asked, looking beyond Alex.

He was looking at Pete's father who was standing behind Alan and Nancy. All the blood had drained from his face and he fell to his knees pleading.

"Loki....I...I couldn't do it, he was just a baby," he said, terrified.

"You weak fool, this is all your fault. My daughter was about to be freed. Oh, the fun we would have had," he hissed.

"You would have destroyed Midgard, I have family here," said Magnus, miserably wringing his hands.

"Family? Pah. My family was taken from me, why should

anyone else have theirs? I couldn't believe my luck when my idiot brother got a human pregnant and triggered the curse. Odin didn't think anyone would defy him but he should have known Thor couldn't resist a good-looking woman with blonde hair. It was all going to plan until that meddling Volva interfered with that damn prophecy about the sword and him," he snarled, looking at Alex. "You had to die Alex. It was the only way my daughter could be freed. If this fool here had done his job properly she would be out and we would rule Midgard together."

"Odin would never let that happen uncle," said Sasha, stepping forward.

"Sasha, sweetness, how lovely to see you," said Loki, turning towards Sasha.

"Sasha?" asked Alex, confused.

"Hey cousin," she said, shrugging.

"Cousin?" asked Matt.

"Yep, my father is Baldur. I was sent from Asgard to keep an eye on you. Make sure our dear uncle Loki didn't harm you," she said.

"Why didn't you say something?" asked Alex, amazed.

"We figured it was better this way," she said. "We weren't sure if it really was Loki who was after you," she said, glaring at Loki.

"We?" asked Alex.

"My dad and I," she said.

"But he's in Helheim, how can you talk to him?" asked Matt.

"Email, they have all the technology down there now," she said, grinning.

"But he's dead, isn't he?" asked Alex, completely confused.

"Your perception of death is different to ours. My mother and father have moved on to another plane. I can chat to them but I can't visit them or touch them, you know," she said, hanging her head sadly.

"Okay this is really weird." he said, rubbing his hands across his face.

"This is weird...really? After all we have been through today?" she laughed.

"Excuse me for interrupting the family reunion but I would really like to take my revenge now if it's not too much trouble," growled Loki, menacingly. "Magnus, he's not a baby anymore. Now can you kill him for me please? You know what happened last time I touched him."

"Loki, I can't, I've known him all his life, he's my son's friend..." said Magnus, pleading.

"Peter, we're good friends now, aren't we?" said Loki, looking at Pete. "Remember what I promised you if you helped me?" he said.

Alex swung around and looked at Pete. He was standing behind Alex holding the sword.

"Pete, what are you doing?" asked Alex, putting his hands up and backing away from him slowly.

"Immortality," Pete said to Loki. "You promised me immortality if I help you."

His hand was shaking and the sword wavered in the air.

"Yes, now finish it, then we can see what we can do about my daughter," said Loki.

"There must be another loop hole to free her," he smiled at Alex and it sent a chill down his spine.

Pete jumped forward and stabbed the sword towards Alex.

"Pete stop," shouted Alex, jumping out of reach. "We're friends."

"Pete, he's lying he can't make you immortal, it's not possible," cried Sasha.

"Silence niece," shouted Loki.

He flung out his hand and Sasha was thrown onto her back. She jumped straight back up and threw herself at Pete's legs knocking him off balance. He fell to the floor and the sword flew from his hands. Alex leapt forward and grabbed the sword pointing the tip of the blade towards Pete.

"Pete, stop. I don't want to hurt you, you're my friend," he pleaded.

"No," hissed Pete. "I want to be a god, he can make me a god," he said, pointing at Loki.

"Pete no," cried Sasha, as he launched himself at Alex with his arms outstretched. Alex tried to swing the blade out of the way but it caught Pete on the arm.

"No," cried Magnus, running forward and grabbing Pete's arm.

"Ha, you'll have to do better than that. You barely scratched me," sneered Pete.

"No, Pete, no," Magnus was crying and hugged Pete to him.

Pete pushed him away.

"It's just a scratch, I'm fine," he said, looking at his arm.

There was a small gash, which was bleeding slowly.

"Pete, the sword, the curse. It brings death to anyone it strikes," said Magnus.

He had tears streaming down his face. Pete looked at his

arm again and then at Dvalin. The dwarf nodded slowly.

"Fix it dwarf," he shouted. "You made the curse, you break it."

"I can't, I can't, I'm so sorry, it's too late, it's starting already," said Dvalin.

Pete clutched his arm and screamed in pain. He rolled up his sleeve and looked at the cut in horror. The skin around it was turning black and spreading up his arm quickly.

"Aghh help me," he cried, looking at Loki.

"No can do buddy, you failed me too, just like your weak father. You're pathetic, all of you," he sneered.

Pete screamed again and fell to the floor writhing in pain.

"Pete, son, hold on," Magnus cried, falling to the floor next to him and cradling his head in his lap.

The blackness was spreading all over his body and they all looked on in horror as he screamed and thrashed in pain on the grass.

"Help me," cried Pete. "It's agony, take the pain away."

"Dvalin what do we do?" asked Alex, desperately.

Dvalin looked stricken. "There is nothing you can do Alex. The slightest wound caused by the sword will cause a slow and agonising death," said Dvalin sadly.

"Alex," Sasha shouted. "The sword."

Alex looked at the sword in his hand and looked into Pete's eyes. He understood what Sasha wanted him to do but he couldn't do it.

"No Sasha, I can't," he said, shaking his head.

"Alex, you have to, he's in agony, finish it quickly," cried Sasha.

"No, I…"

Before Alex could finish Dvalin leapt up and threw his weight onto Alex's hand driving the sword directly into Pete's heart. Alex looked at the sword in his hand in horror and quickly let go. He met Pete's eyes and saw the life and pain leave him.

"What did you do?" shouted Magnus, horrified.

"He was dying, we ended his pain," said Dvalin, removing the sword from Pete's chest and dropping it onto the grass. "He was in agony."

"Quite the heroes," said Loki, sarcastically.

"You murderers," Magnus cried, pointing at Alex and Dvalin. "You killed him, you murderers."

"Magnus, don't blame Alex I did this. I had to, Pete was dying, the sword killed him, not Alex," said Dvalin. "If it's anyone's fault, it's Loki's," he said pointing at Loki.

"He brought it on himself," Loki growled.

"You monster," Magnus said to Loki. "You got into his head. You couldn't make him immortal. You lied to him. You're a monster," he cried.

"Yes, gullible little fool, wasn't he? I'm going to have to find another minion now. How about you," he said, turning to Matt.

Matt backed away from him shaking his head. Suddenly the sky lit up white and a bolt of lightning struck the ground just outside the henge. Everyone jumped in shock except Loki who just looked around casually and laughed.

"Loki," boomed a voice.

A giant of a man with shoulder length red hair and a long red beard stood next to the henge. His eyes flashed white with streaks of lightning and he carried a huge hammer in his gloved hands.

"Brother dearest. You don't write. You don't call. Anyone would think you have been avoiding me," said Loki, smirking. "Please let me introduce you to your son. Look we can have a happy little family reunion."

Thor looked at Alex and nodded. "Hello son."

"Er hello, dad?" said Alex, confused.

"We'll talk later son. I just have some business with your uncle here," Thor said, nodding in Loki's direction.

"Brother, come now, it was a joke. You know me, always kidding around," said Loki, backing away from Thor.

"You took my son from his mother, from me. That is not a joke brother," he spat.

"Thor, come on, all's well that ends well. Look he's a fine young man, no harm done," whined Loki.

"Silence," roared Thor, pointing his hammer at Loki. "He has grown up not knowing who he was, not knowing he had a mother and a father, not having the love of his family. You tried to kill him Loki. That is unforgivable. You have done some bad things in the past Loki but this, this...." he said, gesturing to Alex with his hammer, "This is unforgivable and I will kill you this time," he said furious.

Streaks of lighting blazed from his eyes and static electricity filled the air. Alex's chest started to throb as it reacted to the electricity in the air.

"You can't kill me you idiot, I'm immortal," sneered Loki.

"No Loki, we are not immortal. Remember our brother Baldur, Sasha's father, remember? Was it just a joke to you too when you murdered him?" snarled Thor.

"I didn't know he would die, anyway he's fine. Hel is taking good care of him. He enjoys it down there, Nanna's with him, it's all good," said Loki, looking at his finger nails as though he really didn't care.

"He is stuck in the underworld with your weirdo monster of a daughter," hissed Thor.

"Don't call my daughter a monster," said Loki, through clenched teeth.

"She's a monster and you know it," said Thor, tossing his hammer from one hand to the other.

"Shut up," snarled Loki, stepping towards Thor.

Thor swung his hammer and hit Loki in the chest. He went flying back and hit the central monolith of the henge. His head snapped back against the stone with a crack and he slumped to the floor with a groan.

Thor laughed. "Oh, that felt good. Eric, do you fancy a shot?" he asked, looking at Alex.

"Eric?" he asked. "My name is Alex."

"Alex? Well we named you Eric, Eric Thorsson," said Thor, placing a large hand on Alex's shoulder.

"Well I think something got lost there, everyone knows me as Alex Thornson," said Alex.

"No, it's Eric, a great Viking name. Magnus, was that you? I know you took him as a baby. You put a spell on him didn't you so we couldn't see him?" asked Thor.

Magnus looked up and narrowed his eyes in anger.

"Yes, I changed his name and got a Volva to put a protection spell on him. I was protecting an innocent baby from you freaks," he snarled.

"Yes well, I am still deciding whether to punish you or thank you for saving him," said Thor, looking directly at

Magnus.

Magnus was still sitting on the floor cradling Pete. He looked at Thor with hatred burning in his eyes.

"I should have killed him when I had the chance," he growled, laying Pete's head down gently and rising to his feet. "He murdered my boy. I demand justice," he said, pointing to Alex.

"Justice? He was going to kill my son in exchange for immortality. And you, you stole my son when he was a baby. If anyone should demand justice around here it should be me," shouted Thor.

The sparks in his eyes flashed dangerously.

"Uncle, please have mercy he's upset, he has just lost his son," said Sasha, walking over and standing next to Thor.

"I know, that is the only reason why he is still alive," said Thor, glaring at Magnus.

Loki groaned loudly and sat up rubbing the back of his head.

"That really wasn't necessary brother. I think you broke my skull," he moaned.

"It would take more than that to break your thick head," said Thor, not deigning to look at him. "Magnus, I suggest you take care of your son. As you did not kill my son I will ensure his soul rests in Helheim rather than being sent to Niddhogg. He was intent on murder in his heart so Niddhogg has every right to him," he said.

Magnus went very pale and started to shake.

"Come," said Alan, to Magnus. "Nancy and I will help you with the preparations."

"No, leave me. I want to be alone with my son," said

Magnus, bending down next to Pete and stroking his cheek.

Alex looked at Thor. "What happens to him?" he asked, nodding in Loki's direction.

"Odin will decide, Loki is right I can't kill him but I can make sure his life is miserable for the foreseeable future. Eric..sorry Alex, I'll have to leave you here whilst I sort this out in Asgard. I'll find you when it's done and we'll talk. We have a lot to catch up on," he smiled sadly and grasped Alex by the forearm.

"Sure, no problem. Can we go get my mum too?" asked Alex.

"Your mother? Alex I am sorry but your mother died. She died of a broken heart when she lost you," said Thor, with a tear in his eye.

"But Alan said....." Alex looked at Alan confused.

"Thor, Mathilde is alive," said Alan, looking embarrassed.

"What?" shouted Thor.

A streak of lighting flashed in the sky and a rumble of thunder sounded in the distance.

"Odin made me tell you she had died. He doesn't want gods and humans mixing, you know that," said Alan, miserably.

"She is alive?" asked Thor, looking at Nancy now.

She nodded and smiled weakly.

"My father has a lot to answer for," said Thor, shaking his head sadly. "All this time, I thought she was dead."

He sighed deeply and straightened his shoulders. "Alex, I need to sort this out first and then we will go and find your mother together," he said, smiling widely.

Alex nodded not knowing what to say. He felt like crying

but couldn't in front of everyone. Thor grabbed Loki by the back of his long coat and lifted him up into the air.

"Come brother, you have some explaining to do to our father," he said, glaring at him.

"Ha, I think you'll have some explaining to do yourself, brother," sneered Loki. "You broke Odin's rule and messed with a human. This is all on you brother; do you think he will punish me and not you? You're a fool, always have been."

Thor swung his hammer and knocked Loki out with one blow.

"Peace at last," he grinned at Alex. "I'll be back soon," he said, hauling the unconscious Loki over his shoulder.

Static electricity filled the air and Alex could feel his hair stand on end. A bolt of lightning shot out of the sky and struck Thor. They all shielded their eyes and when the lightning receded Thor and Loki had disappeared.

"Alex, are you okay?" asked Becca, coming over and holding his hand.

He looked at her and tucked a stray strand of hair behind her ear.

"As good as can be expected," he said sadly, looking over at Pete.

"You did the right thing you know, he was in agony and dying," she said.

"I know but I'm still responsible. This damn sword, I have to get rid of it, where's Dvalin?" he asked.

"Picking daisies look," she said, pointing to Dvalin who was crouched on the grass looking for flowers. "I guess he has never seen a flower growing before. This must be quite some experience for him," she said.

"Yeah, for us too. I can't believe it's over, that was pretty intense. Did you see the size of that dog and the bird? I really thought I was going to die," he said, laughing shakily.

"You were brilliant Alex. I don't know what would have happened if you hadn't got the sword in the stone when you did," she said, squeezing his hand.

"That Hel hound nearly had me there, if Dvalin hadn't helped I would be dead. Hey Dvalin," Alex shouted over. "How did you stop Garm? One minute he was flying through the air about to tear my head off and the next he fell over." Dvalin looked up and grinned.

"Dwarf rope," he said. "It's the only rope in existence strong enough to hold a creature like Garm. I originally created it for Odin to bind Fenrir, Loki's other monster child," he said, tucking a daisy into a buttonhole in his waistcoat

"Fenrir the wolf?" asked Becca.

"That's right, when he grew too big Odin got worried so he asked the dwarves to create a rope that would bind him forever. It took a long time but we got there in the end. Fenrir is still tied to his boulder by the rope. Odin help us if he is ever cut loose, he won't be very happy," he said.

"But it looked like a bit of ribbon," said Alex, confused.

"The strongest ribbon you'll ever find. We made it with six things, the noise of a cat's footsteps, the roots of a mountain, the sinews of a bear, a woman's beard, the breath of a fish and the spit of a bird," he said, bending down and picking up a dandelion.

"That's ridiculous Dvalin, you're kidding us," said Alex. "The noise of a cat's footsteps? Yeah right," said Alex, shaking his head.

"No, it's true, just because you can't see things doesn't mean they don't exist," said Dvalin, winking.

"Well I guess it did the job on Garm. Thanks Dvalin, you saved my life," said Alex, patting Dvalin on the shoulder.

"As you saved my life my friend, now we're even," said Dvalin, smiling widely.

"What should I do with sword? I don't want anyone else getting hurt," said Alex, looking at the blade in his hand.

"We need to destroy it before the rest of the curse plays out," said Dvalin.

"What do you mean the rest of the curse?" asked Alex, worried.

"Every time it's wielded, at least three people will die and then the one who has wielded the sword will perish," he said, looking embarrassed.

"Dvalin you didn't mention any of this before," said Becca, horrified.

"Would it have made a difference Alex?" he asked.

"No, I still had to use it to close the breach." said Alex. "It just means I need to destroy it now before it hurts anyone else."

"The only place which is hot enough to melt this sword is in Muspelheim, the land of the Fire Giants." said Dvalin.

"Fire Giants? Great, that sounds fun. Okay I'll go there now. The sooner I get rid of this thing the better," said Alex, determined.

"Unfortunately, it won't be that easy," said Dvalin, smelling the dandelion and grimacing.

"Why? I can just make a door with the crystal..ah, I gave

the crystal to Sven," said Alex, regretting handing over the crystal.

"Yes, and you can't portal in there either, the Volva's won't have anything to do with the Fire Giants, they think they're devils and they keep well away," said Dvalin.

"Well there must be a way," said Alex, exasperated.

He wanted to get rid of the sword desperately.

"Probably best if we ask Thor when he returns, he might know what to do," said Dvalin. "He has been there before."

"Alex, Becca," Alan called over. "Let's get you out of here, we have a lot to catch up on. We can go back to my place, we can get you cleaned up and you can meet your parents there."

"What about Magnus and Pete?" asked Alex.

He looked over at Magnus. He was talking on his mobile phone.

"We have friends who can help him. We can't really explain what happened to the police now can we? Come on they'll be fine, Magnus will take care of his son," said Alan, sadly.

Chapter Seventeen

A short time later they were all sitting in Alan's kitchen drinking steaming hot cups of sweet tea. Alan had called their parents and they were waiting for them to arrive. Alex held onto the sword firmly, he didn't want to risk anyone else touching it.

"Alex, are you hungry?" asked Nancy.

He shook his head, he felt sick to the stomach about Pete and incredibly tired, he hadn't slept in ages. He was trying to process everything that had happened over the last few days and knew he couldn't relax until the sword had been destroyed. His phone vibrated in his pocket and he looked at the screen.

"Cassie," he said, as Matt looked at him quizzically.

She had sent him a Facebook message asking him to call her. He dialed the number provided and she answered straight away.

"Cassie, hi, it's over. We got the sword and sealed the breach," he said.

"I know," she replied. "I saw it."

"You saw it, how?"

"I'm a Volva stupid, I specialise in seeing the future. I saw it all before you even came to me," she said.

"Seriously? You saw all of this happen?" he asked, incredulous.

"Yep, good aren't I?" she said, smugly.

"If you saw it all happen, why didn't you just tell us at the start where the sword was? We have been through hell," he said, his voice rising in anger.

He could feel static electricity prickling the tips of his fingers and took a deep breath.

"Well that wouldn't have been any fun darling. Just think you wouldn't have met Lexi. I hear she has quite the thing for you," she said, laughing.

Alex stood up from the table and moved away from the others.

"Cassie cut it out," he hissed. "What do you want?"

"Lit contacted me, he wanted to know where Sven was," she said.

"He should be back home," said Alex, confused. "He had a crystal to make a door home."

An uneasy feeling started to prickle down his spine.

"Well I guess it didn't work because he didn't get home," snapped Cassie.

"Oh god, this isn't good. The crystal must have run out. He must be still down there," said Alex, horrified.

"Nice way to treat your friend Alex," said Cassie, sarcastically.

"I didn't mean to," stuttered Alex.

He felt hollow inside; he couldn't bear to think about what Sven must be going through.

"Look tell Lit I'll sort it," said Alex.

"You had better Alex or you'll have me to deal with, he owes me a gold bracelet," she said, hanging up.

Alex took a deep breath and slipped his phone back into his pocket.

"Guys we have a problem," he said, looking around at his friends.

"What?" asked Matt. "Don't tell me, Cassie wants to join

you on your date with Maggie?" he asked, laughing.

"Sven didn't make it home, he's still down there with Niddhogg," he said, miserably.

Everyone looked shocked.

"But he had the crystal," said Becca.

"I know but Iduna warned me it wouldn't last forever. I thought it would last longer than that though," said Alex, pacing around the kitchen. "I should've waited, made sure it was okay," he said, rubbing his hand through his hair.

"The door was closing Alex, you had no choice," said Matt.

"I have to go back," said Alex, slumping into a chair at the kitchen table. "I have to go get him, he must be terrified," he said, resting his elbows on the table and putting his hands over his face.

"We all have to go back. We're in this together Alex," said Matt. "I mean Sven's a complete pain but I wouldn't wish that on my worst enemy."

"No, I need to do this on my own. I won't let anyone else get hurt," said Alex, pulling out his phone again.

"Alex what are you doing?" asked Becca.

"Texting Cassie, I need a portal to take me back," he said, dialing her number.

"Why Cassie, why not Maggie?" she asked.

"Are you serious? I already owe Maggie a date and a favour. I need to keep well away from that Volva from now on," he said.

"Alex, we all need to go, we're a team. It was bad enough when you went off to Asgard on your own," said Becca. "We still need to talk about that by the way," she said walking over to him.

He put his arm around her waist and pulled her onto his lap.

"I know, I'll tell you everything. Let me go get Sven first though," he said, tiredly.

"You guys can't go, the only way back is through a portal and we all know the damage that can do," he said, nodding in Dvalin's direction.

"That's not strictly true Alex," said Alan, pushing his glasses up his nose.

"What do you mean?" he asked, looking up at Alan.

"A portal isn't the only way to Niddhogg's lair," he said, mysteriously. "The root of the Yggdrasil tree where Niddhogg lives is directly underneath Helheim. You can get to Niddhogg by going through Helheim and climbing down the root."

"Fantastic, this just gets better and better. How do we get to Helheim then, kill ourselves?" asked Matt.

"Well you sealed a portal to Helheim earlier. We just need to open it again," said Alan.

"Are you serious?" asked Alex.

"It's the only way. We can open it just a crack to let you all through and then seal it with prayers," said Alan, warming to his idea.

"We're doing it," said Sasha, firmly.

"Sasha, no, we need to think about this," said Alex. "Oh, and I haven't forgiven you yet for not telling me we're related."

"We're going, end of discussion," she said, standing up with her hands on her hips.

"If we can get Sven out of Helheim then we can rescue my mum and dad. I never knew you could get into Helheim, or I would have done it before," she said, determined.

"Can you imagine the look on Loki's face if we rescue Baldur?" asked Matt, grinning.

"It will be priceless," said Sasha, laughing. "You saw what Thor did to Loki earlier. My dad is going to seriously kick his butt. I want front row seats to that one."

"Right let's get ready then," said Alex. "I can't believe I'm saying this but we're going to go rescue a dwarf and two gods."

"All in a days work eh Alex?" laughed Matt. "Look on the bright side, you'll get to meet your cousin Hel. This is going to be fun!"

About the Author

Debbie Champion lives in Hinchley Wood, Esher with her husband, three teenage children and two dogs. She started to write as a hobby on her daily commute into London as a means of escaping this crazy world we now live in! She is passionate about history and mythology and enjoys bringing these subjects to life with a modern twist. Whilst her books are aimed at a teenage audience, adults have enjoyed escaping into her world of myth, magic and adventure.

Follow Debbie on:
https://www.facebook.com/DebbieChampionAuthor/
https://twitter.com/Debchamps